"Don't think that because I let you drag me in here like some conquering warlord, that I'm afraid of you. I could put you on your back without stirring a breeze."

Colin leaned closer. "No *woman* could put me on my back unless that was where I wished tae be with her riding astride," he said lowly.

Her eyes widened and her cheeks colored. So her armor was not so thick after all. The lass had a soft underbelly, but he truly wished he hadn't spoken of such things. The words brought to life too many tantalizing images.

"No woman would want you," she spat, and turned away.

He snagged her by the arm and spun her around. She countered by grabbing his wrist and pulled, attempting to throw him off balance so she could jerk free, but he was too quick for her. Snatching her good wrist, he shoved her hand behind her back and leaned against her, imprisoning her in his arms. The moment he felt her toned shapely body pressed against him, he was lost. He could think of nothing, but how much he wanted to taste her.

His lips met hers—hard. He wildly feasted on her mouth as a low growl rumbled in the back of his throat. She answered the call, pressing against him with just as much force, just as much hunger. It stirred his blood to know that she too suffered the same pains as he, the same yearnings.

His hand slid down her back to the odd trews she wore, relishing the way they molded to her firm, round bottom. Cupping her sculpted flesh, he pressed her firmly against his aching shaft. He had to have her. *Now.*

Highlander's Challenge

by

Jo Barrett

Highlander's Challenge

Contact Information: info@thewildrosepress.com

Cover Art by *RJMorris*

The Wild Rose Press
PO Box 708
Adams Basin, NY 14410-0706
Visit us at www.thewildrosepress.com

Publishing History
First Faery Rose Edition, 2007
Print ISBN 1-60154-096-5

Published in the United States of America

Chapter One

Pushing all negative thoughts from her mind, Amelia Tucker, or Tuck as she preferred to be called, lifted her hands out in front of her. Turning her palms in opposite directions as she rotated her arms through the air, she concentrated on her breathing, inhaling deeply as she brought her hands toward her body, exhaling as she pushed them away.

Yin and yang. Out with the aggressive, in with the passive. She pivoted on her toes and raised her arm in a curve to shoulder level while sweeping her other hand toward her chest. Tension left her body as she focused on the flowing movements. Daily she performed her exercises, regardless of where she was or whom she was guarding.

"You look like you're doing the Hokey Pokey," a voice said from the doorway.

Not allowing the smart remark to deter her, Tuck continued executing each action precisely until she was finished. She needed this time, this meditation in motion. It helped to maintain her sanity in an insane world and focus her energies on what was important. Distraction could be deadly.

Lowering her arms to her sides, palms downward, she straightened her legs and equalized her body weight. She slowly relaxed and allowed her arms to hang naturally by her sides and breathed deeply for a few seconds.

The exercise complete, Tuck opened her eyes and pinned her gaze on Jenny Maxwell, her latest client. "For such an educated person, that's the best analogy you can come up with?"

The waif-like woman shrugged as she strolled into the room, her caramel-colored corduroys zipping with each step.

"Can I help it if your exercises look like a slow

1

version of a nursery rhyme?" She sat down on the edge of the bed and clasped her hands between her knees.

Pleasantly relaxed from her workout, Tuck chuckled softly. "I'll bet you've never Hokey Pokeyed in your life. You were probably in a lab somewhere dissecting something while the other preschoolers were wiggling their diaper-clad bottoms."

She crossed to her luggage and changed into her jeans and cable knit sweater. Although she'd never consider herself a clothes hound, the heavy knits were one of the many things she liked about Scotland.

"Actually I was calculating the average number of times my fellow classmates made mistakes in their attempts to follow the basic steps, but eventually I was pressed into performing the dance," Jenny said matter-of-factly.

"I take it that was before they realized you were a prodigy," Tuck replied as her head popped through the top of her sweater, setting her short crop of curls to bouncing.

Jenny sighed and adjusted her wire-framed glasses. "Yes."

Often, Tuck sensed a deep sadness in her client's voice, but pushed it aside, never letting it mesh with her own. They were not friends or confidants. Jenny Maxwell was a job, plain and simple.

"So, where are we off to today? I'm sure there's a pile of rocks or some bushes you've missed on this tour," Tuck asked for the sake of conversation, more than needing any real information. She knew exactly where they were going, the arrival and departure times, and any other pertinent points that would help keep Jenny safe. But she also wanted to be prepared for any of her client's whimsical changes to the itinerary so she could squash them.

Being an avid history buff, Jenny was determined to see everything in Scotland down to the last bit of heather, regardless of the danger. No matter how many times Tuck explained the situation, Jenny would frown at her, and say, "Nobody wants to kidnap me." As if she wasn't worth the bother.

Tuck, however, didn't take her job lightly. There had been kidnapping threats made, and she, as well as

Jenny's father, refused to ignore them. Thanks to her multimillionaire status, Jenny had become some lunatic's distorted version of a hefty retirement plan.

Her charge jumped up from the bed like an eager child. "We're going to the Isle of Mull, and if we don't hurry we're going to miss the ferry. I can't wait to see Arreyder Castle, and Raghnall Castle, and the fishing village, and the gardens," she rambled on.

Tuck held back her moan as she shoved her knit cap on her head and tucked her hateful curls underneath. She despised their walks through old gardens where there were too many places she could get caught unaware.

****

Less than an hour later the ferry pulled into Mull Bay alongside fishing boats and yachts bobbing gently in the water. The passengers disembarked and a few tourists, Jenny included, oohed and awed at the brightly painted buildings lining the streets down to the pier.

Tuck made mental notes of important thoroughfares and businesses as she drove the rental car off the ferry and through the small town, relieved to see the map she'd memorized was correct.

It wasn't long before her client started another of her longwinded lectures, this one on the beginnings of the island and its inhabitants. With a photographic memory, Jenny had a tendency to regurgitate everything she ever read, and, if the number of pamphlets clutched in her hands were any indication, they were in for a very long day.

Resisting the urge to roll her eyes, Tuck took the single-track road toward their first stop. Nodding here and grunting there in response to Jenny's continued chatter, she gave her rearview mirror a quick glance, making sure they weren't being followed. Convinced they were safe, she took a moment to admire the scenery.

She silently sighed in appreciation. The farmlands dotted with sheep and cattle, the moorlands, and sparsely wooded hills, much of the country's ruggedness called to her like a kindred spirit. But this particular island had an unusual soothing quality she hadn't anticipated. An almost coming home feeling. Something she'd never felt before.

3

She couldn't understand why Mull seemed to mean something to her, something personal, but she pushed the sensation aside. Dwelling on it served no purpose. The success of her assignment was her only priority.

"Look, there it is," Jenny said excitedly.

The massive stronghold rose up before them as they neared. Pulling the car into a parking space, she stared at the aged stone structure perched on the rocky point overlooking the sound. Out of the dozens of castles she'd seen on this insane trip, this one sent a faint but definite shiver down her spine. Why?

Stepping out of the car, she turned and carefully scanned the parking area. More likely it wasn't Arreyder Castle but something else raising the hairs on the back of her neck. Yet no one seemed all that interested in her or her client.

"Hurry up, I don't want to miss the start of the tour," Jenny said, trotting up the walk toward the castle.

Tuck kept her eyes on their surroundings as she hurried after Jenny and snagged her arm. "Do *not* do that again. You stay with me at all times," she said.

Jenny's mouth turned down. "Oh, yes. I'd forgotten. You're my bodyguard. It's your job to be with me." She pulled away and walked off, her shoulders sagging.

Tuck sighed and shook her head, despising herself for hurting Jenny's feelings. But Mr. Maxwell hired her to protect his daughter, not to be her companion. She couldn't wait for this job to be over. Guarding someone who didn't want to be guarded and was a wacko genius to boot was hard as hell, but this would get her the recognition she craved. She just needed to get through this one assignment.

Her eyes peeled for any sign of danger, they entered the fortress. The guide's voice echoed off the cool stone walls, explaining the changes that occurred to the castle over the centuries. The crowd shifted across the room toward the huge fireplace, and Tuck's brow rose at the impressive display of claymores and daggers hanging above the mantel, all in pristine condition. She wouldn't mind getting her hands on one of those beauties just to feel the weight of it in her palm, hear the swish of steel as it sliced through the air.

Moving on, the small group was shown a bedroom or two above the great hall, the dungeons, and the kitchens, but the family's private quarters were off limits. She wondered what it was like to live in a castle in the 21st century. Nothing like it had been in the old days, she was certain.

Nearing the end of the tour, they followed the guide up a winding stair leading to the top of the keep. Climbing the worn stone steps, they passed through an arched doorway and stepped out onto the battlements. The wind slapped against her face, and she took long deep breaths of salty air, then flipped up her down vest collar against the chill.

Scotland in June was a lot cooler than she'd anticipated, but the view of the Sound of Mull was well worth the bite of the wind. She intentionally forgot how her fair, freckled cheeks would redden instantly or that the tip of her nose would run a close second to Rudolf the Red Nosed Reindeer.

Slipping her hands into her pockets, she deftly opened the small bag of Gummy Bears she'd stashed there that morning. The jellied candy was her one big weakness. She was a Gummy Junkie. Thankfully, they were extremely popular in Europe. She couldn't go without her Gummies for an entire day, much less a month while touring the country. It was one of the few things she and her client had in common.

The cherry flavored treat slid effortlessly down her throat as she stepped up beside her client. Jenny took her offered handful of candy while taking in the view as Tuck continued to survey the area. The people and their clothes were out of place, almost comical in such an age-old setting, but Tuck easily imagined the former inhabitants, thanks to Jenny's incessant lecturing on how modern man compared to ancient Scots. There was something very appealing about a Highland Warrior.

She hadn't cared too much for the battle stories they'd heard on their previous tours. She'd seen enough pain and blood in her life, one of the reasons she got out of the army. Nor did she wish to relive it through Scottish history. But a man in a kilt wielding a claymore certainly held her interest. She wouldn't tower over that sort of man. A painful lesson she'd learned back in grade school. Men didn't like women bigger than them, no matter the age.

She could almost see him. A dark Highland Warrior surveying the choppy waters below, his long black hair whipping his broad shoulders from the turbulent wind off the water.

"You know, even though this is beautiful, I don't think I could live here. It's too—rough."

The wind carried Jenny's voice to Tuck's ears, snapping her out of her momentary trance. She was slipping. It wasn't like her to daydream on the job. It wasn't like her to daydream at all. What was it about this island, about this assignment?

Internally cursing her momentary lapse, she said, "I don't know. I kind of like it. There are plenty of rougher places to live, believe me."

Tuck watched the remaining stragglers, holding tight to her thoughts. She wouldn't screw this up. With Mr. Maxwell as a reference, she'd be able to stop freelancing and set up a real company, hire some assistants and branch out. She'd be the best in the personal protection business.

"Yes, it does suit you," Jenny said sagely.

Ignoring her client's insightful look, she glanced at her watch. "Time to go if you want to make that other castle before we have to catch the ferry back."

With a nod, they walked to the car.

Tuck looked back at the massive walls reaching up to the sky, one last time. Jenny was right. The roughness of Arreyder Castle was very much like her. It had been beaten by the elements, by wars, by time, and by men, but it still stood, strong and proud, ready for battle.

Shaking off the uncharacteristically poetic thought, she climbed into the car and headed for their next stop.

Once they reached Raghnall Castle, several miles away, they fell in behind yet another group of tourists. They wandered the ornate rooms, while Jenny hung on every word coming out of the guide's mouth.

Tuck held in her sigh. No doubt more lectures on Scottish history were sure to result from their latest excursion.

Ending the tour in the garden, relieved the day of wandering historic landmarks was almost over, Tuck's eyes zeroed in on a gorilla of a man. Did she recognize him? Had he been at Arreyder Castle or on the ferry?

No, she would've remembered him, but his intense perusal of the statues seemed orchestrated, and his constant fidgeting with something in his coat pocket unnerved her.

Every muscle in her body tightened.

It could be a gun or a knife. Or it could be nothing more than his keys. Either way, she had to be ready for anything.

She flexed her calf muscle, comforted by the strap of her knife sheath cutting into her leg. Not her first choice in weapons, but it would have to do. Jenny had a sincere dislike of firearms and refused to be near one even if it might very well save her life. Tuck had almost turned down the job because of that not-so-small stipulation, but she couldn't pass up the opportunity—ergo, no gun.

But damned if she didn't wish she'd brought it along anyway. No one would've been the wiser, and she'd feel a hell of a lot better with her Beretta strapped to her leg instead of her survival knife.

"You aren't listening," Jenny said with a dejected sigh.

Tearing her gaze from the stranger, she glanced at her client. "Sorry, just doing my job."

Frowning, Jenny walked over to a large fountain, her step not nearly as light as before.

Tuck bit back a curse. She wouldn't apologize for the truth. With a glance at the man still studying the statues, she followed, silently slipping up beside Jenny. Keeping her eyes on the milling crowd, she couldn't help but wonder why people wanted to walk all over these old castles. But even she had to admit she liked a few of them.

No. One of them. Arreyder Castle. But this one was too fancy for her tastes. Raghnall Castle had been built in the Baronial style with turrets and steep roofs and decorative doodads all along the roofline. Formal terraces covered with roses, gardens of every type spread over a dozen acres, and a statue walk of life-sized limestone figures surrounded the pale stone structure. Not her style at all.

She liked the rougher castles where the walls were built to withstand invasion and the grounds were laid out for military training, not for strolling through. She could almost picture some dandified man in one of those white powdered wigs shoving snuff up his nose as he trailed after some giggling female wearing a dress big enough to sail a ship.

Tuck shook off the image, disgusted with herself for letting Jenny's obsession with history interfere with her work—again.

"Are you ready to go?" Tuck asked, not liking the way her thoughts repeatedly strayed or the way the man in the long jacket was easing toward them.

"Oh, no. Not at all. This has such a softer feel to it than Arreyder Castle. I could spend hours wandering the grounds, imagining I've gone back in time. Couldn't you?"

"No. I couldn't," she lied, easily picturing herself standing alongside a dark Highland Warrior atop the battlements they'd walked less than an hour ago.

Shaking her head to dispel the image, she said, "Look, I've got an uneasy feeling about this place." And that gorilla, she added mentally, concentrating on her job and not imaginary men. She'd been let down enough by real ones.

"You've got an uneasy feeling about everyplace," Jenny grumbled.

Tuck shot her a look, but remained silent.

Jenny's mouth turned up in a crooked grin. "I think you're afraid. The ghost stories the guide told bothered you, but you won't admit it."

Shaking her head, she said, "I'm not being paid to listen to some local spout off a bunch of tall tales."

"I think you're afraid of the unexplainable." Jenny laughed softly. "I thought you were tougher than that, Tuck."

Tuck snorted quietly at her dig, not willing to let it get to her, although there was some truth in what she said. But who wasn't a little afraid of the unexplainable? She was of a mind that if she couldn't touch it, taste it, or smell it, it wasn't a part of her world. Nor did she want it to be. Just like that imaginary warrior. Men like that didn't walk the earth anymore. Just Amazonian women like herself. Too tall, too strong, and too—freckled.

Crossing her arms, she said, "It's the living I'm concerned with at the moment, not the dead." Another lie. Maybe she needed to find a replacement for this job after all. Jenny and all her dreamy talk of the past was getting to her more than she realized.

The man Tuck had been watching disappeared behind a hedgerow, setting off all her internal alarms. "I think you've seen enough of this place. Let's go." She took Jenny by the arm and stepped away from the fountain, but the woman planted her tiny feet.

"Wait, I have to do something first."

Tuck dropped her hand with a weighty sigh. "Like what, sniff every last flower on the place?"

"I want to make a wish."

She snapped her head around. "You want to what?"

"Make a wish. If you drop a penny in the fountain, your wish is supposed to come true."

Tuck blinked, holding in her snort of laughter at the sincere look on Jenny's face. "You're serious."

Jenny sighed as she crossed her delicate arms. "You never listen."

"Listen to what? A bunch of tourist trap nonsense? They just tell all those stories about fairies and stuff to get you to buy junk. Now, let's go," she said, motioning with her head, setting a few of her short curls loose. They danced around her cheeks, teasing her skin, but she ignored them.

Jenny rummaged around in her massive purse and came up with two shiny pennies. "Here," she said, shoving a coin at Tuck. "We're both going to make a wish."

"I am not tossing a penny into a fountain like some kid."

The man reappeared from behind the hedgerow closer to them than before. Every instinct told her to grab Jenny and make a run for the car, but she didn't want to make a big scene or unnecessarily frighten her client. Jenny was sort of fragile, or she was in comparison to herself.

"Come on, we've got to go," Tuck said, firmly gripping

9

Jenny's arm.

"No. I mean it, Tuck. We're making a wish."

Keeping her eye on the stranger, she said, "You're a doctor, for crying out loud. Medical and otherwise. You've got more PhD's than a sergeant has insults. You can't possibly believe this stuff."

Jenny tilted her chin up as one thin brow rose. "I have also performed years of serious study in psychic phenomena and modern day witchcraft. I've seen things I cannot explain scientifically. Therefore I've decided to never discount any possibility, no matter how ridiculous it may seem."

Tuck sighed heavily. "If I do this, then can we leave?"

"Yes. And please quit staring at the gentleman like he's some sort of underworld hit man. It's embarrassing," Jenny whispered sternly.

Shooting her a frown, Tuck said, "Any possibility, no matter how ridiculous."

Jenny shuddered, although she tried to hide it.

Tuck hated scaring her, but she needed to see how serious this was. Her life could be in danger, and standing at wishing wells out in the open where any yahoo could take a pot shot at her wasn't smart.

"He's just a tourist like the rest of us," Jenny said, but her eyes darted to the man, then to the other strangers milling about the garden.

"He's about as much a tourist as I am," Tuck murmured.

The stranger moved toward the castle without looking back once.

"You see?" Jenny said, the apprehension gone from her voice. "He's just a man enjoying his holiday."

Tuck took a steadying breath, slightly relaxing her taut muscles. Something still didn't feel right about this, but she couldn't deny the fact that the he was strolling toward the building like he hadn't a care in the world.

"As I have said repeatedly, why would anyone wish to kidnap me? It simply isn't logical. I realize my father's status and financial situation is rather monolithic, but if one would look closely, my person is not a part of that fortune. Now," Jenny said, adjusting her glasses. "Before we make our wishes, you need to know the story behind the fountain."

Tuck rolled her eyes heavenward. Not another fairytale. She'd had about all of those she could ever want. She'd not only stopped believing in them a long time ago, she'd wiped them clear of her mind completely. But her client, the somewhat mousy but determined doctor, was doing her best to pump her full of every fanciful thought Scotland had to offer.

And damned if it wasn't working. The imaginary dark Highlander refused to be ignored. The minute they got back to the hotel, she was putting an end to this assignment. She'd just have to find another wealthy client with lots of connections to get her to the top.

"But on the solstice the water sprite returned to the magical waters of the burbling stream, leaving his heart sadly broken. Isn't that a wonderful story?" Jenny asked.

"Yeah, wonderful."

"You're not listening again," Jenny said with a soft scowl.

"No, no, I listened," she said quickly, remembering that a happy client was a cooperative client—and a breathing client. "The, uh, sprite jumped into the water. So, are we ready to toss these coins and beat it?"

Jenny sighed with a shake of her head. "You have absolutely no romance in your soul."

Tuck didn't let that remark go too deep, but knew it would sting for a long while. "I'm a soldier. That's why your father hired me, remember?"

"You're a woman, too." Jenny turned away, a frown pulling down her lips. "But then I guess I'm more scientist than woman. The scientist and the soldier. We make an odd pair, you and I."

Tuck didn't like the twinge in her chest from the pain clearly written on Jenny's face. Or maybe she just recognized something familiar she didn't want to acknowledge. Either way this assignment was over.

"So what are we supposed to wish for?" Tuck asked, eager to get this childish stuff done with and get out of there.

Jenny's lips turned up into a bright smile. "Our heart's desire, of course."

"And this—water sprite is supposed to grant our

11

wish?"

"Yes. Silly, isn't it? What a grown woman will do to—never mind," she said, waving away the rest of her sentence. "Just make your wish and toss the penny into the fountain. And you have to keep the wish to yourself so it will come true."

She watched as Jenny clamped her soft brown eyes closed and hugged the penny to her chest. With her long chestnut braid trailing down her back, she looked like a sweet kid about to blow out her birthday candles instead of a nutty genius pushing thirty. She lifted her lids and tossed the shiny coin into the water, her hopes and dreams reflected in her eyes.

Lonely. Tuck recognized the feeling all too well. Neither of them really belonged to anyone or anything. Always the odd girl out. Jenny's father may want her guarded, but he wasn't really interested in his daughter's life. That was obvious. That was painfully familiar.

"Your turn," Jenny said.

Blinking away the irritating memories, Tuck turned to the fountain, not bothering to make a wish. Wishes never came true. Only hard work got a person what they wanted. Her accomplishments, her performance, gained her the respect and acceptance she needed. Not throwing pennies into fountains and wishing for the impossible.

Flipping the coin from her fingers, the sunlight flashed against the copper, catching her eye. Even if wishes did come true, she didn't know how to make one anymore.

The coin plunked into the water, sending out subtle ripples. Hypnotized, her eyes followed the growing circles as her heart whispered its most secret desire.

Jenny's soft gasp and the scuffle of shoes against stone jerked her head around. The man she'd watched so closely stood by her client, one hand gripping her arm, the other holding a gun at her side.

"Don't do anything stupid. I don't want to hurt her, but I will if I have to," he said quietly.

"You'll be dead if you do," Tuck said coolly. Damn it! How could she be so careless? Her job was to protect Jenny, not be her schoolyard playmate.

He smiled faintly, but as their gazes met and held for

several interminable seconds, he knew she meant business.

His smile fell. "I'm taking her with me. I'll contact you later at your hotel."

"The hell you will," she mumbled as he took a step away.

Tuck lunged for his gun, succeeding in knocking it from his hand without it going off while shoving Jenny to safety. Grappling with the cretin's thick arm, she used his own bulk to keep him off balance.

In a rather loud professorial voice, Jenny moved dangerously close to the man quoting verbatim the many laws he'd broken and what his punishment would be.

"Get back," Tuck snapped. "I have it under control!" Or so she thought.

Using his mass and muscle, and nearly breaking his own arm to free himself from her hold, the gorilla reared back, knocking her off balance. She caught herself on the edge of the fountain and quickly snagged him by the back of his jacket before he could get away. But Jenny decided to help, blast her luck.

Her thin little arms flailing, her voice shrieking, she leapt onto the man's back. "How dare you hurt my friend!"

The gorilla swirled around to shake Jenny off, sending her legs careening into Tuck's chest.

Flying backward into the fountain, the image of Jenny pounding the man over the head with her purse was engraved in Tuck's mind.

The mouse that roared, she thought, as her butt landed in the chilly water and her head connected with stone, sending stars shooting across her line of vision.

Chapter Two

Tuck shook her head, determined to clear the fog blinding her. She had to stop the kidnapper. Her job, her future, and possibly Jenny's life was on the line.

Pulling herself up onto her elbows, she noticed two things. There was earth beneath her hands, not stone and water, and there was no sound other than the birds and the wind in the trees. In a flash, she was on her feet and standing in the middle of a small field.

No castle, no tourists...and no Jenny.

"What the hell?" She spun around and regretted it as the world swayed. Clamping her eyes closed, she fingered the lump on the back of her head. Hissing through her teeth at the pain, she surmised she'd been knocked out and dumped in the woods by the kidnapper.

"But I could've sworn I never lost consciousness." Yet, what other explanation was there?

She shoved up her sleeve, revealing her watch. "Hmm, the time is right." Her gaze shifted to the date. The digital read-out had gone wacko. It had jumped back a couple of months and the year was nonsense.

"Nineteen hundred?" She growled softly. "So much for being water resistant." Which meant the time might be wrong as well. Still that didn't explain how she'd ended up in the middle of nowhere. They'd made one heck of a scene beside the fountain. The creep couldn't have carried her and Jenny off without someone calling the cops. He must have had accomplices.

The thought of Jenny in that cretin's hands churned her stomach.

"No," she snarled. She'd never lost a client, and she wasn't about to start now. She didn't know for a fact that she'd failed in protecting Jenny. She might very well be safe.

"But if she's safe, then what am I doing here?"

There was no way to determine what happened

14

without the facts, but the only one that made any sense was her first assumption. The kidnappers dumped her here after snatching her client.

And all too easily.

Her jaw clenched as she bit back the bile rising in her throat. She needed to act, not stand around like a fresh recruit speculating.

Snatching her cell phone from her pocket, she flipped open the cover and cursed. No signal. Shoving it back into place, she felt her ID, still secure inside her vest. She leaned over and yanked up her pant leg, exposing her knife safely sheathed around her calf.

"Interesting." She slowly straightened, her mind racing over the facts.

Although her phone was useless, she was still alive and armed. They could've easily killed her without anyone being the wiser in such an isolated area. Either the kidnappers weren't too bright, or they really didn't want to hurt anyone, which led her to believe Jenny was still alive.

Knowing that Raghnall Castle sat on the east side of the island, she pulled her knife from its sheath and verified the direction with the compass built into the butt of the hilt. Raghnall Castle was the only place she could go, the only place she could start her search for the vermin who'd kidnapped Jenny.

She slid her knife back into place, jerked up the zipper on her thick down vest and headed off through the woods as she popped a Gummy Bear into her mouth. The icy wind whipped at her cheeks and ears. The temperature had dropped considerably since they'd started out that morning. That in conjunction with her wet butt, the lump on the back of her head, and the knot of anxiety growing in her stomach put her in a foul mood.

"I will not fail," she grumbled, tugging her cap low over her ears and shoving her hair beneath.

Laughter, men's laughter echoed through the trees and she froze. She couldn't be that lucky. The bozos who snagged Jenny had to have more sense than to hang around where they'd dumped her untied and unguarded.

Pinpointing the men's location, she eased in their direction and came across a rutted, muddy road.

Crouching down amid the late afternoon shadows at the edge of the woods, she waited for them to come fully into view as she listened to their conversation. She refused to make any more mistakes.

"I say you shall be bloody miserable," one man said, his English accent thick but refined. An unexpected change from the Scottish lilt she'd been hearing for the last few weeks.

"'Tis the next step, mon," the other replied.

As one of them laughed, she caught her first glimpse of the Englishman. Her mouth fell open, then snapped shut with a soft click.

Riding a white stallion, his black leather boots shone to perfection where they sat firmly in the stirrups. His brocade doublet of deep blue was decorated with gold trim and ties and fit his broad torso snugly. A riding cape cast off one shoulder and draped the horse's hindquarters. The sun glinted off his fair hair, pleasantly disheveled by the wind.

His charismatic smile made her suck in a breath. He looked and sounded like he'd walked right out of a fairytale.

"If Jenny could see this guy she'd bust a gut," she whispered to herself. He fit perfectly into one of her silly stories, but even Tuck had to admit he was more than easy on the eyes.

Her brow furrowed as she studied him. What was he doing wearing that getup?

"You plan and plan, my friend, but 'tis a waste of time. When will you learn you cannot control your destiny?" the Englishman asked, glancing at the man riding alongside him.

Her eyes followed his and there they stayed. Tuck swallowed hard as her knees gave out, and she tipped forward in the brush. Barely catching herself with her hands before she landed on her face, she mouthed a curse but didn't tear her gaze away from the dark haired giant.

He was amazing. A breathy sigh slipped from her lips, something she never did where men were concerned. Why expel the energy on being attracted? They were never attracted to her. But with this man she couldn't help herself.

16

She examined him from the tips of his leather clad feet, up muscular bare legs, over his woven plaid wrapped around his waist, to his midnight hair stirring over his massive shoulders. The rough angles of his face, almost hidden by several days' growth, gave him a menacing air. He wasn't pretty like his English friend, but unbelievably striking.

Now—that—is a man.

His dark brows pinched together at the sound of his friend's laughter, his thick full lips pulled into a grim frown. "You are one tae talk. Whether I wed the lass or no, 'tis nothing compared tae what you've done."

The Englishman's smile faded, and he shot him a dark look.

A smile, if it could be called that, it was so dour, eased over the burly Scot's face. "You canna deny you left your homeland tae avoid the destiny your father laid out before you."

The pretty one's back stiffened at his words. "My father and I were not of like minds. However, my fate did not include wedding a woman I've never laid eyes on. She could be a shrew for all you know. Some toothless harridan sure to drive you mad."

Tuck shook her head. Men were the same the world over regardless of their shape and size. They all wanted pretty little petite things that would fawn all over them while they played Tarzan. It made her sick to her stomach.

Realizing they were obviously part of some reenactment thing, she could be fairly certain they had no part in Jenny's abduction, but she'd keep her wits about her just the same. She stepped out of the brush and onto the road.

They both jerked back on the reins, coming to an abrupt halt several feet in front of her. If she thought the frown the Scot threw pretty-boy earlier was bad, the one he shot her was deadly. But she held her ground without flinching. She was more than used to glares from men, yet this one had an edge to it, and she found that extremely interesting.

She glared back at him and was satisfied when one lone dark brow rose. Apparently the hairy Scot wasn't used to being faced down. Of course his size alone would intimidate anyone who had any sense, but she never backed away from a challenge—ever.

"Do either of you have a cell phone I could borrow?" she asked. "I can't get a signal on mine and it's an emergency." They gave each other a quick glance, then looked her over from head to toe. Something wasn't quite right about these two, she could feel it, but she needed information. "Okay. Then how about giving me some directions to Raghnall Castle?"

The Scot squeezed his muscular legs, urging his horse closer. She cursed her hormones for standing up and taking notice. The fact that he looked too much like the man she'd imagined at Arreyder Castle, with the exception of the beard, didn't help any either.

Telling her libido to take a hike, she took a cautious step back. Being attracted to some wacko doing an imitation of a long dead ancestor was not on her agenda, but she couldn't deny how good it felt to stand before a man who didn't bolt with his tail tucked between his legs from one of her intimidating glowers.

His eyes narrowed to sharp slits. "From where do you hail, lad?"

Lad? Well, doesn't that just make my damn day?

Her thick down vest and cable knit sweater more than aptly hid her average sized breasts, and she'd be the first to admit she didn't come anywhere close to what appeared on the cover of Vogue, but his unintentional slight to her womanhood stung just the same.

"Just point the way," she said, not bothering to curb the acidic tone of her voice.

They looked at one another again, then pretty-boy spoke. "I believe you are somewhat confused, my good fellow. There is no such castle."

With a huff, she shoved her hands in her pockets. "Taking your roles a little too far, aren't you?"

She knew, thanks to Jenny, that Raghnall Castle didn't exist until the early nineteenth century and judging by these two throwbacks' clothing, they were doing an earlier imitation of the Isle of Mull inhabitants. But she'd had about all the fun she could stand for one afternoon and shook her head at their bewildered silence.

"Never mind. Forget I asked." She stepped into the brush at the edge of the road, determined to keep on an easterly track well out of sight, but more so because she didn't want to share the road with these two clowns.

Nice legs or not.

Blast it! She really needed to get a grip and stop taking these mental side roads. Jenny and all her fanciful talks of long dead knights and ancient warriors had warped her brain.

"I knew I should've turned down this job," she grumbled.

"Hold there," the Scot said, his booming voice echoing through the forest.

With a backward wave, she picked up her pace, not willing to waste another minute chatting with them. They'd only manage to get her off track again. She couldn't waste anymore time. Jenny was out there somewhere and it was her job to protect her.

She'd barely made it a few yards before the sound of horse hoofs thumped behind her, snapping twigs and crushing long dead leaves. Spinning around, ready to tell them to beat it, she spied a man crouched on a tree limb above the Highlander. And he didn't look like he was up there admiring the view.

Reflexively, she reached up and snagged the Scot by his belt and jerked him from his horse as the man leapt from the tree. Not sparing a glance at the Scot as he landed at her feet with a grunt, she pivoted to take care of the attacker.

He landed awkwardly on the vacant saddle, spooking the horse. Rearing up, the animal tossed him to the ground then bolted away.

Whoever took Jenny had changed the game and was tracking her, although she could swear she hadn't been followed. Whether they wanted her dead or not, she couldn't be sure, but the sunlight glinting off the goon's knife was enough to get her moving. She wasted no time in nailing the little weasel.

Her forearm across his throat, the other pinning his knife hand to the dirt, she leaned her knee into his chest.

"What have you done with Jenny?"

His brow crinkled as his eyes shot to hers, then to

something behind her. In one swift motion she snatched the knife from his hand, rolled away and up onto her feet to face whoever thought they'd get a drop on her. She hoped it wasn't the Scot.

The man she'd pinned rolled to the side as a sword sliced through the air, cutting brutally into his upper arm, barely missing his head. He yelled and clutched at the gaping hole in his flesh where blood poured out of his body, then staggered off into the woods.

Tuck swallowed hard. That was meant for her. Apparently they'd changed their minds and wanted her dead after all.

"What I wouldn't give for my gun," she whispered hoarsely.

The unknown swordsman turned his black eyes to her. "Ye clootie!"

She barely had a second to take in the chaos exploding around her, the sound of steel against steel, men shouting, horses whickering. The two she'd encountered on the road were battling with everything they had, while the huge swordsman with murder in his eyes bore down on her.

As he heaved his claymore over his head in a mighty swing, she took her best and only shot. One powerful kick to the groin followed by a roundhouse kick to the head. His eyes rolled back as he fell to the ground, his sword landing in the dirt with a heavy thud behind him as it slipped free of his hands.

Surveying the others, she immediately realized they were outnumbered. But she'd gotten these reenactments guys into the middle of something that didn't concern them, and she had to protect them as best she could.

She quickly assessed the situation. The Scot she'd unhorsed was holding his own, sword-to-sword with two men.

Impressive. If she had the time, she'd take a moment to admire his form, but pretty-boy was having some difficulty. Three men had surrounded him, two with swords and one with a knife. He was barely keeping them at a distance and had already taken a blow to the shoulder.

She tucked the knife she'd snatched into her belt at

her hip, not wanting to kill any of them since they were her only link to Jenny. Silently, she eased up behind the men surrounding the Englishman. Swiping her leg wide, she put the one closest to her on his back and promptly knocked him out. She would've rather tried to get some facts out of him, but didn't have time. The other two seemed hell-bent on murder.

One of the attackers noticed her success in taking out his comrade and turned on her. He gave her a sinister grin displaying several yellowed teeth as he weighed his dagger in his hand, then lunged straight for her.

Stupid move.

Knocking his knife arm to the side, she struck him under the chin with the heel of her hand then followed with her elbow. One arm locked behind him, she jerked up her leg, slamming her knee into his face. He slumped to the ground with a groan.

She spun on her heels to lend the Englishman a hand, and ground her teeth together. Pretty-boy had managed to stick the last man clean through with his sword before slumping to the ground at the base of a tree, his doublet covered in blood.

Grumbling, she hurried to his side. She wanted them alive, but that couldn't be helped now, the Englishman was wounded.

She dropped to her knees beside him and examined his shoulder. His electric baby blues rolled around in his head before focusing on her as she applied direct pressure to the wound.

"It doesn't look too bad," she said, ripping away the sleeve of his shirt to use as a bandage.

"'Tis glad news," he said with a dazzling, somewhat lopsided smile.

Sitting there with a gash in his shoulder, he could still make her breath catch. A regular Prince Charming. He had it all. The hair, the eyes, the build, the bone-melting accent, even the smile. If anything, he proved she was still a woman, her type or not.

His eyes suddenly widened. Someone was bearing down on her, but she couldn't roll away and leave him exposed. Pivoting on her toes in a crouched position, she barely managed to block the thrust of a knife to her back.

Apparently the one she'd taken out first had come around a lot sooner than she'd anticipated.

Deflecting his hand, and sending the dagger tumbling into the dead leaves, she knocked him to the ground. He took her with him. Rolling in the dirt, she took a few swift blows of his meaty fist to her side. But she refused to lose.

Grabbing him by the hair, she yanked his head back from where he lay atop her. His howl echoed in her ears, then was abruptly cut off when the heel of her hand slammed against his chin. She rolled his limp body off hers then jumped back to her feet.

Ignoring the pain in her side where the thug had pummeled her, she rushed back to the Englishman.

"Unusual fighting technique," he said, his eyes studying her closely as she resumed direct pressure to his shoulder.

"Whatever it takes, I always say."

The absence of steel clashing against steel caught her attention. She chanced a look back at the Scot, hoping he was still alive. She couldn't fail these guys as she had Jenny.

No, I did not fail. I will not fail.

Thankfully, the Scot was okay, but now two assailants lay dead and the rest had disappeared into the woods like wraiths. Even her most recent attacker. He apparently had a very hard head.

Twigs crunched beneath heavy feet. Her eyes flashed to the Scot and those muscular legs as he marched in her direction. Traveling slowly up his body, she nearly swallowed her tongue at the size of him. He was as big as a hundred-year-old oak and likely as solid.

Forcing her gaze away, she gave the dead man laying beside her a cursory glance. But she didn't recognize him. He wasn't one of the tourists she'd seen earlier and neither were any of the others.

This was too weird. Why didn't they come at her with guns? Why the antique clothes and weapons? Pretending to be a part of a reenactment group would be good cover, but why not hide guns on them somewhere? The guy at Raghnall Castle had a gun. And why didn't she remember reading anything about a reenactment event when she and Jenny were planning this trip?

Things just weren't making any sense and neither were these two nutcases with her. They fought entirely too well for playacting and didn't seem all that surprised to be battling for their lives.

Putting aside the questions she couldn't yet answer, she concentrated on the Englishman's wound. Wrapping the makeshift bandage around his shoulder, she pulled tight to slow the bleeding.

Powerful fingers wrapped around her upper arm and jerked her to her feet. She hid her wince at the sudden stab of pain in her side.

"Who the devil are you?" the burly Scot demanded, staring down at her with the most amazing eyes she'd ever seen. Golden amber, like a lion's, drilled into her.

She'd known men taller than her before, but they'd all been long and lanky like basketball players. This was a whole new experience.

His eyes narrowed and warmed as he looked more closely at her face. She felt her skin flush slightly with his perusal. This attraction thing was getting way out of hand. She never ever blushed.

Slowly, his gaze cooled, and he shook her—hard. "Answer me, mon!"

She shot him a glare. Although it was her fault he was caught up in this mess, she'd saved the ungrateful bear's ass, and he still thought she was a man!

"The name is Tuck," she said, her voice filled with enough venom to make any normal person take a few steps back. This man barely blinked.

"You lured us into the woods, didna you?" he snapped, his hand tightening on her arm. "Didna you!"

"I didn't lure anyone anywhere, you idiot! Now, let me go so I can finish dressing his shoulder or he'll bleed to death." She jerked free as the Scot's gaze turned to his friend.

She quickly knelt beside the Englishman and finished what she'd started. The wound was worse than she led him to believe, but he'd be okay after a few days in the hospital.

The Scot lowered to one knee beside him. "Damn you, Ian. You're a better swordsman than that."

"I'm afraid I was...distracted."

She felt their eyes on her and lifted her head from her work. They were looking at her like some specimen under a glass.

Assuming they wanted answers to why they'd been attacked, she said, "I'll explain later, but first we need to get you to a doctor." Her paramedic skills were excellent, but they couldn't compare to what a doctor and a fully staffed hospital could do.

Tuck wished Jenny was there with her. She could sure use her medical expertise right now, and her client would no doubt enjoy taking care of the blonde Adonis.

The Englishman laughed roughly. "A physician? The last thing I need is a bloody leech."

She sat back on her heels, her limited patience at an end. "Would you drop this stupid reenactment stuff? This isn't a game. This is real blood, those were real weapons."

They exchanged frowns then pinned their gazes on her once more.

"I'll ask again, lad. Who are you?" the Scot snarled.

With a muttered curse, she stood. "This is ridiculous. We've got to get Prince Charming here to a hospital." She reached for his good arm, while continuously scanning the area for any sign of another attack.

With a sudden push against her shoulder, the Scot knocked her on her butt.

"He isna a prince, you dolt, and his name isna Charming."

Grumbling beneath her breath, she scrambled to her feet. Her blood-covered fists on her hips, she stuck her face in his—almost. He was too tall to intimidate properly, blast her luck. "I don't care if he's the friggin' King of England! He needs a doctor."

The Scot lowered his head with a growl until their noses nearly touched. "No thanks tae you."

She wanted to scream at the top of her lungs, but held it back. "You listen to me, you stupid, ignorant—"

Grabbing the edge of her vest near the collar, his dark expression changed to confusion as his gaze dropped to the slick material, then returned to hers. "You watch your tongue, lad, or you'll be finding it on the ground."

"You'll be the one eating dirt, Sasquatch," she hissed.

The Englishman burst out laughing.

The giant released her with a shove and looked to his friend. "What do you find so amusing, you bleedin' Sassenach?"

He shook his head with a wide smile. "The lad does not appear to be afraid of you, Colin. I find that enormously humorous."

Tuck let out a long puff of air, noting the thick bead of sweat covering pretty-boy's upper lip. He was in a great deal of pain, but still managed to jerk his friend's chain. She figured that was a good sign as to his recovery, but it would be short-lived if they didn't get him the medical attention he needed. And standing around arguing with a big stubborn ape wasn't getting the job done.

"Unless you want some help intae the next life, you'll shut your yap," the Scot said, but his wounded friend merely laughed harder.

She shook her head. These two were beyond weird. Handsome, but weird.

Shoving aside her irritating observations, she reached down for the Englishman's good arm and slung it over her shoulder. "Come on, we've got to get out of here before they regroup and comeback. You boys can play later."

"We'll not be going anywhere until I have some answers, lad," the Scot said.

If he calls me lad one more time..But they didn't have time for a little heart to heart about her true gender. They needed to put some distance between them and the kidnappers.

"I'll explain as we walk," she said, then pulled pretty-boy to his feet.

With a grunt from King Kong, he shoved her out of the way and took his friend's arm. "I dinnae know what you're blathering about, but we'll not be walking."

He pierced the air with a sharp whistle. Barely a second passed when his horse came trotting toward them through the woods, the white stallion not far behind.

Tuck sniffed. "Nice trick, Tarzan. Now, get him on his horse. I'll ride behind to keep him steady."

The tip of his sword came dangerously close to her throat. "Dinnae go thinking I trust you, lad. I am not convinced you didna have something tae do with this, but you've done what you can for Ian's wound, so I'll put up with your lip. For now."

Her gaze followed the edge of the finely honed steel, across his massive fist, up to his face. He was serious. She knew that look all too well.

One of her fingers twitched, eager to reach for the knife at her waist, but she knew she'd never be able to retrieve it before he separated her head from her shoulders. And yet, she wondered if he'd really do it. Somehow she didn't think so, but that was one theory she wasn't foolish enough to test.

Narrowing her gaze, she stared at him, determined to make it crystal clear that he didn't intimidate her in the least. "I don't have any warm fuzzy feelings for you either, but at the moment neither of us has much choice."

His jaw clenched beneath the thick black stubble. "Aye," he said, lowering his sword. "But I'll be taking the dagger."

He sheathed his sword and held out his hand. She reluctantly relinquished the weapon. Two was better than one, but she'd allow him this small victory.

A satisfied smirk touched his lips, setting off a small spark inside her. Why did he have to have such a sexy mouth? And why did I have to notice it? Argh!

He easily heaved his friend onto his horse.

She did her best to ignore the feminine voice in her head, the one that was usually quiet as death, as it cheered the flexing muscles of his forearms and legs.

"I must have hit my head harder than I thought," she muttered, making her way to the stallion.

Chapter Three

Something about the lad bothered Colin. He was too fair of face, for one, and he was too puny to have unhorsed him so easily. And yet he'd done just that.

He growled softly as he tossed Ian the reins. "I'll wager the lad can hardly sit a horse," he grumbled.

"Now is not the best of times to taunt him, my friend," Ian said roughly, his voice showing signs of his pain. "You are not the one depending upon his horsemanship."

"The name is Tuck, and I know how to ride," the lad said snippily.

Colin snorted at his continued bluster. More mouth than muscle, yet he had fought alongside them and aided Ian. But did he have something to do with the ambush?

He watched the boy slip his foot into the stirrup and toss his leg over the horse. The lad's jaw clenched as he let out a silent hiss of air. He'd taken his share of blows during that last fight before winning. Colin admired his bravery against bigger and stronger opponents, and his determination to put Ian's welfare before his own. This was no whining stripling, but he refused to trust the lad as of yet.

Satisfied with the boy's skill in the saddle, Colin mounted up. "Follow me." He kneed his horse into a steady gait toward home.

He'd been gone too long from Arreyder Castle, but his friend had asked him to accompany him to visit his sister who had recently made him an uncle. A prouder peacock could not be found, he was certain.

Several months passed in Caroline's home while Ian strutted around the estate. When a missive arrived from Colin's father, he realized he'd stayed away too long. His duty lay before him at the end of the muddy road, at Arreyder Castle.

It was time to marry.

Regardless of Ian's remarks, he would do what was expected, what he'd planned for most of his life. He would not leave his future and the future of his clan to chance. Not as his friend did.

Ian Southernland had no direction in his life. As a younger son of an English gentleman, his father pressed him to seek a profession. Ian, however, always managed to sabotage his situation and was repeatedly sent back to his father. Now, a man who possessed an odd smattering of schooling from law to religion, he rode alongside Colin because he simply had nothing better to do.

Their unlikely pairing after a rather raucous brawl in a pub where they'd found themselves on the same side had lasted for almost three years. Together they'd found themselves in more than a scrape or two, and genuinely enjoyed one another's company. But today, for the first time in their acquaintance, Colin worried over his friend. A sensation long forgotten and one he did not care for in the least.

He slowed his horse until he rode side by side with Ian and the lad. "How do you, mon?"

His friend smiled crookedly, sweat more pronounced upon his upper lip than before. "I have had better days." He swayed dangerously, but the stripling caught him tight to his chest.

Ian sucked in a sharp breath and straightened.

"Mind you take care, lad," Colin said, leveling his gaze on the boy. No one would harm his kith or kin. Not even a mouthy bairn with less fuzz on his cheeks than sense in his head.

Tuck returned his cold stare. "Let's pick up the pace, Sasquatch."

With a grumble, he moved ahead once more, and Tuck fell in behind.

"You okay?" she asked the Englishman.

"I believe I shall survive, *lad*."

She sniffed at his tone. So, Prince Charming had finally figured out she wasn't a he. She'd seen the confusion on his face as he studied her closely earlier, yet he refused to believe his own eyes. It figured it would take feeling her breasts slammed into his back to do it.

"Tell me. Where did you learn to fight?" he asked.

"The army mostly."

He jerked his head around, his face twisted with confusion.

She rolled her eyes at his obvious dislike of women in service and promptly changed the subject. "So, if you're not a prince, then who are you supposed to be?" she asked, curious as to whom he was portraying. She figured it was better than getting into one of those men versus women arguments or sitting here grinding her teeth about the brawny giant she couldn't seem to stop thinking about.

He smiled, erasing the puzzled expression from his face. "Now that is a rather daunting question, as it would depend on to whom you posed the query."

"Uh-huh. What's your name, hotshot?"

He chuckled softly and attempted to hide his wince of pain. She tightened her grip on him, cursing herself for wasting his strength with conversation.

"I rather like the sound of that," he said taking a shallow breath. "Hotshot. Yes, I like it very well, but I doubt 'twas intended in a kind light."

"Name," she said with a shake of her head. How could he stay in character when he was bleeding all over his costume?

"Ian Southernland, at your service," he said with a mock bow followed by a somewhat deeper steadying breath. "And the one you so guilelessly called Sasquatch, another name I am certain 'twas not meant to be complimentary, is Colin MacLean."

It took her a second to connect the name to Arreyder Castle, the clan who built and lived at the massive fortress. But she could swear there had been no reenactments planned. She would've remembered that all too clearly. It would've drawn huge crowds and made her job ten times more difficult.

But you failed anyway.

Ian carefully glanced back over his shoulder for several seconds, distracting her from the nagging voice.

"Amazing," he said with a hoarse whisper, then turned back around. "A female who can fight."

"Yeah, well, you'll get over it. Now, stop talking and save your strength."

Jo Barrett

He chuckled roughly. "I can hardly wait to see Colin's face when he learns you're a woman. 'Twill be the most fun I've had in a great while."

She clamped her teeth together. "Yeah. A real barrel of laughs."

"What is your true name?"

She sighed, and said, "Amelia Tucker. But I prefer Tuck."

"Amelia. A beautiful name." He glanced over his shoulder again. "For a beautiful woman."

She nearly choked on her snort of laughter. "Listen, buddy, you can cut the crap. Sucking up to me won't get you anything. I know who I am, what I am, and I don't need some nutcase Prince Charming trying to butter me up."

"Your speech is quite unusual. Where do you hail from, my lady?"

"Tuck. Not my lady, and I hail from the U.S. Now, quit talking."

"I am not familiar with this U—S. Is it far?"

She shook her head with a low chuckle. "You're too much. Don't you ever get tired of this reenactment stuff?"

"If you are referring to our altercation, nay, I do not particularly care to relive the event, but one never knows what sort of cutthroats one will meet when traveling."

"Oh, I give up," she muttered.

He finally fell silent, and she knew he was struggling against the pain. She hoped he wouldn't pass out on her. He wasn't as big as Sasquatch, but big enough to make things difficult. If he conked out, she'd have a rough time keeping him in the saddle.

MacLean slowed his horse until they rode side by side once again. She watched him look Ian over carefully. He never said a word, but she could sense the worry he skillfully hid.

"Is it much farther?" she asked.

They hadn't seen a single sign of civilization since they started down the road. It was eerie. She knew she couldn't be that far from Raghnall Castle, but couldn't understand why she'd seen nothing familiar. Not even a road sign.

MacLean turned his amber eyes on her, suspicion

written along the rough lines of his face. "Around the next bend," he said, pointing ahead of them.

She nodded. Good, much more riding and Ian was sure to fall out completely.

They rounded the corner and the trees lining the road ended abruptly. Her gaze followed the muddy rut up the hill to a fortress.

"What the—" The air rushed from her lungs.

Arreyder Castle stood before her like a sentinel overlooking the sound. But where was the gift shop, the parking lot, the tourists?

People dressed in plaid and hard worn wool, many barefoot, gathered at the edge of the road, their curious eyes examining them as they made their way up the hill. Small cottages dotted the hill, and stood in the shadow of the massive fortress.

No, this had to be a different castle. There were several on the island, but she'd understood that all except Arreyder and Raghnall were in ruins. Maybe she was on another island. Yes, that had to be it.

She called after the Scot. "Hey, MacLean." Pulling Ian's horse up closer to his, she didn't miss the scowl he shot her. "Where are we?"

He cocked his head, his brow furrowed. "You mean tae say you dinnae ken what's before your eyes?" With a grunt, he looked back to the road, muttering insults beneath his breath.

She pulled the horse to a stop, frowning at his back.

Ian's head bobbed slightly. "We are at Arreyder Castle," he said. "The home of the clan MacLean, and I hope to God, a soft bed for my weary bones."

Her mouth slid open as her eyes widened. "But that can't be. It isn't—it doesn't look—no, no, no. Something is very wrong here. You two are just jerking my chain, right?"

He slumped over, distracting her from the mass of confusion in her head. Regardless of how determined these two were in keeping up this silly game, the man had a hole in his shoulder. That much was very real.

Gripping him tighter, she nudged the horse onward and followed MacLean through a large arched gate into the bailey. It couldn't be the same gate she'd walked through with Jenny several hours before. It just couldn't be.

Her eyes darted from left to right, taking in everything, and finding more and more evidence to the contrary. A sickening tingle snaked down her spine.

"This isn't happening. This isn't real. I must have hit my head really hard on that fountain. I'm probably unconscious and in a hospital somewhere," she muttered.

She squirmed slightly in the saddle, her wet jeans chaffing her legs. A very real sensation. Either she'd missed the bedpan or she was lying in a fountain half dead and delirious. It was the only logical explanation.

MacLean barked orders, nearly jarring her from her horse. People scattered and men came and took Ian from her tight hold. All Tuck could do was stare.

An older woman wrapped in a woolen shawl bustled out of the keep. "Colin, 'tis good tae have you home." Reaching up, she cradled his rough face in her hands and pecked him on the cheek.

"'Tis good tae be home, Elspeth, but Ian is wounded. We need tae tend him quickly."

"Ach, the poor lad. Take him tae his bed and be quick about it," she said, waving at the men. She spun to follow them and paused. Her eyes surveyed Tuck curiously.

MacLean's eyes turned to her as well, and Tuck shivered. For the first time since she was a kid, she felt real fear. This was all too genuine to be a delusion. She felt the cold of the wind biting her cheeks, the smell of leather and horses teasing her nose, and the unintelligible chatter of Gaelic mixed with English from the people around her echoed in her ears. And there was blood, Ian's blood. She knew the smell, the feel, the taste all too well. No one could imagine such accuracy.

"Who is this then?" the woman asked.

MacLean marched over to the stallion, snagged Tuck by the arm, and jerked her to the ground. She managed to land on her feet—barely—her body semi-numb with shock.

"'Tis a lad with less brains than a newborn babe." He yanked her up to his face. "You will help Elspeth tend Ian's wound since you seem tae have the skill, but I'll be watching you."

Elspeth's fine brows rose, her lips pursed. "Lad, is it?"

Snapping her scattered thoughts in line, Tuck tore her gaze from the lion's eyes and looked at the woman. "Take me to Ian."

Whatever was going on, the man needed a doctor, and as it looked, she was as good as he was going to get. Whether she was delirious and lying in a hospital bed or caught up in some lunatic reenactment party, she couldn't take a chance. She wouldn't risk a man's life in an imaginary world anymore than she would in a real one.

****

Colin grumbled as he followed the strangely dressed boy and Elspeth. The lad was an undetermined, unpredictable part of a puzzle, and he sorely disliked puzzles.

He entered Ian's bedchamber, the only home his friend had known these last years, just as Maighread finished removing his doublet and the remains of his shirt.

"That's fine, I'll take over," the lad said, and elbowed his way between her and Ian.

His cousin huffed, her eyes narrowing. "And who are you tae be ordering me about?"

Colin observed closely, curious to see how the boy would deal with Maighread. His cousin may be a bonny lass on the outside, but he knew there was more to her than she let the world see, having known her since she was a child.

Never taking his eyes from Ian's shoulder, the lad said, "Look, sister, I don't have time to play nice. Now, move."

"Sister? I'm not your sister, you oaf!" Although smaller than the boy, Maighread lifted her hand to cuff him smartly on the ear, but the lad snatched her wrist out of the air and shoved it away with lightening speed.

Maighread teetered on her feet, her mouth agape.

Colin's cheek ticked, urging his grim lips to smile at his cousin's sudden loss of words. Not a sight he could ever recall having seen before, but he refrained from grinning. The lad may be quick, and he grudgingly admitted that he was agile, but he could not be trusted.

33

"Would someone get her out of here?" the boy grumbled with a muttered curse.

Maighread's fury grew, and Colin feared he would have to step in. But Elspeth quickly took the matter in hand.

"Maighread is our healer," she softly explained. "She knows what needs tae be done."

The lad straightened, planting his bloodstained fists on his hips. "Look, I'm sure she's real good at home remedies and stuff, but this isn't a simple scratch."

"Not to worry, Elspeth. Tuck has many unusual talents," Ian said, a wry grin on his face.

The boy's eyes narrowed at his friend, but Ian said nothing more.

Elspeth glanced back over her shoulder to Colin, and he gave her a nod.

"'Tis all right, lass," Elspeth said to Maighread. "You go and see tae your other duties. I'll tend tae Ian."

Maighread spun around with a huff, a sharp frown on her face that vanished the moment she laid eyes on Colin.

He held back his groan. When would the woman leave well enough alone?

"Colin, I've missed you terribly," she cooed, latching her bony arms around his neck. Her raven hair caught in his beard as she burrowed her face into his shirt.

He heard a snort from the other side of the room and locked eyes with the lad. "Dinnae you have something tae tend tae, you dolt?"

The boy turned back to Ian, a sour smirk on his face.

Prying his cousin loose, he said, "Do as Elspeth tells you, lass."

"But Colin—"

"Go," he said firmly, and she scurried out of the room.

Crossing his arms over his chest, he watched the lad remove the last of the bandages.

Elspeth examined Ian's shoulder with a tsking sound. "A jealous husband, no doubt, finally caught up with you, you rogue."

Ian chuckled and winced. "Now, Elspeth, my sweet, why would I tarry with another woman when the most beautiful one is here." He took her hand and kissed it soundly.

"Ach, even bloodying up my good linens, you still have a need tae tease me."

"I need alcohol, and plenty of it, sutures and clean bandages," the lad rattled off.

"Alcohol?" Elspeth asked, shaking her head. "Sutures?"

The boy looked up at her, his face grim. "Oh, uh—whiskey and, um, needle and thread. They'll have to do."

Colin barked out into the hall for the supplies and feet scurried bringing a scowl to his face. Maighread was likely hovering about waiting for him. The woman would never leave him be. She dogged his steps day and night with her wooing nonsense. Surely she must realize his father intended him to marry Aileen MacKenzie. There'd been a verbal agreement between the clans since he was a lad.

He stroked his new beard with the thought. As soon as he was certain Ian was well taken care of, he would seek out his father. If he was to marry Aileen, then why had her kinsmen attacked him? Or had the lad been their real target?

Within moments Fiona, one of the kitchen maids, appeared with the drink and other items. The boy snatched the bottle from the young girl's hand, and to Colin's surprise, poured it directly into Ian's wound.

Ian bolted up in the bed with a vivid curse. "For the love of God, are you trying to kill me?"

"Stop being such a baby," the boy said, pressing his forearm against Ian's chest to hold him down as he continued his unusual torture.

Colin crossed the room in two strides and snatched the lad's wrist, tilting the bottle away from Ian's shoulder. "Have you gone daft?"

The young idiot glared hotly at him. "It has to be thoroughly cleaned. Now either let me go so I can sew him up or you can do it yourself."

He clenched his teeth, at a loss as to whether or not he should risk leaving his friend in the hands of this stranger or toss him out on his arse.

"Let her finish, my friend," Ian said through clenched teeth, his eyes bright with pain. "I have the oddest notion she knows what she's doing."

"All 'tis well, Colin," Elspeth said, her hand gently patting on his arm.

He withheld a shudder, easily imagining his friend's pain by the grimace on his face and the tone of his voice, but he trusted Elspeth's intuition. If Ian was in any danger from this stranger, she would know.

Releasing the boy's hand, Ian's words cut through his anger. *She?* His pain must indeed be great to mistake the lad for a woman. Unless...

Colin stepped back, looking the stranger over carefully, noting the smattering of freckles, the pert nose, and deep green eyes. The face he'd done his best to ignore in the wood, as he'd found the lad uncomfortably attractive.

The devil take him. He was a she!

A faint bit of relief that he was his usual self settled over him with that truth. The unusual covering she wore hid her bosom well, or else he would've noticed from the beginning. Moving his gaze down her body, over firm long legs, he felt a stirring deep inside, but adroitly shoved it aside. He had no time for such things.

She gave what was left of the drink to Elspeth, then turned and threaded the needle. Holding her hands over a basin, she said, "Pour some of the whiskey over my hands, then give it to him, he'll need it."

Elspeth did as she was told without a word, then handed Ian the bottle.

Colin observed as the woman clad in dark blue trews gently shook the excess moisture from her hands, then spoke over her shoulder. "Drink up, Prince Charming. This is going to hurt a hell of a lot more than the whiskey."

Her voice, he noted, was firm and strong. Not the irritating twitter he was used to hearing from females like Maighread, with the exception of when his cousin was stewing over something. But not only was her tone different, the words this woman used were strange. Her speech vaguely similar but not exactly that of a Sassenach. He found himself struggling to understand much of what she said. He grumbled lowly as the puzzle twisted and turned.

Watching her slender fingers as they skillfully worked at Ian's torn flesh, he remembered those same hands snagging him by the belt and tossing him to the ground. His anger rose with every stitch. Luck had been more than kind to her that afternoon. She could've been killed by any one of those men.

Although, he thought while scratching at his scraggly beard, she had been quick and sure.

He dropped his hand to his arm, his scowl deepening. She was still a woman. One he intended to learn more about, like what was she doing on MacLean land dressed as a lad, and what connection did she have with the ambush? What purpose could she have for traveling in disguise?

Several minutes later, she dried her hands on a bit of cloth. "There, the worst is over. You'll survive."

Ian, now several shades paler than when he'd first been brought into the room and likely a bit light in the head from drink, grinned. "Thanks to your tender loving care, my dear."

She sniffed and shook her head. "You're a real piece of work."

Lifting her head, she looked at Elspeth, who had watched her with utter fascination.

"We need to keep the wound clean," Tuck said. "The bandages will need to be changed regularly. Never touch his shoulder without first washing your hands thoroughly with strong soap or whiskey. The last thing we need is for an infection to set in. Assuming there aren't any antibiotics lying around."

Elspeth shook her head slowly.

"No, I didn't think so," she said with a heavy sigh. "Then I've done all I can. Let's just hope it's enough."

"If you are quite finished, *woman*, I'll have a word with you," Colin snarled, growing more irritated by the minute. *An-ti-bi-ot-ics? What was she blathering about?*

Ian chuckled softly and took hold of her slender fingers. "Ah, so the truth comes to light. Do not be afraid, dear heart, he's harmless." He pressed his lips to her hand. "Most of the time," he added with a broad smile and a wink.

Her mouth opened a fraction then snapped shut as

she pulled free of his grasp. "Not much scares me."

Crossing her arms, she turned and met Colin's gaze openly. "And the name is Tuck. Not lad, not woman. Tuck. I suggest you use it, or you'll find yourself becoming better acquainted with the floor."

Clenching his jaw, he bit back the urge to throttle the shrew. He traversed the room in a breath and towered over her. "I'll call you whatever I like...*woman*." He hated the twitch of pleasure he got from the deep green fire glinting in her eyes. "Tell me what you have tae do with the MacKenzies."

Her brow furrowed, and he took note of the spark of confusion on her face before she expertly hid her thoughts behind a blank mask.

She dropped her fisted hands by her sides. "I don't have a clue, nor do I care who the MacKenzies are."

"They're the ones who ambushed us, you taupie!"

He ignored Elspeth's soft gasp, she would know the details soon enough. First, he had to deal with his present problem.

The irritating woman growled, her rosy lips parting over her perfect white teeth. "You listen to me, Sasquatch. I was minding my own business, when you followed me into the woods. And, I might add, if it weren't for me, you'd be dead right now!"

"You'll be wishing I were, if you dinnae watch your step."

"As amusing as this is, I think I would prefer it if you took it outside," Ian said with a soft chuckle.

Their heads snapped to the side, facing the bed.

"I have caused enough grief for poor Elspeth here," he continued, patting her hand. "I do not think she would appreciate any more blood being spilled on her fine linens."

"Ach, my, no." Elspeth glided to the woman's side and took her by the arm. Pulling her toward the door, she said, "Come with me, lass, and we'll get you cleaned up and proper."

The bothersome female shot Colin a look over her shoulder as Elspeth led her from the room.

Ian grinned like a buffoon as the door closed behind them. "She's amazing, is she not? Never in my life have I met a more captivating woman."

"You've gone daft from too much drink, mon. That—" he pointed toward the door, "—isna a woman. Not in the way you mean."

Ian grinned broadly. "I can see you like her as much as I. Well, my friend, you shall have to wait until I am fully recovered before we can fight over her."

"If you weren't already wounded, I'd be happy tae break your nose."

"Come now, Colin. Even you have to admit, she has an unusual fighting skill. And she did do you a great favor by pulling you off your horse," he said with a chuckle, then winced. "A sight I never dreamed I would see. Colin MacLean, unhorsed by a woman."

"'Tis not funny, and you'll not mention it again."

"Quite right, quite right, but 'twas so—" he gripped his side with laughter.

Colin spun on his heels and stormed from the room. "Damn Sassenach."

Chapter Four

Tuck followed the woman down the hallway, her thoughts jumping around in her head like Mexican jumping beans.

Where was she? How did she get here, wherever here was? And why did she feel the oddest urge to grab that stubborn, bull-headed Scot by the shirt and—no she wouldn't finish that thought. If she did it meant she'd finally gone over the edge. Sex had no place in this delusion. If it was a delusion. That explanation was rapidly losing its validity. Everything felt too real. All of her senses, and a few she rarely ever used, were operating at peak performance. She could smell, touch, taste, see, hear everything around her. And those unused senses, the ones her hormones ruled, were doing some very bizarre things. But she was determined to ignore them.

It was bad enough that Ian's teasing and that kiss to her hand had thrown her for a loop, but MacLean was a different story entirely. Parts of her body were tingling eagerly. It was enough to make her stomach twist into knots.

"Are you not well, lass?" Elspeth asked.

"Oh, um, sorry. I guess I'm just a little tired. It's been a rough day." A fatigued sigh escaped her lips. She hadn't felt this drained since boot camp.

"We'll get you cleaned up and in some proper clothes then you'll feel like yourself again."

"Proper clothes?" She glanced down at her jeans, not happy with what the woman was insinuating. But if she was being inducted into this reenactment thing then proper clothes meant a dress of some sort. Women didn't go around in jeans in the—whatever century she was supposedly in.

She took a deep breath, letting that thought settle into place, but her rational side didn't exactly buy it. Nor did it buy the only other explanation left to her.

Time travel.

She snorted. *Right. Time travel. I must be insane.*

She could not, would not accept that possibility. It wasn't tangible. It scored right up there with fairytales, wishing wells, and water sprites.

"Water sprites," she rasped, stumbling to a halt.

"What's that, lass?"

"Oh, nothing. Just thinking out loud." What had Jenny said about the fountain and a water sprite? There had to be a connection. Or was she really going off the deep end?

She rubbed at her temple where one doozy of a headache was forming. Her only option at this juncture was to go along with whatever came her way and adapt as she saw fit. The blood was real, and so was that finally honed steel MacLean had held at her throat.

Regardless of where or *when* she was, whether she was crazy or sane, she had a job to do, and the best way to accomplish that was to gather all the information she could. She needed to know whom she was dealing with before she could plan her next move.

"So, Elspeth. What's your relationship to MacLean?" she asked, making her tone as light as she could, which was just this side of a demand, but for Tuck it was as good as she got.

The woman's soft honey eyes glittered with warmth. "He's my nephew, the dear."

Dear? "Right. And he's been gone a while, I take it."

"Aye, nearly six months. I expect they'll have many an adventurous tale to tell." Elspeth shook her head with a small grin.

"I'll bet," Tuck muttered, holding back her snicker. Their stories would likely rival the ones her old army buddies used to tell. There'd be so much exaggeration, they couldn't be believed.

And his claymore was—this—big. She cleared the chuckle from her throat. Making stupid jokes wouldn't get her back where she belonged.

She glanced at her watch then discretely slipped it back under her sleeve. "What's the date? I lost track of time on my, uh, travels."

"'Tis the twentieth of March. Have you been

41

journeying long?"

"Yeah, you could say that. Um, and the year?"

Elspeth stopped in front of a chamber door and lifted a worried gaze to hers. "You poor lamb. I knew it the first moment I laid my eyes upon you. How long has it been since you've had a place tae call home?"

Tuck cleared her throat, surprised by the small lump that formed from the genuine sincerity glittering in the older woman's eyes. She'd never had a real home, not one worth remembering, anyway. "A while. The year, Elspeth. What is it?"

She shook her head with a soft frown. "'Tis fifteen hundred and eighty-four."

Tuck swallowed the panic rising in her throat as waves of dread roiled through her. If she were crazy, why would she choose that specific year? Had her subconscious plucked it out of one of the tour guides' talks? Even if it did, how would that explain the names of these people? Sure MacLean was an easy pick, but Elspeth, Maighread, and what about the Englishman, Ian Southernland? She knew she'd never heard them before. And her watch. If they were a reenactment group gone schizoid, then why did her watch have the supposedly correct date? All except the year? If she'd been knocked out, they could've tampered with watch. But why?

Unless...the computer chip couldn't calculate before 1900.

Elspeth grasped her gently by the arms. "Are you ill? Can I get you something? Ach, dear me. Should I call for Colin?"

Tuck nearly leapt from her arms. "No! I mean, no thanks. I'll be okay. I just hadn't realized that I'd been on the road for so long." *For more than four hundred years.*

No, it wasn't possible, and yet the evidence continued to pile around her.

"Aye, perhaps a wee rest will do you good," Elspeth said as she ushered her inside the chamber.

Tuck scanned the room, missing nothing. A heavy curtained bed with an embroidered cover faced a fireplace. Several pegs dotted one wall while the other walls were covered with woven rugs and small tapestries. A pair of chairs flanked the hearth and alongside one sat a small chest with Celtic inscriptions decorating the top.

Sunlight streamed in through the window, distorted by the glazed glass, and danced on the rough wooden floor. The planks creaked as she crossed the room to look outside while Elspeth started a small fire in the hearth.

The room faced inland, and she could see for miles. The landscape was not the same one she and Jenny had traveled. No paved road, no modern houses, no sign of anything familiar, but she was on the Isle of Mull. There was no mistaking the mountains in the distance.

Her eyes shot to the sky and the soft wispy clouds, not a single jet vapor trail. In the woods, a faint sign of spring touched the trees. It wasn't June. Her watch hadn't been tampered with.

Tuck's shoulders slumped with the weight of the facts before her. She was not where—when she belonged, and she had no idea how she got here.

The sound of hinges squeaking brought her attention back to Elspeth. The woman pulled a skirt of dark burgundy, a cream colored bodice, and a few other items from a large chest sitting in the far corner near the door.

"I think this will suit you. 'Twas my sister's." She eyed Tuck for a moment, then said, "Take off your waistcoat and let me have a look at you tae be sure."

Acting on the side of caution, Tuck turned her back. As quietly as possible, she unzipped her down vest, not wanting to frighten the woman.

Holding the vest over one arm, she faced Elspeth once again.

"Aye, 'twill suit you fine. You are about the same size. A big bonny lass, she was, just like you."

Tuck snorted softly. *Bonny?* She'd been called a lot of things in her life, but that definitely wasn't one of them.

Elspeth laid the items on the bed then moved to help her with the rest of her clothes.

"I think I can handle it," Tuck said. She may have managed to get out of her coat okay, but her blue jeans and sport bra were a different story. The way her luck was running, she'd send the woman running into the hills screaming she was a witch. Not a happy thought. Didn't they burn witches in the sixteenth century?

Elspeth's hands lingered on her cable knit sweater. "I

have never seen such a fine weave. Did you craft it yourself?"

"Yeah, right," she said with a derisive chuckle.

The older woman cocked her head, her dainty brows crinkled.

"I mean, no, I didn't. Look, I'm not exactly the kind of woman—what I mean is, where I'm from women don't weave and sew and stuff. Well, some do, but..." She sat on the edge of the bed and ran a hand over her face. "Look, I'm what you would call a soldier or warrior. I don't have any of the skills a normal woman would have." The truth left a bitter taste in her mouth.

Elspeth eased down on the bed beside her, the leather straps groaning with the added weight, and gently clasped her hand. She gazed into her eyes for several minutes, raising the hairs on the back of Tuck's neck. The few that weren't already snapped to attention.

A smile eased over the woman's round face. "Aye, you are different, and you have come from far away. With a bit of help from the fey folk, no doubt, but I dinnae ken what I'm seeing."

"Seeing?"

She laughed softly and patted her hand. "Dinnae fash yourself, lass. I have the gift of second sight. Not as strong as my sister's, but a gift nonetheless."

"Uh-huh." Tuck dropped her head into her chilled hands. She was losing it. She hadn't traveled back in time, and she wasn't sitting on an antique feather bed in sixteenth century Scotland talking about second sight and fey folk of all things.

"All will be well." Elspeth patted her shoulder as she rose. "I'll have some water sent up so you can wash, then we'll leave you tae rest." She paused at the door. "What is your name, lass?"

"Amelia Tucker."

"Amelia. Aye, 'tis a fine name."

Tuck spun around on the bed. "Elspeth?" The woman paused with one foot in the hallway. "Why doesn't my being different...frighten you?" she asked with a small shrug.

Elspeth smiled softly, oddly warming Tuck's insides. "I have seen many strange things in my years with both these eyes and with the sight. Things I dinnae understand. I have learned tae accept them since I canna change them. You have a good heart, Amelia, and a skill with healing. I have nothing tae fear from you, lass."

First Jenny and now Elspeth. Tuck shook her head, thoroughly bewildered. How had she managed to find two women years apart both in age and centuries, who were capable of accepting the unexplainable so easily? She almost envied them. They wouldn't feel like their heads were about to split open trying to deal with the possibility of time travel.

"Rest a bit, lamb. Then we'll have supper tae welcome our Colin home." With that, the woman slipped out, pulling the door closed behind her.

"Oh, joy. Dinner with the beast. I can hardly wait," she said to the grey stone walls as she yanked her knit hat off her head, ignoring the slight increase in her pulse.

Tuck eyed the pile of fabric lying beside her. Warily, she stuck out a finger and poked at the skirt and bodice.

"Fabulous. I'll look like a dinner theater refugee. One of the ugly stepsisters from Cinderella, no doubt."

The door squeaked open and the same young girl who'd brought the medical supplies—well, the whiskey—to Ian's room, eased inside.

"I brought you some water. 'Tis warm," she said, scurrying to the fireplace, her voice quivering. With shaking hands, she filled a basin sitting on a small bench. "I also brought soap and a soft bit of cloth."

She laid the items down, then lifted her head and smiled tremulously. "Will you be needin' anything else?"

Tuck shook her head, a little disappointed that she was obviously frightening the girl. "No. But thanks."

With a nod, the girl hurried to the door, her skirt swishing around her ankles.

"Wait a minute," she called.

The girl jerked to a halt and peered over her shoulder. "Aye?" she squeaked.

"What's your name?"

"F-Fiona."

Tuck attempted a smile, which probably resembled more of a grimace, but it was worth a shot. She couldn't stand the fact that this kid was terrified of her. "I don't

45

bite."

Fiona's eyes widened.

She ran a hand over her face. "Christ. I mean I won't hurt you or anything. Understand? I'm just a visitor, a traveler."

The girl nodded warily then rushed for the door. She chanced one last panic-filled glance at Tuck before pulling it closed.

"That went well," Tuck grumbled. What had she done to scare her so badly? Shaking off yet another mind numbing question, she stashed her phone and wallet in the little Celtic box by the chair then peeled out of her clothes.

She quickly untied her knife sheath from her calf and wrapped it in her sweater for the moment. Somehow she'd have to conceal it beneath that thing Elspeth had laid out for her. She was not going anywhere without her only weapon.

Moving closer to the fire, she slid out of her damp jeans and draped them over the back of the chair to dry then turned to the basin of water. She washed away the mud and grime, trying not to dwell on her situation.

Shivering, she rubbed the back of her panties while standing in front of the fire, hoping to dry them before wriggling into her new duds.

"Oh, the things we take for granted," she murmured.

****

With his mind on other matters, Colin nearly plowed Elspeth down. Mostly on how badly he wanted to strangle Ian. Fight over that she-devil? The man was daft, no doubt about it.

"Where did you put the shrew?" he demanded.

Her lips pursed as she splayed her hands on her ample hips. "I placed her in your mother's auld bedchamber, but I'll not have you upsetting her. She needs her rest. The poor lamb has had a bad time of it."

He growled deep and low. First his best friend sided with that female and now his aunt. That witch had turned a goodly portion of his life upside down in less than a day.

She had to go.

"Aye, and she's not done with it." He pushed past

Elspeth, ignoring her small huff of outrage.

"Colin MacLean, you'll be nice tae Amelia or you'll answer tae me," she called after him.

His steady gait faltered at the sound of the woman's name. The beauty of it didn't fit the harpy he knew, but he didn't let that deter him. He wanted her out of Arreyder Castle, off MacLean land, and as far away from him as possible. By sheer luck, she'd aided them that afternoon, but something deep down inside told him she would bring more trouble into his life than he cared to deal with.

Without a knock or word of warning, he threw open the chamber door and froze in his tracks.

She stood before the fire. Miles of creamy fern-tickled skin filled his eyes. Slowly, he lowered his gaze to the pebbled peaks of her breasts straining against the odd fabric, then down her firm stomach to the patch of cloth barely covering her woman's mound.

His mouth went dry at the sight of her unexpected beauty. He'd never seen a woman so firm of flesh and yet unbelievably feminine at the same time.

"Are your eyes full yet?" she snapped.

Colin jerked his attention to the heated green eyes glaring at him from beneath a wayward lock of red curls. At his continued silence, she cocked her head, barely brushing her shoulders with her unruly main.

His fingers, rough and callused, rubbed against one another, imagining the silkiness of her hair and the softness of her skin. His constricted throat prevented him from speaking. The only word his lips could form was Amelia, but he dare not put a voice to it. He knew if he should speak it, his control would slip. Something he could not allow to happen. Ever.

She stomped across the room to the bed and snatched up a frock. "Fine. Watch. I could care less. But close the door. I'm freezing my butt off."

Unable to tear his gaze away, his fingers flicked the door shut. As she turned, he noted several large bruises forming on her ribs and hip and felt a slight pang of concern before remembering that this was the woman who'd unhorsed him.

His growing desire was temporarily squelched,

although his curiosity was peaked. She had more than bruises and freckles on her body. A long jagged mark rose up over one pleasantly rounded hip, while another circular scar marred her left shoulder. But these were old wounds, long since healed, and now was not the time to question her about such things.

Cursing softly, she struggled with the bodice laces, bringing a slight grin to his lips. By the look and sound of her, one would think she'd never worn skirts, which upon closer inspection could very well be the case. She didn't act like a woman nor talk like a woman, but if he kept staring at all that skin, his body was sure to prove that she was very much a woman.

His moment of humor disappeared with that thought. He had no time to get involved with this or any other female. He stomped up beside her, snatched the bodice from her hands, and tossed it back to the bed.

Her body stiffened as she lifted those fiery emerald eyes to his. "Touch me and you're dead meat."

Gritting his teeth, he said, "I have no desire tae ravish you, you twit." No, he wanted much more. He wanted to savor every inch of her freckle-laced skin, to watch her faceted eyes spark with passion, and feel her long firm legs wrap around him and hold him tight while he slid into heaven.

He growled softly as he took the shift from the bed. He'd been too long without a woman. Being attracted to this witch was proof of that. Yet barmaids and the like were, of late, not to his liking. Nor did he wish to scatter the countryside with his bastards. He would have to wait until his wedding night to relieve his discomfort, a good plan, albeit a painful one.

"This goes on first." He shoved the undergarment toward her.

One reddish brow rose, as did her chin. "I knew that."

The corner of his mouth twitched with the desire to grin at her blatant lie. He admired the woman's spirit, but couldn't allow his feelings to soften toward her. He knew nothing about her, other than she stirred his blood and his ire to the point of insanity.

Her head popped free of the shift and his eyes latched on to her bouncing ringlets as the glow from the hearth set fire to her hair. How on earth had he mistaken her for a lad?

"Somehow I get the feeling you're not here to play valet," she said, crossing her arms firmly beneath her breasts.

He narrowed his eyes, tamping down the urge to throttle her. "You are not tae leave this room. There will be a guard posted at your door in case you've other ideas."

She shook her head slowly, her jaw tight. "You can't keep me prisoner. Not indefinitely."

He leaned closer, tempting his resolve not to wrap his fingers around her pretty little neck. But to strangle her or to simply feel the softness of her skin? "I have no intention tae, but I'll not have you roaming about the castle until I know who you are and why you're here."

"I already told you."

He snorted. "You were looking for a castle that doesna exist. Which means, you're either daft or lost. I have not ruled out the first, but you dinnae seem like the kind of lass tae lose her way."

She smirked. "Gee whiz. That almost sounded like a compliment. My heart's all a flutter."

He breathed deeply, reining in his anger. "You need tae curb your tongue, woman, before you find yourself in trouble."

"And who's going to make me? You?" She snickered softly. "I seem to remember taking you down without any trouble."

"Luck."

"Ha! You're just too proud and too stubborn to admit you were bested by a woman. Typical." She turned back to the bed and gathered up the skirt.

He snagged her arm and jerked her back around, his nose mere inches from hers. "You'll do as I say, and I'll not have any of your sass." He noted the well-toned muscle surrounding strong bone before she pulled free. And her scent, heaven save him from the soft womanly fragrance teasing his nose.

"Listen carefully, Sasquatch. I don't take orders from you or anybody else. Those days are long gone. If you don't like it, I'll be happy to leave."

"And go where? Back tae your henchmen in the

49

wood?"

He didn't know why he said it, he felt certain she wasn't in league with the MacKenzies, her confusion earlier said as much. But he couldn't seem to hold his tongue where she was concerned. Or perhaps he was trying to convince himself she was trustworthy because he wanted her. Either way, the woman was going to cause him nothing but grief.

With an exasperated huff, she threw up her arms and stomped toward the fire. "I did not have anything to do with that ambush!" Spinning around, she fisted her hands on her hips. "I saved your stubborn hide and that pretty-boy friend of yours. A fact you seem to have conveniently forgotten."

He used every ounce of his strength to ignore the silhouette of her shapely body clearly displayed through the shift from the firelight behind her.

"I forget nothing." But he sorely wished he could. Storming out the door, he heard her throw words at him no woman should know, much less use.

What in the name of Heaven had possessed him to confine her to the bedchamber? He wanted her out of his life and far away from Arreyder Castle. And yet, wasn't it wise to keep his enemy close where he could watch them?

Raking his fingers through his hair at his vacillation, he barked down the stairs for one of his men and gave him explicit instructions to guard their guest.

He would discover her real reason for being there soon enough. She was hiding something, she had to be. Why else would she travel dressed as a man? Then again, perhaps she was running from someone. The MacKenzies? Nay, it didn't make sense. Her confusion when he'd mentioned them was too clear, or else she was a fine performer.

Disgusted with the mounting questions he could not answer, he turned down the corridor toward his father's quarters. He needed to find out what had transpired since his absence. The puzzle of the she-devil would have to wait.

"Pretty-boy," he snorted softly, her words coming back to nag him. All women found Ian handsome, especially in comparison to his own rough visage. It wasn't anything new, but it rankled just the same.

Chapter Five

Tuck stared at the door MacLean had slammed in his wake. "Ogre," she grumbled, having used up all her more colorful names to call him.

Yanking the skirt up over her hips, she grimaced as she brushed her fresh bruises with her knuckles. What she wouldn't give for a hot soak and a jumbo size bottle of painkillers.

She belted the skirt into place then struggled into the bodice. Although she loosely tied the laces, the stupid thing cut her air off. Apparently Elspeth's sister was a bit on the small size in the chest.

Realizing she'd have to lose the sport bra for the extra room, Tuck stripped down to nothing but her panties. She stretched and shivered from the chill still lingering in the air, then dressed in a hurry, keeping an eye on the door. She wasn't sure if her jailer would burst in again.

The way he'd stared at her, cataloged every inch of skin, warmed her in ways she'd never dreamed of before. Never had she reacted so strongly to a man, but then few men had ever bothered to look at her twice.

She'd been on a few dates over the years, usually army acquaintances, but she'd never given them much thought. They were good company, they had a lot in common, but she never let things end up in bed.

As if, she thought with a small snort. They weren't really interested in getting into her pants. She was more like one of the guys to them, a buddy, a pal. But even if they did have sex on the brain, she would never ever let a man take control of her that way. She'd won her freedom, and she refused to hand it over to anyone.

Convincing herself that her sexual reaction to the ogre had been a fluke and wouldn't happen again, she finished dressing. Her ensemble complete, Tuck glanced down at her chest, amazed to see so much cleavage.

"Wonderful. An antique push-up bra."

She gazed longingly at her comfortable sport bra draped over the chair, but figured breathing placed higher than general comfort, and resigned herself to her new rig. For the moment. She was not traipsing around in a dress for longer than her clothes took to dry, regardless of what the locals thought.

She quickly tied her knife sheath high on her thigh then patted down the skirt. Not bad, but if she bumped into someone they'd feel it, so she'd have to be extra careful.

Lifting the tartan from the foot of the bed, she draped it over her shoulders as she'd seen Elspeth do. At least she'd be warm, with the exception of her nether draft.

She looked down at her hiking boots sticking out from beneath the skirt with a smirk. They didn't exactly go with the outfit, but there she drew the line. Quaint little leather slippers in place of her boots and thick wool socks were not going to keep her feet warm.

How the villagers she'd seen with no shoes at all could stand the cold was a mystery, but then she'd been in some pretty uncomfortable situations herself over the years. A person could get used to a lot when they didn't have a choice.

Trudging through mud and muck, over desert and through jungles, she'd had more than her fair share of roughing it. This was a tea party compared to some of the places she'd been. With the exception of the date.

Tuck shook her head at the thought. It just didn't make sense, and yet that ambush was like nothing she'd ever encountered. Those men weren't the kidnappers, and the landscape wasn't what it should be. Nothing was. But time travel?

Even if it was possible, why would she travel back to 1584? What was so special about that year? And why her? Was someone guiding this kooky train she was on or had she fallen down a wet version of a rabbit hole?

Letting go of questions she couldn't answer, she focused on the facts. She had to find a way back to where she belonged, and to do that she had to escape. But go where? That stupid fountain at Raghnall Castle was her only lead. But assuming she was actually in 1584, the

Jo Barrett

darn thing didn't even exist yet. Her only option was to inspect the small field where this nightmare had started.

Moving to the door, she gently eased it open and came face-to-face with a guard. He looked at her blankly then casually crossed his arms as he took a firm stance in the doorway.

Tuck sized him up and, although he was a big one, she knew she could take him out. However, she needed to do a little recon before she made her move, and decided it wouldn't be wise to jump the gun on her escape. The castle didn't appear to be laid out exactly as it had been when she toured it with Jenny, and she was currently in the section that had been off limits. She didn't need to come up on a dead end with the ogre of the hill in pursuit. A hike through the woods in a dress didn't sound very appealing either.

With a slight nod, she closed the door, then wandered over to the window and waited. Looking out over the landscape, her thoughts went back to the moments before she landed in the fountain. She'd listened to Jenny tell her fairy story then they'd tossed pennies into the fountain.

"I couldn't have wished myself here," she mumbled. No, that would be too easy, and her gut kept telling her it had something to do with that fairy story.

"Oh, if only I'd paid closer attention." But then how could she have known that Jenny's lectures would ever be of any help to her? Being tossed back in time wasn't exactly an every day occurrence.

Or was it? Had others traveled through the centuries? Was she one of a select few? If so, why her and why now? She didn't like the idea that there was an unknown agenda somewhere with her name at the top of the page.

Leaning against the windowsill, she let out an exasperated breath and plopped her chin in her hand. A curl dangled in front of her eyes and she blew at it, but it only bounced back into place.

Taking her frustrations out on her hair, she ruthlessly shoved it back, trying to put it in some sort of order. But no such luck. With her cap still damp from the rinsing she'd given it, and without a hair band to pull her

54

curls back into a stubby pigtail, she was stuck wearing it down.

She hated wearing it down, and the damp air only made it curl more. She felt like Shirley Temple. One more thing to irritate her already frazzled nerves.

Crossing the room to where her jacket hung on a peg, Tuck pulled out several Gummy Bears. At least they'd survived the trip. It would've been hell to go through this wacko ride without her addiction. Once she checked on Ian, she'd do some of her Tai Chi exercises as well. She had to steady herself before she made her next move. Holding on to her sanity was a must, if she wanted to get back to her time. Her job, her future, and Jenny's life were at stake.

****

Colin entered his father's chamber, bewildered to find Maighread at his side by the fire urging him to sip some concoction she no doubt had brewed. Douglas's gaunt face and weathered features struck him hard. This was not the man full of life and vigor Colin had left behind months before.

"What ails you, Da?" he said, taking the chair opposite him before the hearth.

Glazed eyes looked up from the flames. "Colin? Is that you, lad?"

"Aye. I have returned."

"Returned, you say? Were you gone? I canna seem tae remember." He rubbed his forehead where his brow creased deeply.

"You must drink," Maighread said, holding the tankard to his father's lips.

He shook his head. "Leave me be, woman." He shoved feebly at the brew.

"He's terribly ill, Colin. You must make him drink," Maighread said.

"You need tae do as the lass tells you, Da, if you are tae get well."

The old man continued to rub his wrinkled brow. "I must think, but I canna. And I'm so tired."

"Come lie down a bit," Maighread said as she helped him to his feet. "You must rest."

He felt at a loss as to what to do. Seeing his father ill

55

was a new and unwelcome experience. He quickly stood and helped his da into bed, closely watching his face, the old man's confusion evident by his twisted features.

"What ails him?" he asked Maighread.

She adjusted the coverlet and lifted her dark eyes to his. "Did you not get word of what's happened then?"

He shook his head as he watched his father's eyes glazing over as her brew performed its magic.

"I am sorry, dear. I thought you knew," Elspeth said softly as she entered the room. She crossed to the bed and rested her small hand gently on his father's brow. "We sent word, hoping 'twould find you before you returned home."

"Nay, I received word tae come home, but not because of this."

Taking Colin's arm, Elspeth pulled him back to the chair by the hearth and urged him to sit. His body fell onto the seat with a weariness he'd never known.

His eyes on the flames, he asked, "How long has he been like this?"

"For nearly a fortnight," Elspeth said. "His mind seems tae come and go. We canna do more than keep him comfortable." She took a deep breath and met his gaze. "There was a battle in the middle of the night with the MacKenzies. Reiving, they were, and your father was determined tae put a stop tae it."

He shook his head slightly. "We have always lived peacefully with the MacKenzies."

"Aye, and your father tried tae talk tae them, but auld MacKenzie wouldna meet with him. We still dinnae know why they began raiding the outlying farms. They have had good years and are not in need. It makes no sense."

She lifted her watery eyes to the bed. "'Twas the blow tae the head that left him this way. Fergus brought him back that night, his own wounds grave. He—he didna survive."

Colin's gut clenched unexpectedly. He hadn't noticed Fergus' absence when he'd arrived, he'd been too distracted by Ian's wound and the woman. The thought of never seeing his father's old friend again, never hearing his rumbling laughter, or receiving a cuff on the ear, although he stood taller than his mentor, sliced at his heart.

He clenched his fists where they lay on the arms of the chair. Grieving would do him no service.

"Colin?" his father muttered.

Elspeth rose and went to his side. She waved Maighread out of the room then stroked his wrinkled brow. "Rest, Douglas."

Colin stepped to the bed and leaned closer. "I am here, Da."

He turned his hazy eyes to Colin's. "Where's your mother, lad? Why have I not seen her?"

Elspeth silently withdrew her hand from his forehead.

Closing his eyes for a moment, Colin let out a deep breath. His mother had been dead since he was barely more than a babe, her face often no more than a shadow on his memory. Looking down at his father now, he could see her lying in another bed, her skin ashen, her breast still.

"No tears, lad. No good will come from a bunch of weepin'. 'Tis womanly," his father had said. "You have tae be strong." He squeezed Colin's shoulder firmly. "You'll be the MacLean one day. 'Twould be a sign of weakness tae let the men see your tears."

He swallowed the small lump in his throat from the memory and straightened. "She'll be along soon, Da," he said lowly.

The old man nodded vaguely and closed his eyes.

He watched his chest rise and fall with each shallow breath. His father was dying.

"The clan needs you, Colin," Elspeth said, wringing her hands. "I know 'tis not proper tae take your father's place before he's gone," she choked on the words, her fist flying to her mouth. She took a small breath and lowered her hand. "Something must be done about the MacKenzies. Some of our people have been hurt, some killed. Families have lost their homes."

His jaw ached from its repeated clenching, as did his head. Soon he would be the MacLean, but he hadn't expected it to fall on his shoulders so quickly and so heavily.

"The MacKenzies ambushed us in the wood. On MacLean land," he said, the taste of vengeance tempting his tongue.

"Aye, so you said earlier."

"I didna know the men, but they wore the crest of the MacKenzies on their bonnets."

She clasped her hands tightly beneath her breasts. "I didna foresee any of this. What are you going tae do?"

His gaze snapped to hers. "End it."

Spinning on his heels, he left his father's chamber in search of a quiet place to think. Women clad in trews, Ian's shoulder wound, his father's pale fragile body barely holding on to life, all of it had to be pressed from his mind. Getting to the bottom of the unrest between the clans was where his energy needed to go.

And what of his impending marriage? Was he to wed Aileen MacKenzie or not? Had something happened to negate the verbal contract between the clans? If only his father were well enough to tell him.

Without thinking, his feet carried him to the battlements. He stood for more than an hour, embracing the bite of the wind. His callused hands idly rubbed the stone wall as he watched the churning waters of the loch.

If auld MacKenzie would not meet with his father then there was little left for him to do except train the men, make them stronger, better warriors. Then they would strike back at those who dared to harm his kith and kin.

Chapter Six

Tuck's door opened and in waltzed the woman who'd practically drooled over MacLean when they'd put Ian to bed. Her long dark hair had been brushed out carefully since she'd seen her last. Probably because her boyfriend was back.

"I was sent tae fetch you tae supper," she said, her tone dripping with contempt.

This woman, Maighread, Elspeth had called her, wasn't afraid of her in the least. Interesting, considering the way Fiona had run off. But then this one seemed to be made of sterner stuff.

Tuck crossed the room, slightly uncomfortable with the brush of the skirt against her bare legs. But it was that or go naked. "First, I want to check on Ian."

Maighread sniffed then spun around. Her pride was obviously bruised in regards to Ian. Well, tough cookies. She wasn't about to let the local witchdoctor kill the man with her homegrown remedies.

She followed Maighread out into the corridor, noting the guard falling in step behind them. They walked briskly down the hall to the chamber where Ian lay.

Maighread stood aside while Tuck nudged past her and pushed open the door. Crossing to the bed, her patient lifted heavy lids and gazed at her through an alcohol-induced haze.

"Ah, my sweet Amelia. You're lovelier than ever," he said with a distinctive slur.

"And you're loaded to the gills." She pressed her hand to his forehead, then to his cheeks, trying to determine if he had a fever. As best she could tell, he was all right for the moment, other than being soused. She peeled back the edge of the covers and checked his shoulder, relieved to see the bleeding had stopped.

He smiled crookedly as he battled to keep his eyes open. "The tartan brings out the fire in your hair. I should have known you would be a redhead."

Tuck shook her head. "I feel like a fire engine."

His brows knitted together, then smoothed as he captured her hand while she readjusted his covers. "When I am healed, I shall bring you flowers, quote poetry, and court you well."

Ridiculously pleased with his silly flirting, she eased her hand from his. "Get some sleep, Romeo. You're going to need your strength to do all that."

"Ah, you refer to Shakespeare, the new playwright's work. A fitting name, but I think I prefer Hotshot," he said with a soft chuckle that faded as he fell asleep.

A faint smile touched her lips. For the first time in her life a man, a very handsome man, didn't look at her like she was some sort of freak. Or had two men looked at her that way?

She shook her head, setting the question aside. It didn't matter. She wasn't the least bit interested in getting involved, especially with a man who'd been dead for more than four hundred years.

Turning for the door, she paused and took a moment to look out the window. Thick vines of ivy clung to the side of the keep, well within reach.

"How convenient," she muttered softly. The drop was steep, but with a few lucky toeholds in the vines, she could make it without any trouble. Her plan of escape began to form as she left the room.

She followed her unhappy escort down the stairs toward the great hall. As her foot left the last step, Maighread clamped down hard on her arm. It took all her energy not to toss the woman on her ass. But Tuck didn't think her bear of a boyfriend would care for that idea. The last thing she wanted was to go another round with the hairy beast. She didn't need to have her quarters moved to the lovely dungeon she recalled from the tour she'd taken in her own time. She'd never be able to escape from there and find a way back to Jenny. Her job was her top priority, not putting some irritating witch on her rump.

"You can have Ian, but dinnae be thinking you can have Colin. He's mine, you ken?" Maighread said with a sneer.

"He's all yours, sister." Tuck slipped easily from her

grasp, wanting to laugh her head off. How could this bitchy but beautiful woman think she was competition?

The idea she was in an insane asylum was beginning to sound better and better as the day wore on, and was a lot easier to swallow than time travel. What with Elspeth and her second sight nonsense, Ian and his courting—although he had a good excuse, he was drunk—and now this. Honestly, to think she was competition for MacLean was too much. Men just didn't think of her that way.

The woman's dark eyes narrowed. "I dinnae trust you."

Tuck shrugged, resolved to deal with the crazies around her, considering she might very well be one of them. "Fine. No skin off my nose. Just lead the way to chow," she said with a jerk of her head.

As they crossed the large room, the buzzing of voices stopped and all eyes fell on her.

Elspeth tottered over to her. "Amelia, you're looking well. Did you have a good rest?"

"Yeah, I feel fine," she said, scanning the room. "And call me Tuck."

She couldn't figure out why everyone was staring at her. It couldn't be her shoes. Although they were unusual, the skirt hid them. Surely Elspeth hadn't been telling them a bunch of junk about her traveling with fairies and stuff.

"Come and set yourself down." Elspeth gently tugged on her arm.

Moving toward the table, Tuck whispered, "Why is everyone staring at me?" The men didn't seem to be afraid of her, merely uneasy, but from the women she sensed fear. She noticed Fiona, especially, refused to meet her gaze.

"'Tis likely because they have not seen such a bonny lass in a long time."

She shot Elspeth a look. "Ease up on the bonny bit. I'm not buying it. There's more going on here than a bunch of guys checking out the new girl."

She twittered softly. "You are a different one, I'll grant you. But you forget, they saw you ride in looking for all the world like a mon. 'Tis a bit of a shock, I imagine."

The tension in Tuck's shoulders eased. She had a

good point. Not only were these guys taking in the fact that she was a woman, and a big one, she hadn't resembled a female in the least when she'd arrived. At least not by their standards.

Of course she wasn't sure she did now, but the antique push-up bra was helping, and the skirt belted at her waist accentuated her hips. Still, she didn't make the grade in comparison to Maighread or any of the other women she saw buzzing about the room. Did they see her as competition too?

She snorted softly. Not likely. That whack on the head must have really done a number on her. The most logical explanation was the one she always faced.

She was *different*. A fact her father never let her forget.

Ignoring the pinch of an old pain, she took her measure of each of the dozen or so men, noting their size. For once in her life she wouldn't tower over everyone in the room. That, at least, was a good feeling.

"What took you so long?" MacLean barked.

Her gaze zeroed in on her host, seated at the head of a long table. The sight of his face cleanly shaven, put a catch in her step.

Her fluke reaction theory went right out the window. The man was more amazing than when she'd first seen him. The harsh angles of his face, the broad set of his shoulders, he was everything she'd imagined a true warrior would be. But he was also a man who was more stubborn and irritating than any she'd ever met before.

Maighread shot her an icy smile as she slinked up beside him. "I had tae look in on poor Ian."

The woman was waging a war she didn't know she'd already won. Even if Tuck wanted to fight her for MacLean, a thought that was as foreign to her as wearing pantyhose and high heels, she wouldn't have a clue how to go about it. That sort of battle was one she'd never been trained to fight.

Tuck nearly stumbled as she moved to her seat, unable to keep from looking at him. Why couldn't the man have been ordinary?

Colin had trouble keeping his eyes off her. Although he'd seen her in nearly nothing and had been deeply affected by her visage, dressed in skirts with her crimson curls framing her face, the top of her supple breasts mounding slightly above the bodice, she was remarkable. Traveling alone, she'd been safe dressed as a man. The sight of her now was a testament to that fact. He wondered if that was the only reason she did so, and why was she alone?

As she moved closer to the long table and took a place by Elspeth, he noted the silence thickening in the hall. He turned his gaze to his men and studied their faces. Some stunned to see that she was female, others merely curious, and a few interested in a way that was more than irritating.

"Eat, you bampots! 'Tis only a woman," he bellowed.

Everyone jerked their attention from his unwanted guest and went back to their meal. He glanced up and down the table, satisfied, until his gaze found her again.

One fine brow arched high on her forehead, a smirk on her rosy lips. He could see her desire to make some comment, a need to put him in his place, but thankfully she remained quiet. He did not wish to flail her hide in front of the whole clan, although she already deserved a beating. The woman had called him names no man would live to repeat if he tried.

"Colin, your cup. 'Tis nearly empty. Let me fetch you more drink," Maighread said, brushing her ample breasts against his shoulder as she reached for his tankard.

He wouldn't have taken note of his cousin's none-too-subtle attentions if it weren't for the she-devil sitting beside his aunt. A sturdy, well-toned, pleasantly rounded body with nimble reflexes and creamy skin lay beneath her borrowed skirts. The memory taunted him to distraction, but he could not allow his urges to rule him. Other, more pressing matters plagued him.

The clan's safety, the men's training...the press of his manhood against his sporran. He mentally groaned at his sorry state. Perhaps he should seek out some comfort from a willing lass after all.

Maighread filled his cup to the brim. He took a hefty gulp of ale to cool his ardor and idly noticed the spices she'd added. She was constantly putting herbs and such in everything he ate and drank. Hoping, he assumed, that

Jo Barrett

he would look pleasingly on her, but he didn't care for the flavoring nor her continued attempts to snare him.

Setting the drink aside, he picked at his meal. Obviously disgruntled that he hadn't commented on her fare, Maighread sidled closer to him on the bench, her large black eyes peered at him questioningly.

Heaving out a weighty sigh, he asked, "How does Ian?" He hoped for some bit of good news and something to pacify the lass. Much closer and she'd be in his bleedin' lap.

She shook her head, her long dark locks scraping against his arm. "Not well, I fear."

The news took him by surprise as did the pinch in his chest, but he kept his features calm. Though Ian was a good friend, he could not waste his time fretting like a woman over his condition. His energies had to remain focused on the clan and its needs.

"She knows not what she's about," Maighread said, cutting her eyes to the side toward the stranger. "Poor Ian will likely die from her hand. She is no healer, but a bad omen."

His brow furrowed deeply, adding to the ache in his head. Looking toward his unwanted guest, he watched her, weighing Maighread's words. Had he brought a viper into his midst? She had a keen talent for stirring his anger, of that there was no doubt, but he'd seen her with Ian. She seemed genuinely concerned over his health, and Elspeth had taken her to heart as well.

"She isna what she seems, Colin," Maighread said, her voice tight with suspicion.

"No woman is," he muttered.

His guest's red-capped head lifted, and she steadily returned his gaze. He saw strength, determination, and vast amounts of courage reflected in the emerald depths.

No, he did not believe she was a murderess, yet he could not trust her. The welfare of the clan was at stake.

"Dinnae worry over Ian. He is young and strong," he said, breaking the unusual connection with the woman. He shoved a bit of bread into his mouth. "Elspeth will watch over him. You tend tae the laird. He needs your skills now."

Maighread smiled up at him, and he withheld a

64

frustrated groan. She'd seen his comment in too fair a light, as it seemed to renew her pursuit.

"I will do all I can for your da, Colin. He is like my own." She rested her hand on his thigh beneath the table then ran her tongue over her full lips.

It was all he could do not to roll his eyes at her blatant invitation. Although beautiful, she had never held any appeal for him. He'd explained time and again that he would not wed her nor bed her, but she persisted.

He ruefully recalled the day she appeared on the steps of Arreyder Castle. A more bedraggled waif he'd never seen in his life. But there had always been something about her that ate at him. To this day he felt wary around the woman. More than likely due to the stories surrounding her mother.

His own father swore she was a witch, that she'd cast a spell over his cousin to lure him to her bed. The bed in which he'd died. Some say of an illness, other's say it was murder.

His father was more than pleased when Maighread informed him of the old crone's death. Yet, regardless of his dislike for her mother, he'd welcomed Maighread into his home, and the infernal woman had been Colin's shadow ever since.

Removing her cool fingers from his leg before she saw fit to explore beneath his kilt, he said, "I have things tae tend tae."

He left the hall. His determined stride took him to the room where his father lay quietly sleeping. Although he sorely missed his counsel, Colin refused to disturb his da's peace. Nor would the old man be able to aid him in his current state of mind.

Elspeth appeared at his side, a worried frown on her face. "You didna eat much. Are you not well, Colin?"

He turned and studied her closely. "Da didna summon me tae wed Aileen." It was a statement, not a question.

"Nay. 'Tis I who wrote the letter, bidding you tae come home and do your duty."

Nodding, he moved to the far window and peered up at the stars. "Another vision. I should have known." When his aunt saw something, she could not let it be. She felt duty bound to act, and often against his father's advice.

Colin looked over his shoulder. "Did Da know of your vision?"

She wrung her hands together, her gaze darting about the room. "Aye. He knew." Moving toward the hearth, she grasped the back of a chair firmly and lifted her head. "He didna want me tae summon you. He said I was a worrying auld woman."

"What did you see? I'll have all of it. Now." He didn't hold much trust in his aunt's visions, although they often came true. He preferred not to think that things were destined to be, were out of his control, but he would be a fool not to hear the tale.

Her shoulders sagged as she exhaled deeply. "I canna see it all clearly. A wedding, of that I'm sure, but I dinnae know for certain if 'tis Aileen. I only assumed 'twas her because of your father's wishes. But there is treachery and a fierce battle of which I canna see the outcome. 'Twas the reason Douglas ordered me not tae summon you. He feared for your life and the future of the clan."

She turned to gaze upon his father. "But you are our only hope now. 'Tis glad, I am, that I sent for you against his wishes."

"Aye. I'm glad as well."

Although he'd known what his future would hold most of his life, he always felt in command. He believed that his decisions and duty would lead him there, not some vision by a sweet old woman, and yet, she'd been in the right to summon him, for was likely he would have received her second missive too late.

"Goodnight, Aunt." He quietly left the room, feeling his future, the one he'd expected and planned for his entire life, dissolve amid the mist hanging over the loch.

Chapter Seven

Tuck looked in on Ian one last time after putting on her nearly dry clothes. She performed a quick check of his shoulder to be sure before she left. It looked no different, a relief considering the lack of medical supplies. He was strong, and he had Elspeth to take care of him. He would recover in time.

Opening the window as quietly as possible, she stuck her head out into the cold night air. A few guards walked the battlements, and at least one stood by the gate. It wouldn't be easy getting past them, but she had to try.

She glanced back at Ian, and whispered, "Thanks for everything, Romeo." And she meant that sincerely, although, when he woke up with a roaring hangover, courting her would be the furthest thing from his mind.

Climbing onto the windowsill, Tuck took a deep breath. She popped a Gummy into her mouth then lunged for the vine. The large glossy leaves helped to cover her descent and provided just the sort of toeholds she needed.

Close to the ground, she jumped, rolling as she hit to ease the impact. Using the shadows as cover, she made her way across the bailey then climbed the stairs to the outer wall, hoping she could scale the other side without killing herself.

Stealthily, she crept up behind one of the guards, knocked him out then dragged him back into the stairwell. She checked to make sure the area was clear before easing over the edge at what she hoped was the lowest point on the wall. She'd done her share of free climbing, but on much rougher surfaces. The blasted wall was nearly smooth.

"Where's a good vine when you really need it?" she whispered.

She eased over the edge and began her descent. Halfway down she lost her footing and fell a good ten feet.

Cursing beneath her breath, she checked herself for damage.

Thankfully, a sprained wrist seemed to be her only injury, but she could've broken her leg. Having a bone set was not fun. She'd had that delightful experience before, and she didn't want to imagine it without major painkillers. Well, at least her wrist wouldn't keep her from hiking to the clearing.

Jumping to her feet, she hurried toward the woods before the guard woke up or was found. She made her way east, avoiding the rutted road, with particular care. She didn't relish the idea of running into any MacKenzies. Not after her close call with a claymore. They wouldn't be so easy to beat by herself, especially with only one good hand. If only she had her gun, she'd feel like the odds were more in her favor.

"No sense wishing for the impossible. But then I'm living the impossible," she grumbled as she retrieved her knife from her calf. The cord-wrapped handle fit her palm perfectly, giving her a small sense of comfort.

Moving deeper into the woods, the cold crisp scent of the forest teased her nose, and she took a deep cleansing breath. It was so similar to the one in her time, she could barely tell the difference. Tuck had noticed the day she and Jenny stepped off the boat that the pollution and bustle of the modern world had barely touched the isle. At least some things hadn't changed over the centuries. She remembered how odd she'd felt when she'd drove off the ferry. How the island had called to her, touched her in some way. Strange, how it was even stronger here in this century.

Shaking off the weird thoughts, she trudged forward. All this time travel stuff was making her batty. She needed to get back to her own time and find Jenny. Imagining the island was some magical place calling to her like a siren was beyond absurd. She had a career in the twenty-first century, and it had nothing to do with quaint little Scottish isles or overbearing Highlanders with lion eyes that made her want to do things she'd never wanted to do before.

She scowled as she moved swiftly between the trees. The big overgrown ape was not on her agenda. "No way, no how," she grumbled.

Nearly an hour later, she sank to the ground against a large tree trunk, the weight of failure too heavy to bear any longer. She tilted her knife so that the compass caught the moonlight. With a disgusted nod, she rested it in her lap.

She'd found the right clearing, but nothing happened. She laid her head back against the trunk and considered devouring her entire stash of Gummy Bears. Her wrist ached, her ribs hurt, her fingertips burned from her climb on the wall, and she was bone tired.

What now? The field had been her best shot. She thought if she found the exact spot where she'd appeared there would be some sort of portal for her to step through. Then poof, she'd be zapped back to Jenny. It was the only idea she could come up with. Clicking her heels three times and wishing she were home didn't sound like much of a plan.

Her only other option was to recreate everything that had happened just before she found herself in the field. But having someone knock her upside the head didn't hold much appeal. She hurt in enough places as it was.

"Jenny said something about a stream," she whispered.

She shook her head at the lunacy of it all. What was she thinking? She wasn't a water sprite, for crying out loud. She was a soldier, lost in time, with little idea as to how to get home.

The night sounds grew around her as she rested, reminding her of other cold nights spent among the bushes, and hating every minute of it. And dang it, she was freezing her butt off. She fumed, cursing herself for taking the assignment in the first place. Somehow she'd let that loony scientist get to her. Jenny had seeded her mind with all sorts of fairytales, surely the catalyst to this insane trip.

A sardonic grin slipped over her mouth. Shame Jenny hadn't fallen into that stupid fountain with her. At least then she'd know whom her client needed protection from. Ian and his wooing. If that sixteenth century womanizer so much as grinned at Jenny, she'd have been down for the count.

A twig snapped, stiffening every muscle in her body. Thoughts of Jenny were quickly relegated to the back of her mind. She listened as blood pumped faster through her veins, but all was still. Her heart pounding in her chest was the only sound she heard. Even the creatures of the forest had fallen silent. Something wasn't right. Focusing on her surroundings, she cataloged every shadow.

There. Alongside a fallen tree, several yards away, was something that didn't belong. It was a man, of that she was certain from the outline of his body against the faint shafts of moonlight, but was he a MacLean or a MacKenzie? She waited for him to make a move, something to give away his reason for being there.

As the night sounds slowly returned, she took careful note of each one, mentally identifying their source. All belonged in the forest except for her and the unknown man.

Waiting, she nibbled a few Gummies until another man joined him. After a discussion she could barely hear nor understand, they started to move. Crouching down along the undergrowth, they headed west.

To investigate or not to investigate?

Elspeth's sweet smile popped into her head.

She had to follow them. MacLean may not want her help, but she wasn't going to stand by and do nothing.

A soft chuckle tickled her throat. Want her help? Hell, he didn't need her help. She remembered, all too well, the sight of him battling the ambushers. His skill with a claymore was far better than any she had ever seen. She wondered if he was as adept with a knife.

Expert swordsman or no, she couldn't risk any of the MacLean clan getting hurt if she could stop it. Her trip back to Jenny would have to wait, as if she had a choice since she was clueless as to how to get back in the first place.

Stretching out her legs, getting the blood circulating again, she paralleled the men's progress, her knife clutched in her hand. She needed to be ready for anything.

In the distance, she detected the soft squeak of leather and the faint jangle of harness. Almost imperceptible, but there nonetheless. Whoever these new players were, they were making their way through the woods as stealthily as possible on horseback.

Geez, doesn't anyone ever sleep at night in the sixteenth century?

The two men moved closer to the horses, hiding and shifting in the shadows, but never moving into an attack position. Only watching. She hadn't seen so much covert activity since the army, but who were the bad guys and who were the good guys?

She continued to parallel the two men as they moved closer to the others, wishing she knew which side they were on. Putting them out of action would be a snap, but she didn't dare take the risk. They may be on recon duty for MacLean, and as far as she was concerned, the MacLeans were the good guys.

Okay, so she had a soft spot for a few of them, like Elspeth and Ian, although he wasn't a real MacLean, but *not* Colin MacLean. No siree, she did not care a whit about that man.

Still, she couldn't let anything happen to him either. It was obvious how much Elspeth loved the big ape. The thought of his sweet aunt hurting because he'd gone and gotten himself killed or something simply wasn't acceptable.

Shaking her head, she couldn't believe how soft she'd gotten in so short a time. With a silent sigh, she crouched low in the brush as one of the horsemen dismounted and studied the ground.

A tracker. But whom was he tracking? Her or these two bozos lurking in the bushes beside her?

The man stood as the moon slipped from behind a bank of clouds. The dark strands brushing his shoulders appeared blue-black in the meager light.

She sucked in a silent breath. *Colin.*

Although nothing more than a silhouette, he did something to her, and she hated it.

He pointed in the direction of the clearing. "She's gone that way," he said softly, then mounted his horse.

He was looking for her. A small spurt of pleasure shot through her, but died quickly. Had she lost her mind? He wasn't tracking her for some romantic midnight rendezvous. The ogre was no doubt ticked because she'd escaped.

He and his posse started to move again. She glanced at the two men hidden in the shadows, then back to her former jailer.

Should she nab these two spies or should she just slip away and let him deal with them himself? If he'd managed to locate her trail so easily, and she knew darn well she'd done a good job of covering her tracks, it wouldn't be long before he realized he was being watched.

But he wouldn't be out here at all with two unknowns circling him, if I hadn't decided to take off in the first place.

She stifled a curse and carefully made her way to the nearest spy. Honor could really ruin a girl's day.

Slapping her hand over one man's mouth, she promptly knocked him out and laid him on the ground. She moved on to the other one and knocked him out as well, but he managed to make more noise than the other.

"Colin," one of his men whispered harshly, pointing to the small hedge disguising her presence.

Her luck was running thinner by the minute. She wouldn't be able to sneak off and leave the goodies behind now.

Eyeing them through the bush, she noted each of his men had a hand on a weapon. The way things were going for her lately, they'd pin her to a tree with their dirks first, then ask questions later.

With a defeated sigh, she silently sheathed her knife at her calf and stood up very slowly.

"Out for an evening stroll, fellas?"

MacLean vaulted down from his horse and stomped toward her. As he churned the earth beneath his heavy feet, the musty smell of the forest teased her nose. She kept the hedge between them, knowing full well from the look on his face that he was not a happy man.

"You've caused me enough grief for one day, woman. I suggest you hold your tongue."

She crossed her arms, hiding her wince at her injured wrist. "Ah, gee. And here I thought you'd be happy to see me."

His low growl rumbled through the tense night air,

sending waves of electricity coursing down her spine.

Not good. Not—good—at—all.

Colin's jaw clenched so tightly, he was certain he'd cracked one of his back teeth. He was too damn happy to see her alive and well with the moonlight kissing her creamy skin, and that galled him to no end.

He snagged her by the arm and jerked her through the bushes. She didn't bother to struggle, making him pause. Why did she risk her capture? Why did she not simply make off in another direction as they passed? She'd obviously circled back on him and he'd not known it.

Holding her against his chest, steeling himself against the pleasure it brought, he looked into her eyes nearly black in the dim light.

"Why did you not run?" he asked, his voice low but firm.

The corner of her mouth quirked up. "What, and miss all the fun?"

He lowered his face closer, barely stopping before he tasted her. "I want a real answer."

Her tongue darted out and dampened her lips, leaving them glistening. A sweet, quivering breath caressed his skin as she stared up at him, her expression warm. White-hot heat surged through his body and pooled in his groin.

He wanted her...and no other woman.

A low moan split the tense silence. For a moment he thought the sound had come from him, until he noticed his men rushing through the hedge behind him.

"There are two men here," Michael, the youngest of his guard, called.

She tilted up her chin, her look much cooler than before, but just as tempting. "I bring you a present and this is the thanks I get?"

Pulling his gaze away, he looked toward his men.

"They're not wearing any crest. I dinnae think they're MacKenzies," Michael said.

All eyes focused on the unsettling female at his side.

"What do you know of them?" he asked, jerking her slightly.

"They were following you, so I followed them. Once I realized who they were following, I decided you might want to talk to them."

"Aye." Abruptly releasing her, not willing to openly credit her for her sound reasoning, he spun on his heels and faced the captives. "Who are you, and what are you doing on MacLean land?"

"Our boat sank in the loch and we washed ashore. We were lookin' for a safe place tae camp for the night, when one of yer men attacked us."

"Oh, brother," Tuck muttered. "I got the jump on you, you moron."

Colin shot her a look.

She folded her arms and shrugged with a smirk so lissome, he nearly smiled. God, help him, he was beginning to actually like the woman!

He quickly turned back to the captives before he made a complete fool of himself. "I'll ask you again and I suggest you answer truthfully this time. Who are you, and what are you doing on MacLean land?"

Their gazes darted about, nervously taking in his well-armed men, but they said nothing more.

Colin motioned in the direction of the castle. "Take them back tae the keep. We'll finish this there." Looking at the female thorn in his side, he said, "You will ride with me."

Holding up her hand, she shook her head and backed away. "Oh, no, Sasquatch. You got your little present, now I'll be on my way."

She ducked to the side as quick as a hare, but he was quicker. He caught her by the collar of her odd coat before she could disappear into the shadows.

"You'll be going back tae the keep, whether you like it or no."

"I suggest you let me go, if you don't want to be embarrassed in front of your men," she said with a snarl.

Whirling her around, he pinned her to his chest, his arms wrapped tightly around her. "You can ride astride, or you can ride with your backside in the air, but you are going."

She looked beyond his shoulder at his men awaiting their next order. They hadn't been over pleased with this hunt. Someone had started a foolish rumor that she was a kelpie or some such nonsense. That she would bewitch them and take their souls. He'd never heard so much grumbling in his life, and these his best men. But they would cut her down, of that he had no doubt.

"Fine. But this isn't over," she hissed.

"I dinnae dare have a hope."

Thankful to see she would not fight him, unnecessarily risking her life, he dragged her to his horse. He placed one hand around her wrist and stilled at her sharp hiss of breath.

He gently slid his grip up her arm and examined her hand in the dim light. "What have you done to yourself, you daft woman?"

A small sense of relief eased some of the tension from his neck. He was afraid, for a brief moment, that he'd been the one to hurt her with his rough handling, but he'd not touched her wrist until now.

"Nothing you need to worry about." She moved to jerk free of his grasp, but instantly stiffened. With her eyes clamped shut, the grim press of her lips, there was no doubt she was in pain.

"Maighread will look at it once we return," he said.

"The hell she will," she said, her tone venomous.

"For the love of—! Bloody nettlesome shrew," he finished on a murmur.

"Overbearing ogre."

He clamped his hands around her waist and hoisted her onto his horse before their asinine relay could continue any further then seated himself behind her.

He set his teeth at the feel of her legs brushing against his, her backside nestled between his thighs. His arms wanted to close in around her and pull her back against his chest, while his lips wished to seek out the side of her neck and taste her fair skin. Luckily, she wore her knit cap, her hair carefully secured beneath, or else his nose would surely find its way into the curls, exploring their scent and texture.

Stifling his groan, he kneed his horse on. As they moved toward the castle, she settled against him, seemingly comfortable while he was aching in the worst possible way imaginable.

"You realize that if those men aren't MacKenzies then there's something fishy going on around here," she said.

"Fishy?" he asked, hiding, as best he could, his continued annoyance at her use of words he did not understand.

"You know, suspicious, underhanded, sneaky." She turned slightly, displaying her profile, her chin tilted high into the air. "Untoward," she added haughtily.

He refused to allow himself to smile at her playfulness, but the lass had a point, blast her hide. "'Tis none of your concern."

She twisted to look him in the eye. "Of all the—I hand you those two lowlifes on a silver platter and that's the thanks I get?"

"Cease your prattle, woman." He jerked her back around, unwilling to test his willpower with her lips so close to his. He'd gone daft, to be sure.

"The name is Tuck," she growled.

He swallowed hard against the sensual rumble. What sin had he committed to deserve such torment? He could not possibly want this irritating female!

"You just can't stand it that I escaped and caught those two."

"What I canna stand is a woman who doesna know her place."

"Oh, I know my place, all right. And it sure as hell isn't here."

He snapped his jaw shut, nearly taking off the tip of his tongue. He despised the truth in her words. She did not belong with him or to him. His life, his clan's future, did not include a woman who had more grit than some men he knew, and who constantly refused to behave as she ought. He still knew little to nothing about her. She could be in league with his enemies, although he wanted to believe otherwise.

Once they arrived at the castle, he pulled her down from his horse. Taking her by her uninjured hand, he firmly guided her to her room. He discounted how perfectly her long slender fingers wrapped around his. She was not to be his.

"Sit," he said, pointing to the bed.

She tilted her chin and propped her hand on her hip, blatantly disobeying him.

"By the saints, you're a stubborn woman."

He turned to the door and ordered one of his men to bring him some cloth to bind her with. Her eyes widened, and he quickly realized what she thought he intended to do. He almost smiled.

She slowly edged away. "If you think I'm going to let you tie me up, you've got one seriously rude awakening coming, buster."

"You're in my keep and on my land. I'll do what I like with you, and there's no one tae stop me."

"I'll stop you."

He chuckled. "I know your tricks, lass, and you'll not be using them on me. I'll not give you the chance tae catch me unawares."

Michael appeared with an armful of rags and Elspeth on his heels. She bustled up in front of him, placing her round body between him and his female tormentor.

"I'll not stand by and let you harm the lass, Colin. I've put up with your bad manners, but you'll not touch a hair on her head."

He gently took her by the shoulders and placed her in Michael's care, then snatched the rags from his guard's hands.

"I'll not do anything she doesna deserve. Now, off with you, Aunt. I've work tae do here." With his back to the woman, he gave Elspeth a wink.

She sputtered and blustered a moment, her gaze darting back and forth between them. Eventually, she allowed Michael to take her out of the room.

The door closed with a solid thud, echoed by his guest's small squeak of disbelief.

"Will you sit, or do I have tae use force?" he asked.

Her eyes narrowed. "You'd lose."

Oh, but she was a fiery female. He had to admire her spirit, her determination, but it was based on such utter codswallop. She had no chance against him. She had to see that.

He took one step in her direction, and she shifted into a defensive stance. Her weight properly balanced on both feet, her hands in an odd, but obvious fighting position. The woman was fully prepared to stop him whatever the cost.

Jo Barrett

He ran a hand down his face, exhausted with this game. "I only wish tae bind your injured wrist, you taupie. Now, sit down!"

"Oh." Relaxing her stance, she straightened. "I prefer to stand, thanks just the same." Turning away, she removed her odd coat and laid it in the chair.

With a sigh, he crossed to her and gently took her hand. "It doesna look bad. 'Tis only sprained, I'm thinking."

"Gee thanks, Doc. I'm so relieved," she said flatly.

He shook his head and tossed most of the rags aside. "You're a mouthy woman who doesna know when 'tis wise tae watch your tongue. You wear my patience thin." He wrapped her wrist, and did his best not to think of the skin he was touching, but on the task he was performing.

"Oh, poor baby," she mewled snidely. "Like I asked to be here. You should've let me alone. I was fine out there. It's not like I haven't roughed it before."

"You're a madwoman, tae be sure. Are you not afraid of the beasties that roam the wood? 'Tis said lassies are their favorite."

She snorted. "Right. Tell me another one. The only beastie I know is you. I want out of here, MacLean. And I want out now."

His head snapped up from his chore. "You'll not leave the keep for any reason. Not until I learn who you intended tae meet in the wood."

He wanted to trust her, but didn't dare. Although she'd been good to Ian, had handed him two men who didn't belong on MacLean soil when she could've escaped, it may have all been planned to gain his trust. But he prayed it was not so.

"You're so off, it isn't even funny," she snapped.

He gripped her shoulders firmly. "Where were you going? Why were you traveling dressed as a mon? The truth, damn you, or I'll put you in the dungeon with the others."

"You wouldn't know the truth if it bit you on the butt. How many times have I got to tell you? I don't have anything to do with your stupid little war. I don't know the MacKenzies. I don't know those two jerks downstairs, and I happen to like my clothes!"

He dropped his hands to his sides. "You will stay. You have no choice."

She tilted up her chin. "We'll see about that."

"Dinnae test me further, woman. You wouldna like the outcome." He turned and marched to the door. "And dinnae leave this chamber again wearing those bleedin' trews," he bellowed as he slammed the door closed.

Chapter Eight

Tuck awoke with Colin on her mind. It would've helped if he'd been an ogre for real. But he had tended Tuck's wrist with the gentlest of touches. And since he could've thrown her in the dungeon and forgotten all about her, he'd proven himself to be a compassionate man. A trait she had little experience with in men. And he was strong, virile, handsome, honest—there was little she could fault him for. She had to admit it to herself. He was irritating because she was attracted to him.

Sick of dwelling on thoughts of him, Tuck tended Ian's shoulder and made a trip or two to the garderobe, all with a guard on her heels. She considered escaping again, but it wouldn't be nearly as easy as before. They'd posted a guard beneath Ian's window, and her sprained wrist didn't allow for much in the way of scaling walls. Not to mention, she wasn't too sure where to go. Since the field was a bust, she had no idea how to get back to Jenny.

She tried to keep herself busy, but there wasn't much to do for Ian as he spent the majority of the day sleeping off his liquid painkiller. Checking on him, however, was better than sitting around doing nothing. That's when her brain took more of those dangerous little side roads involving a certain irritating Highlander.

Elspeth visited, tsking about Colin's manners. She checked to make sure Tuck's wrist was bound properly, and to deliver the repeated order from his high-and-nastiness that she was to wear a dress.

"What is his hang-up with women in pants?" she asked.

"'Tis not seemly tae be wearing men's trews," Elspeth explained. "Have you not noticed the looks the men give you?" She grinned mischievously.

"Uh, no. What kind of looks?"

"With your legs so clearly displayed, what do you think?"

"Oh. Well, I'm still not putting that thing back on. It's too...drafty," she said, waggling her hand in the air.

"Well, you do as you like, lass. I'll not ask you tae put the dress on, although it does look fine on you. You would almost think 'twas made for you." Elspeth slipped out the door with a distinctive twinkle in her eye.

Tuck shook her head as she examined the outfit the scheming little Scot had laid on the bed. She couldn't possibly look good in all that frilly stuff, regardless of what Elspeth thought. She had enough unpleasant memories on that score. Dressed up like a Barbie doll on steroids got her nothing but snickers when she was a teenager and a backhanded slap from her father. She clenched her teeth against the twinge somewhere in the vicinity of her heart.

Nothing had changed. Just because she was in a different time didn't mean she could pass for a regular woman. The men looked at her because their medieval mentality didn't know what to make of a woman in pants, not because it got them all hot and bothered. Nobody ever got that way around Amelia Tucker.

Her finger slid along the bed until it touched the dress. Some of the outfit wasn't so bad, though. The shift was actually kind of nice, comfortable. She eyed the door, then quickly shed her clothes and slipped it on.

"Ah, freedom." It was a lot like the men's shirts she wore at home. Women's nightgowns were hard to find in her size that weren't frou-frou'd to the hilt, so whenever she happened across some men's extra large tee shirts on sale she grabbed them up. It wasn't a sexy look, by any means, but it wasn't as if anyone would ever see her.

Moving to the center of the chamber wearing only the shift and her panties, she began her Tai Chi exercises, relishing the unbound comfort.

There was a soft scratch at the door.

"Come in," she called on an exhale.

Fiona's dark head peered in through the crack, her gaze darting around the room.

Tuck waved her in as she followed through on another movement.

The girl hurried across the chamber and set a bowl of warm water on the table as she'd done the previous evening for her use. It wasn't much as a bath went, but Tuck figured she couldn't be too picky considering where she was.

The girl's skirt quivered with her trembling as she laid a small towel alongside the basin.

Having had about all she could stand, Tuck dropped her arms. "Okay, that's it. I don't know what the deal is or why you're so afraid of me, but I am not going to hurt you. How many times do I have to say it?"

The girl darted for the door, her trembling hand groping for the latch.

Sitting down on the bed, Tuck tried her best not to look intimidating. But it wasn't easy considering she was almost twice the girl's size. When she'd learned Fiona was only eighteen, she'd been more than surprised. She was so small and petite, she barely looked older than twelve.

Tuck blew out a puff of air. "I haven't hurt Ian, have I? And Elspeth isn't afraid of me. I haven't done anything that I know of to make anyone afraid of me," she said, shaking her head. "Well, okay, so I bonked one guard on the head, but he's fine now, right?"

The girl eased away from the door, her dainty brows pulled together.

Tuck took that small bit of progress and ran with it. "Look, just because MacLean is mad at me and put me under house arrest, isn't a reason to fear me. He's just not used to women who show him up." She grinned cockily.

Fiona opened her mouth to say something then shook her head, apparently not understanding.

Tuck whispered conspiratorially, "He can't stand the fact that I saved his butt then slipped out right under his nose."

The girl's eyes widened, and she took a step closer. "Then 'tis true. You are a warrior. But how is that possible, unless..." She jumped back to the door, her hand blindly searching for the handle. "You must be a kelpie or a witch," she said with choked horror.

"Whoa, whoa, whoa. Uh-uh. I'm not a witch or a kelpie." She didn't even know what a kelpie was. "I'm just a woman who knows how to fight. That's all. I swear," she said, holding up her injured hand. "See, I can even get hurt. Kelpies can't get hurt." At least she assumed they couldn't. What the heck did she know about this fairy stuff? "Look, Fiona. Here's what happened."

Tuck explained the events of her first encounter with MacLean as if she were telling a child a bedtime story, making sure not to make any sudden moves, and definitely avoided mentioning time travel.

As the girl relaxed, she added her little foray into the woods, meeting up with the two spies, and why she was currently under guard. "So, you see I'm not a supernatural being. Just a woman who has some uncommon fighting skills that got a little off course. That's all."

Fiona's heart-shaped face slowly brightened and the fear disappeared from her eyes. "Elspeth tried tae tell me, but I wouldna believe her. You are different, verra different, but you're no kelpie." She shook her head, her long dark hair shifting perfectly over her shoulders as she moved closer. "I should've known better than tae listen tae Maighread and her tales."

Tuck's mouth pulled tight. "Maighread. I should've guessed." Still worried about her as competition, the woman had cooked up a bunch of horror stories to keep the locals in line. "What a bitch."

Fiona gasped then giggled behind her hand. "Aye, she can be that."

She sighed. "Well, at least now you know that I'm no threat. To you or anyone else."

"But you are." She sat down on the opposite side of the bed. "Maighread has loved Colin since she was a bairn. She's not one tae have as an enemy."

Tuck's gut pinched sharply. She must've eaten something that didn't agree with her. She wasn't jealous. Really. "Well, whoopee for her."

The girl grinned, her eyes alight with more wisdom than she should have for her age. "'Tis in the way he looks at you, that has her pea green."

Tuck snorted. "Yeah, right. If looks could kill, I'd be long gone."

"For one so auld, you dinnae know men verra well."

"Great. Just what I need. Advice from an adolescent," she muttered. "Well, thanks for the info, Fiona. But I'll be okay. You don't need to worry about Maighread. I can take care of myself. I'm just glad we got this straightened out. And I'm not that old," she added over her shoulder as she returned to her exercises. She wasn't even thirty yet.

"Nay, you dinnae understand. Colin doesna want Maighread, but she'll not stop trying tae snare him."

Tuck's heart did a happy dance to rival the most complicated military drill, dang it. Idly fingering the edge of her shift, she placed one knee on the bed, knowing full well she shouldn't ask. "You say he doesn't want Maighread?"

She shook her head. "Nay."

"Well, um, too bad for her. She'll get over it." Determined to change the topic before she started jumping for joy like a stark raving lunatic, she asked, "So, what is a kelpie, anyway?"

"'Tis a water sprite."

Wonderful, back to water sprites again. "What's so bad about a water sprite? I thought they were the good guys."

"Ach, no. They're devils that take pleasure in drowning their victims. But..." Fiona leaned closer. "...now, that I look at you, you dinnae have the eyes. Your skin 'tis fair, but your eyes are green. Not blue."

"Did Maighread give any reason as to how she knew I was a kelpie?"

"Your trews were wet when you arrived, and 'tis said you were not near water when Colin found you."

"Just to set the record straight, he didn't find me. I found him. Anyway, Fiona, I'm glad we had this little talk. But don't say anything to Maighread. I'll deal with that little problem myself, okay?" She winked then moved back into the first position of her exercises.

Fiona's smile widened. "I'll not be speakin' a word. I swear it." She rose from the edge of the bed and went to the door, then stopped. "Those motions you make. Are they part of your training? Like the men do in the lists?"

"In a way."

Fiona glanced at the door and lowered her voice. "Could you teach me? Tae fight like you?"

Pausing in mid-turn, Tuck said, "Well...sure. A little, I guess. But why? From what I can tell, the women around here aren't into that sort of thing."

Wringing her hands, she eased back toward the bedside. "If the MacKenzies should come and take the castle, Robert will be free tae—tae do as he wishes with me."

"Robert being a MacKenzie?"

"Aye. He asked for my hand last winter, but thankfully my father knows he isna a kind man and wouldna give me tae him." She clenched her tiny fists at her sides. "Robert is nearly twice my age, with yellowed teeth and a stench that would turn the stomach of a hog. I would rather die than give myself tae him." Her voice and face softened. "'Tis Michael I want and no other. We hoped tae be wed by now, but with the laird on his death bed, he thought it best tae wait."

Tuck grinned at Fiona's fervor, but understood what she was saying. "Okay. I'll teach you what I can. At least it'll give me something to do other than sit around all day and watch Ian heal."

Fiona sighed with relief. "I thank you." Grinning brightly, she scurried out of the room.

Tuck dropped her head back, closing her eyes with a weary sigh. "I am such a pushover."

At this rate, she'd never get back to her time. Of course she still had no idea how to get back. Then again, wasn't time on her side? Jenny wouldn't be kidnapped for another four hundred years.

She flopped down on the bed and focused on the story Maighread had cooked up. All the talk about kelpies and water sprites filtered and shuffled around in the back of her mind. There had to be a connection to the legend Jenny'd told her and that fountain.

Jenny's voice echoed in her thoughts. *The water sprite returned to the burbling stream.*

The corner of Tuck's mouth curled up. A stream or spring must feed the fountain in the twenty-first century. She just needed to find it in this time and jump in. That was the true gateway, the way back to Jenny. It had to be.

Leaping off the bed, she moved to the basin of warm water with a light step. Soon, she'd be where she belonged. She could only hope the stream took her back to the moment she left so she could stop the kidnapper in time. While bathing, she planned her next escape attempt.

****

Colin avoided any contact with the woman and concentrated on training the men, but knew he couldn't ignore his duty much longer. He had to speak with her and learn what she knew of the men in the dungeon. There had to be more than what she spoke of the previous night. No woman could take two men as silently as she had. It simply wasn't possible.

His fingertips scraped against the rough stone of the battlements as his chest tightened. She had to be working with them. What other explanation was there?

Yet she had overcome one of his men on the wall and displayed some fighting skills against the MacKenzies. She was of a considerable size to lay a firm blow to a man and deftly used surprise as her weapon. Could she have used those same tactics to take the two spies? Could she be telling the truth? He had heard of such things as women warriors, knew of some who were Scottish, but had never given much credence to the tales. In his mind, little of the truth was left amid the stories he'd been told.

His head ached with the questions, the evening wind off the water failing to ease him as it usually did. He longed for the days when his future, his duty was clear. When his only fight was against himself and the foolish whispers from the shadowy corners of his mind. His clan needed a strong leader, one who would keep them safe in the years to come, not a weak man who longed for more than the title of Laird. The one thing he could never have. A heart.

He turned from the churning waters and made his way to the solar. It was time to discover some truths. He prayed they would be of help to him and his clan

Chapter Nine

Flanked by two guards, Tuck was taken to the solar. Surprised to be out of her room, even on a tight leash, she relished the moment of freedom. Elspeth smiled warmly at her from where she sat by the hearth stitching. Maighread, however, shot her evil glances while she hovered liked a big fat housefly around MacLean where he reclined in a large chair. The woman was certifiable. No doubt about it.

Tuck stood her ground in front of MacLean, waiting to hear what it was he wanted. The man never did anything without a reason and letting her out of her prison for an hour or so wasn't for grins and giggles.

He stared at her openly, and with each breath she became more agitated. What was it about this man that unnerved her in a way that no other man, not even her commanding officer at his most fierce, could? Was her attraction to him that strong?

"Tell me of those men," he grumbled lowly.

Ah, so that was why she'd been allowed out. Apparently he'd failed to get any information from them.

No surprise there. She may not like the man, but he wasn't cruel. He wouldn't torture those men. It just didn't seem to be his style.

Turning her head to the side, she feigned interest in the tapestry on the far wall while observing him from the corner of her eye.

"I already told you," she said coolly, although she felt anything but. "I came across two men acting suspiciously and followed them."

He waved off Maighread as she offered him more drink. "And you heard nothing? You observed nothing else?"

She turned to face him, surprised he was asking since he considered her more a pain in the butt than someone who could be of help. He still didn't trust her, but could she really blame him? He had no clue where she was from, she broke all the girlie rules, and she didn't back down from him. The man simply didn't know what to do with her.

"I heard a lot, but it was in Gaelic. I don't speak Gaelic," she said with a casual shrug.

He nodded as he steepled his fingers at his chin.

"I will tell you this, since you asked." She sat down opposite him in one of the straight-back chairs, stretched out her jean-clad legs, and crossed her feet at the ankles. "They were tracking you, but not to kill."

A single dark brow rose as his gaze traveled up her legs to her face. She managed to keep from flushing at his open perusal. It wasn't a sexual look. At least she didn't think it was, having never really received one before. He was obviously not happy about her disobeying him and wearing her jeans.

Maighread scoffed. "What would you know of tracking? Dinnae listen tae her lies, Colin."

"Be quiet, cousin." His voice was low, almost a whisper, but Maighread obeyed.

Tuck held in her smirk and the ridiculous desire to stick out her tongue.

"What makes you think they didna wish tae kill me?" he asked.

"They followed you for several minutes, but never moved into an attack position. Besides, a full assault without claymores and backup would've been suicide. My guess is they were sent for something else. A little recon. You know, checking out the area, determining the enemies' weak points. Spying."

He studied her for several minutes, then rose and left the room. Maighread grinned smugly and followed.

Dream on, sister. But then Tuck didn't really believe MacLean wanted her either. Fiona was imagining things.

"He is behaving verra badly," Elspeth said.

Tuck rose and explored the solar. "No big deal. I know it's no picnic around here right now." She paused and glanced back at her. "And I'm not much of a guest. But thanks, Elspeth. You've been more than kind to me. I appreciate it."

The older woman smiled with a nod, then returned to

her sewing. Some sort of chair cushion, Tuck guessed.

"Sit down, lass, and keep me company," Elspeth said.

She glanced at the woman sitting by the fire burning in the hearth. It was a sight too serene to be real, and yet it was.

Settling in the large padded chair, Tuck held in her sigh of relief. She was so tired. Getting no sleep last night hadn't helped, but everything was still sore. Her body, her wrist, her brain, and parts of her she'd rather not think about. They just ached for something she couldn't have.

She jumped up and started pacing once more. How could she plan her escape when all she could think about was sex? It was like she was making up for lost time. Years of working to be the best, refusing to stop until she reached whatever goal she'd set for herself, she never had the time nor the inclination to think about men.

Raking her hand through her hair, she grumbled softly, "Fall through one little crack in time and my brain stops functioning." But the rest of her was working just fine.

She drew her fingers over her arm where Colin had held her the night before. Although his grip was like steel, he hadn't left a single mark on her skin. She could still feel the warmth of his broad chest pressed against her. The minute he'd pulled her to him, she forgot all about being tired and cold.

During their ride back to the castle, she'd tried to talk shop and get his take on the two men who'd been following him, hoping it would distract her from how wonderful it felt to have him warming her back with his arms stretched out around her. Then he ticked her off.

A weighty sigh eased past her lips. Yep, she'd totally lost it. She was attracted to a man who thought women had a place.

"What's troubling you, lass?" Elspeth asked.

She turned to find the woman's eyes full of concern. Concern for her well-being. She couldn't remember the last time anyone cared about her. Come to think of it, no one ever had. It was a lot to take in.

Clearing her suddenly constricted throat, Tuck said, "Nothing, I'm okay." She couldn't tell Elspeth what was going on inside her, especially since she wasn't too sure she knew herself.

"I gather you're homesick. I should've known," Elspeth said with a slight shake of her head.

"Yeah, homesick," she replied, although she'd never felt that way in her life. Oh, there'd been times when she wished she were back in the states or in a soft bed instead of camped out on the ground, but never really homesick. There was no such place.

"Tell me about your home. Perhaps 'twill make you feel better. I know 'tis far, with many wondrous things I canna put a name tae."

She chuckled roughly. "Things like smog, noise, people."

"You dinnae sound as though you care for it."

She shrugged, not really sure whether she did or not. But it was her world, regardless of how she felt about it. "What about you? Do you like it here, Elspeth?"

"Why would I not? 'Tis my home."

"But it's so isolated. Wouldn't you rather live on the mainland? Spend time at court, or whatever they call it?"

"Ach, nonsense. This is where I belong. I have my family and friends around me. I couldna ask for better. I am verra lucky."

Tuck nodded as she rubbed her arms and peered out the window. Torches flickered here and there, but beyond the keep all was dark. She couldn't blame Elspeth for wanting to stay put. The world could be a nasty place.

An odd sense of security crept over her as she stared into the darkness, a feeling she'd never experienced in her own time on any continent. The closest she'd ever come was two days ago when she drove off the ferry and onto Mull Island with Jenny.

She turned from the window with a jerk. She didn't belong here. She was needed back in the twenty-first century. Here she was nothing but an oddity, a freak.

She sniffed. Well, maybe that part wasn't much different, regardless of the year, but this wasn't where she was supposed to be.

Taking a greater interest in the room, forestalling the wave of melancholy before it could take hold, Tuck noted the differences from when she toured the castle. The massive fireplace looked to be the same, but the far wall was different. A set of unvarnished shelves housing several papers and books stretched across the stone, catching her interest.

Moving closer, she perused the manuscripts, but didn't take one aside to read. She doubted they were written in a language she was familiar with. Instead, she let her fingers brush along the thick leather bindings until she was lucky enough to find a book in English.

Not ready to return to her chamber and with nothing better to do, she pulled it from the shelf. How often does a person get to read a four-hundred-year-old first edition?

Returning to the chair beside Elspeth, she opened the heavy tome and began to read. It was slow going at first, the classical wording throwing her off a little, but eventually she settled into a slow, steady pace.

"Bless my soul. You can decipher the scratchings," Elspeth said with awe.

"Mm-hmm," she murmured, her eyes still on the page, struggling to determine a flamboyantly scripted word.

"Will you not read tae me? 'Tis been some time."

She lifted her head at the sound of longing in Elspeth's voice. The lack of such a fundamental skill, something she used every day of her life, struck her with an intense wave of sadness.

Taking a deep, steadying breath, she said, "I'd be happy to read to you."

Although she'd never been one for poetry, the words were comforting in the way they fit together, and Tuck found herself actually enjoying the verse. Relieved the disquieting gloom threatening to settle around her had dissipated, she moved more adeptly across the pages.

The door opened, but she paid little attention, her concentration solely on the text, not wanting to trip over any of the words. This moment seemed too important to Elspeth. Or was it important to her?

A faint memory, so faint it was nearly nonexistent, teased her mind. The sensation of sitting in someone's lap, a soft pretty scent surrounding her. Her grandmother perhaps, but it was short-lived. Someone, her father she recalled, jerked her up and ordered her to go to bed. She'd complained and received a slap. Like all of her other childhood memories, it ended in pain.

"Continue," a deep voice said.

She jerked her head up, unaware she'd stopped. MacLean sat across from her, his lion eyes peering at her over his large hands, gently cupped together and resting against his chin.

"Please," he said softly with a faint nod.

Caught in his gaze, she couldn't find the strength to deny him, yet she couldn't look away.

"Aye, lass," Elspeth said. "Please go on."

She turned to Elspeth, grateful for the distraction and gathered her wits. With a nod, she cleared her throat and picked up where she'd left off. She shoved down the haunting memory while doing her best to ignore the man sitting opposite her and the disquieting feelings he let loose with his presence.

Colin took in her bowed head as she read the words on the page. A woman who could read. Not an impossible feat, but an improbable one. He wondered if she could write as well.

He vaguely shook his head. So many things about her were different than other females, he could hardly believe it, and yet he knew her to be a woman beneath her crusty shell. No force on earth could wipe away the memory of her before the fire with nary a stitch of cloth to cover her distinctively feminine traits. Some of which his men could plainly see because of those damnable trews.

Perhaps he should let her go, removing the temptation once and for all. She could be innocent as she claimed, but so many lives rested on his shoulders, he didn't dare take the risk. She was far too puzzling, her way of speaking, her odd comments about a castle that didn't exist. The woman herself was as confounding as anything he'd ever encountered.

How could she sound so angelic as she read when he knew she was anything but? This woman fought him at every turn with her sharp tongue and strange words, and yet this voice, this one he'd not heard her use with its soft and gentle tones, soothed him greatly. Passage after passage, the taut muscles in his body relaxed and his weary lids closed.

As she ended the verse, he could not find the

wherewithal to move, as he was nearly asleep. The soft pop and crackle of the fire echoed off the stone walls. Comforting though it was, he missed the sound of her voice. He attempted to rally his strength to ask her to read more, when she softly broke the silence.

"I think your nephew's asleep."

"Aye, the poor dear," Elspeth said with a weighty sigh. "'Tis a difficult time for him. For us all." She sniffled and gently cleared her throat. "Tell me of your family, Amelia."

There was that name again. The sound of it achingly sweet. He yearned to roll the word across his tongue and taste its honeyed tone, but didn't dare.

"No," she said. "No family. My father died some time ago."

"'Tis sorry, I am."

"Don't be," she said quickly. "He wasn't much of a father."

"And your mother?"

"She died when I was born."

"Then who took care of you, child?" Elspeth asked, her face pinched with sympathy.

"My grandmother, but she died when I was very little. After that it was mostly just me and my father."

He stored that piece of information in his mind carefully. It was all he knew of her history and was a glimpse into how the woman came to be as she was. She'd no doubt had to learn to take care of herself and at a very young age.

"Colin's mother died when he was a lad as well," Elspeth said softly. "I dinnae think he ever quite recovered from the loss."

He managed not to flinch at the truth in his aunt's words. His mother had been loving and warm, and he missed her sorely, but he could not allow his feelings for her or his loss to show.

"So, this thing with the MacKenzies. What's the story there?" the woman asked, her voice hard once more.

He wondered how much of it was intentional, now that he'd heard her speak in what he surmised to be her natural tone. What had happened in her life to make her this way?

"They've been reiving along the border. 'Tis a dreadful business," his aunt said. "I'm afraid 'tis war we'll be having. Such a waste of life. I shall ne'er understand why."

"Reiving?"

"Stealing our cattle. Douglas, Colin's father, took some men and tried tae stop them. They were outnumbered. Not all of them survived. Douglas—" Her words were choked off.

"I'm sorry, Elspeth."

"Ach, dinnae mind me. I've become such a watering pot of late," she said with a forced chuckle.

His guest let out a long breath. "As much as MacLean ticks me off, I have to admit, I admire him. Taking over any command is rough enough without all the family stuff added into the mix. I guess I can't blame him for not trusting me. I know I wouldn't, if the roles were reversed."

One of his brows rose sharply, but he quickly calmed his features. He may learn more of her by pretending to sleep than with his direct questions. But how did this woman know so much about his plight? She spoke as if from experience, not observation.

Her reasoning where the two captives were concerned was amazingly logical, proving her to be intelligent, but he couldn't understand how she was so keenly knowledgeable of his situation.

He restrained his growl. More cursed puzzles to add to the growing list.

"Come, lass. We'll leave Colin tae rest. Tomorrow will be another busy day, I warrant," Elspeth said.

He listened to their steps, the soft shuffle of his aunt's slippers, the heavy clomp of his guest's boots. A sardonic grin stole over his lips. The woman was a paradox. But she admired him.

He found that intensely satisfying.

Chapter Ten

"You do not look well, my friend," Ian said quietly from the bed, rousing Colin from his light rest.

He lifted his head and caught sight of the day dawning through the window. He'd stalked the keep for some time, thoughts of the woman sleeping in his mother's chamber and the other matters weighing heavily on his shoulders making him restless. Finding himself in Ian's room, he'd promptly fell into a chair by the fire.

His friend's snoring told him he would recover, despite Maighread's dire warnings, but Fergus would not. The old fool should've known better than to go after the MacKenzies.

Although older by far than his father, Fergus never saw himself as anything but fit. In his last years, he continued to challenge the young men, to train them as best he could to fight, but he would never accept that he was getting old. The man thought he would live forever.

If only Colin had been there when his father needed him, when Fergus needed him. He would've made sure the old man stayed behind, and that his father had not ridden into the fray, which he was certain, he did. He, too, thought he would live forever.

Climbing to his feet, his body weary from lack of a good night's sleep and the pressing matters weighing on him, Colin said, "Fergus is dead."

A long hiss of air slipped past Ian's lips as he propped himself up in bed. "I am sorry. I shall miss him, as I know you will."

Crossing his arms, Colin moved to the window and watched the sun gently kiss the tops of the trees. "He was an auld mon, and is no longer my concern."

"Ah, yes. Just a bit of old baggage," Ian said snidely.

Colin glared back at Ian, his arms tightening over his chest. The man would goad a raging boar to make a point. Determined as always to prove Colin did indeed have a

95

heart, contrary to what he resolutely showed the world. But he was overtired and did not wish to spar with his friend. He would grieve silently for the loss of his mentor, as he did all things of that nature. To show his true feelings would make him weak and vulnerable. He could not take such a risk. The clan needed him to be strong. But he wished, more often of late, that he could face the world as Ian did, with a smile and a laugh...or a tear.

Dropping his hands to his sides with a sigh, he said, "The MacKenzies killed Fergus, and my father, or so it would seem. He lies on his deathbed as we speak. His mind fading as is his body."

"Good God," Ian rasped. Reaching to throw back the covers, he winced. "Have someone saddle my horse. We shall find them. They shall regret their actions."

"You're in no condition tae fight." Although he appreciated his friend's determination to do so, he wouldn't allow him to endanger himself further for his cause. The MacKenzies were his problem, and it was his duty to handle the matter.

"The hell, I'm not." Ian managed to teeter to his feet as the door flew open.

"Have you lost your mind?" his unwanted guest said, as she stormed across the room.

Shoving at Ian's shoulders, she easily put him back into the bed, although Colin suspected she wouldn't fail to use whatever force necessary in order to have her way.

"Amelia, I am not—a—babe," Ian said, his voice broken with pain. "Although I do appreciate your attentions, welcome them in fact, I—must get out of this bed."

"You'll get out of bed when I say you can and not a second sooner. Now lie down." With a final shove, he was back against the pillows and being tucked beneath the covers.

Colin covered his grin, struggling to resist the urge to chuckle.

She shot him a look over her shoulder. "This has your name written all over it."

His humor vanished. "As usual, you make little sense, woman. But tae make certain you're clear on the matter, the mon has a right tae do as he pleases. I am not his keeper."

She spun around, her eyes snapping furiously. "He's got enough problems in this germ farm without you coming in here and blowing reveille. Now beat it before I toss you out on your ear." Pivoting back to Ian, she surveyed his shoulder.

"Colin, you shall not leave without me," Ian said.

"Tell that tae the harpy."

Tuck flinched slightly and her back stiffened, but she remained silent. He cursed himself for wanting to retract the insult. He had no time for female sensibilities.

Ian took her busy hands from his shoulder and held them firmly against his chest. "Amelia, my sweet. I am sorry for being irritable, but I must get out of bed." He grinned with the familiar devilish gleam in his eyes that made women swoon. "Unless you wish to aid me in donning my clothes, a sight to surely bring a blush to your beautiful face, I suggest you leave."

Colin ground his teeth together. A day did not pass that the man failed to do his best to seduce some unwitting female. And yet the woman before him was far too intelligent to fall under his charms, or was she?

He growled softly. What did he care what the woman did? She was an exasperating female who refused to keep to her place!

"I'm not going anywhere, buster," she said. "Now, give me back my hands before I have to hurt you."

Ian chuckled. "Amelia, you are a treasure."

"Whatever. Look, I don't know where Sasquatch is going, but you aren't going with him. You've been lucky so far. No fever or infection, but I'm not taking any chances. Got it?"

Ian's smile faded as his gaze met Colin's. "Will you wait? I wish to be at your back, my friend. As always."

"Aye. There is still much planning tae be done. I will not make the same mistake as my father and have my head bashed in."

The woman's head snapped around, her brow pinched. They exchanged a long unsettling look before he turned and left Ian to her care, but he couldn't remove her puzzled frown from his mind. Was she curious or concerned?

The answer shouldn't matter, but then he shouldn't have asked himself the question in the first place. She was a dangerous distraction. One he feared would grow and fester with time. Whoever she was, she had to leave, yet he couldn't bring it upon himself to cast her out.

He had no proof of her working with the two men in the dungeon, more proof to the contrary in fact, and yet he was afraid. But was he afraid of her or for her?

****

"What was that all about?" Tuck shook her head and busied herself with changing Ian's bandages. "No, never mind. I don't want to know." She didn't want to get any more involved with these people than she already had.

Ian took a laborious breath, but she could see he was much better, despite his attempts to get out of bed. Another few days on his back and some good food, he'd be back to his usual roguish self. If she could keep the locals from screwing up her work.

Pulling his gaze from the closed door, his worried frown turned up devilishly. "You're sweet to worry over me, dear heart. I shall treasure these moments immensely."

She smirked. "Would you cut the sweet talk? You're wasting it on me. Why don't you aim it at Maighread? I'm sure she'd be happy to oblige you, batting her lashes, sighing, and all that stuff." She kept from biting her lip. Why had she said that?

"Amelia, my love, there is no other to compare to you. And Maighread has set her heart on Colin. The girl won't so much as look at another man."

She chuckled. "Struck out, huh?"

He frowned. "If you mean, did I fail to win her affection, you are correct." He rubbed his cheek thoughtfully. "I remember the sting of her hand quite distinctly."

With a snort, Tuck tied off his new bandages then adjusted the covers.

"'Tis not a laughing matter." He grabbed her hands and pressed them to his chest. "But you, Amelia, would never be so cruel."

She sighed softly. "Ian, you're a nice guy. I like you, but I'm just not interested."

He eyed her suspiciously for several moments. "Ah, I see," he said with a weighty sigh, releasing her hands. "You have already chosen between us. Pity. I was so looking forward to courting you."

Ignoring his comment, she concentrated on straightening every wrinkle in the covers. "You can't keep trying to get out of bed. You'll pull the stitches and you'll never heal. Not to mention it might bring on infection. And would you please stop calling me Amelia. It's Tuck, remember?"

He clasped her hand and kissed the backs of her fingers. "Fear not, my sweet. I shall not utter a word about your feelings for Colin, but you should know that he will not be an easy triumph."

She met his steady gaze, successfully burying any silly notions that had seeped into her demented brain about Colin MacLean. "I don't know what you're talking about."

He smiled, his bright blue eyes twinkling. "You are a very skilled liar, my sweet. But never fear, I shall keep my vow."

Tuck blew a frustrated breath at a lock of curls determined to tease her brow. "I've got to get out of here," she muttered.

"And where would you go? Home? Back to, what was it, the U.S.?"

She placed her good hand on his to lift it off her sore wrist. "Close enough."

"Wait. What have you done, dear heart?" He gently lifted her bound wrist and examined it closely. "Who has done this to you?" His bright blue eyes flared as he sat up abruptly in bed. "Did one of the men—did Colin—"

"Whoa there, hotshot," she said, pressing against him. "Nobody did this to me. I did it myself. Now lie down."

"You are certain? There is no one I must kill?"

She chuckled. "No. No one needs to die today." Amazing. Such a show of indignation on her part and even against his best friend. She couldn't remember anyone ever bestowing such an honor on her before. This chivalry stuff was pretty good for what ailed a girl.

"Then I shall lie here and bask in your beauty," he

said, and pressed his lips to her injured hand with the gentlest of kisses. His touch was almost as gentle as Colin's when he bound it.

She clamped her eyes closed. *I must have left my brain back in the twenty-first century.*

"I brought you something to break your fast, Ian. 'Tis hoping you have a healthy appetite, I am," Elspeth said, bustling into the room. She placed a tray by his side upon the bed and clasped her hands beneath her ample bosom. "My, you look fine. No doubt due tae Amelia's skilled hand."

"Yes, she is very skilled at healing, and other things," Ian said with a wink.

"Ach, you rascal. You aught not be teasing her after she's taken such good care of you."

She chuckled. "It's okay, Elspeth. I give up. He's got sex on the brain."

Elspeth blushed furiously while Ian laughed.

A noise, a bellow actually, caught Tuck's ear and she turned toward the window. Stepping into the small shaft of sunlight, she looked down into the bailey.

MacLean stood in the center, yelling something, while everyone around him scurried to do his biding. He looked like a general. Waving toward the lists, he marched across the courtyard, pulled his claymore, and began a mock battle with one of his men.

A soft sigh slipped unbidden from her lips as she watched him wield the hefty steel. He was all man and then some.

Remembering his words about not getting his head bashed in, she looked over her shoulder at where Elspeth sat beside Ian, happily spooning some sort of oatmeal into him.

"Think he'll get his head bashed in?" she asked.

Elspeth shuddered, nearly toppling Ian's breakfast to the floor.

Tuck grimaced at her blunder. "Ah, geez, I'm sorry, Elspeth."

The woman shook her head.

Ian took her quivering hand and kissed it. "There, there, my sweet. You know as well as I, that nothing will happen to Colin." He grinned broadly. "The man simply

100

won't allow it."

A grim smile on her face, Elspeth rose. "I pray you are right, Ian. I pray you are right," she said then disappeared from the room.

"I didn't mean to spit it out like that," Tuck grumbled.

He sighed. "'Tis not your fault. The woman loves Colin as though he were her own son and has loved his father for years, but the old man has never noticed. Now, 'tis too late for them. Colin tells me his father is dying."

She took a deep breath. "I know, but still, I didn't have to put my foot in my mouth. I just wish I could—" Tuck let the words die in her throat. These people weren't her responsibility.

Ian pinned his thoughtful gaze on her. "You should be out there training those men. Your added skill would be a great advantage."

"You're off your nut if you think those men would listen to a word I have to say. I'm just a woman, remember?"

Turning back to the window, she crossed her arms and leaned her shoulder against the wall, watching their impressive show of strength. A good group of men, but they used only brute force to overwhelm their opponent. A quick way to wear yourself out and lose your edge. Then again, that's how the other clan would fight. They knew nothing of martial arts and they didn't have a foray of techno dreams to take out the enemy from a distance.

Still, remembering Colin's skill in the woods, his ability to track her when she'd been pegged as "the ghost" in her last platoon, spoke volumes. His determination to bear his clan's problems, to protect them all was the noblest thing she'd ever seen.

"They don't make men like that anymore," she whispered, riveted by his swordsmanship.

"You are more than a woman, Amelia."

Pulled from her thoughts, she shot Ian a look over her shoulder.

"Tuck," he said sheepishly. "You are also a warrior."

"It won't work," she said, shaking her head.

He grinned ruefully with a soft sigh. "You are so like him. Stubborn to the core. I have seen you battle. You cannot deny your skill. Do you think I received this wound by chance or poor swordsmanship?"

He rubbed his shoulder. "Hardly, dear heart. I was indeed distracted. Stunned to be precise. The way in which you avoided a fatal blow from behind and swept to your feet, held me in awe. I have never seen a man, so I assumed you to be at the time, move so swiftly and gracefully. It caught me quite unawares. Thusly, I received this blow for my moment of vacillation."

"Okay, I'll admit that I can fight, but that doesn't make me a teacher."

"Any knowledge you could provide would be of help." He paused, a soft hum rumbling deep in his chest. "I wonder where they obtained the extra men. The two clans have always been somewhat equal in size."

She shrugged, trying not to show her interest, but this was how she made her living. Explore and extrapolate the enemy's strategies and discover their weaknesses. Prepare for all possibilities, train to fight, and fight to win.

"Recruitment," she said, unable to remain silent on the subject.

"Not likely. The only others on this island are MacLeans or a relative of sorts."

"What about the mainland or another island?"

His brow shot up. "The idea has merit. Banding with another clan would give them the upper hand, and yet the question that remains unanswered is why? What would they have to gain?"

"Do you really have to ask? People want only one thing in this world. Power. The more they have the more they want, and so on."

"A rather cynical view, and one I do not wholly agree with, but you have a point. If the MacKenzies have decided they want the entire island to themselves, they've chosen the only way to obtain it. A clan war, a decisively one-sided war if they have in fact found an ally, and if so who? And what are they offering in exchange for this alliance?"

He paused with a soft chuckle. "You know, I rather like this discussion. I do not believe I have ever had such an intelligent conversation with a woman in my life."

The corner of her mouth quirked up as she shook her head. "That's because you have only one thing on your mind when you're with a woman. I just happen to be immune to it, leaving you no alternative but to find something else to do."

He nodded sagely. "You have a point. But I do not believe you are immune to my charms. I think you've simply found what you want. And when a woman with your determination makes up her mind about something, there is little I or anyone else can do about it. I do know how to be a pragmatist, when the situation calls for it. Now, as for training the men..."

She shook her head, her gaze still on MacLean. "This isn't my fight, Ian."

"But 'tis yours, if you truly want him."

Her head snapped around with his words. "Me and Sasquatch?" she snorted.

"Although my heart is sadly broken, a state I may never recover from..." He pressed a hand to his chest, so full of drama, she nearly laughed. "I honestly think the two of you make a good match. A formidable laird with a rather formidable lady by his side."

She touched his forehead, making a big show of searching for a fever. "What did Elspeth slip into your food?"

He sighed. "Very well, I shall leave the topic alone. For now."

"Glad to hear it."

She turned back to watch the men train, doing her damnedest not to let his crazy talk get to her. Even she hadn't let her silly daydreams get that far. Admiration, respect, a little female appreciation for the masculine form, and maybe a few warm twitters in her gut, okay a freakin' bonfire, but that was it. The idea of them together was ludicrous.

But isn't MacLean the reason you're still here? A voice whispered in the back of her mind.

"Christ," she growled.

Her ridiculous stomach acrobatics had sabotaged her brain, sucking every ounce of common sense right out of her head. For hours she'd lain awake the previous night rethinking her plans, finding more and more ludicrous reasons to postpone her escape, never once admitting she wanted to stay because of that irritating ogre.

She had to get back to Jenny, which meant she had a spring to find. Spinning on her heels, she marched to the door.

"You have a fierce look about you, dear heart. What are you going to do?" he asked.

"My job."

She slammed the door closed behind her, turned on her guard, and punched him dead in the nose. He sprawled out nicely on the stone floor. "Sorry, Michael."

Shaking her hand to relieve some of the pain, she strode toward her room to retrieve the rest of her things. It was time to leave never-never land.

Chapter Eleven

Michael rushed across the bailey holding his nose and came to a dust stirring halt before Colin.

"The woman, she's gone," he sputtered behind his bloodied fist.

A snort, followed by several small bouts of laughter, sounded around them, but Colin ignored it.

Eyeing the lad carefully, he asked, "What do you mean, she's gone? And what happened tae your nose?"

"She caught me unawares," he said, his eyes darting to the side as the choked laughter grew. "She must have had a bit of stone in her hand or such," he muttered.

"By the saints, not again." Colin rubbed his hand down his face, wearier than he should be for so early in the day. "Where was she last?"

"With Master Southernland."

He ignored the sudden knot in his stomach. The fact that she'd spent so much time in Ian's room was of no concern. She was tending his wound and nothing more. But his thoughts continued conjuring heated images in the back of his mind.

Michael's voice, full of remorse, snatched him back from his silent brooding.

"I have searched the entire keep and canna find a trace of her. She's vanished," the young man said with awe.

Renewed mutterings about kelpies and deviltry, her strange dress, and her odd manner of speech, and something about a witch's dance, circulated among the men. If he didn't put a stop to this idle gossip, there would be no end to their foolish fears.

He knew her to be a woman, his lust for her was proof of that, but moreover, he didn't believe in kelpies and the like. His aunt may often times know things, see things, but he refused to believe there were creatures roaming about the earth with nothing more than mischief on their minds. He'd seen too much in his travels to believe such childishness.

Nevertheless, the lass had managed to turn Highland warriors into a band of sniveling children muttering of witches and fearing their own shadows.

"Enough!" he bellowed.

The garrison fell still.

He pointed to Michael, still holding his nose. "Come with me."

Gritting his teeth, Colin stormed back inside the keep with murder on his mind. It was a sad day when one of his men was so easily overcome by a woman. He knew her to be stealthy, her ability to turn back on him in the wood without his knowledge was proof of that, but in broad daylight?

"Elspeth!" He stomped his way through the great hall toward the kitchens.

His aunt bustled out of the larder, wiping her hands on an apron draped around her plentiful hips. "Stop your bellowing before you bust a gullet."

He glowered down at her. "Where is she?"

"She who?"

His voice laden with grit, he said, "None of your nonsense, woman. Where is she?"

"Dinnae woman me, Colin MacLean. I changed your nappies and swatted your behind. And I'll swat your behind again, if it needs doing."

He sighed and looked to the ceiling. "Tuck. Where is she?" He refused to call her by her given name, the sound of it silently torturing his mind and tongue.

"If you mean Amelia, in her room, I imagine." She glanced around him to Michael and grinned. "Ach, I see now. Well, then I suppose the wee lass has left." She straightened, clasping her hands in front of her as she gave him her sternest look. "No thanks tae your hospitality, I'm sure. Keeping the lass under guard," she said with a shake of her head. "Ashamed, I am."

"That *wee lass* has been nothing but trouble since the moment I laid eyes on her. And once I find her, she'll get the beating she deserves."

She laughed softly, a teasing gleam in her eye. "*If* you find her." Turning, she waved Michael onto a bench. "Sit, lad and let me tend your nose. I'll warrant there's no real damage. Amelia's not the kind tae hurt you overmuch."

"What do you know of her? Tell me," Colin snapped.

She glanced at him, where he stood seething. "She has traveled a long way. I'm thinking she was homesick, although she wouldna say as much."

"She's a kelpie," Michael muttered, his eyes wide. "Ouch!"

"That'll teach you tae talk that way about dear sweet Amelia. She's no kelpie, and I'll not be hearing anymore of that," she said, a determined frown on her face.

"I dinnae think she's a kelpie nor a witch," Fiona said, easing up beside his aunt with a clean damp cloth. "She's far too nice tae be such a thing. I like her verra much."

Colin glowered down at her, not believing his ears. *Nice?* That woman had bewitched the entire keep. He looked back to his aunt. "Did you see anything that would help me find the taupie?"

She cocked her head, as she took the cloth from Fiona and dabbed more gently at Michael's nose. "'Tis too far for you tae travel, I'm sure. And there was water. Bright and clean it was."

His head ached with her vague reply. "'Tis all?"

She nodded and continued tending his guardsman.

With a growl to match his growing frustration, he spun around and stormed the stairs to Ian's room, hoping he had some real knowledge of where the woman had gone. He'd had more than enough babble to last him for some time.

"Water," he muttered, steadily climbing the stone steps. "Too far tae travel," he snorted softly. No land was too far to travel to find that shrew and bring her back.

He stopped, his left foot landing squarely on the upper landing alongside the other.

What was he doing? What did he care if she'd left? It was what he'd wanted all along. Wasn't it? Although he hadn't decided that she was innocent, wouldn't it be best to let her go and be done with her?

His feet slowly moved once more, guiding him to Ian's room. He entered and walked directly to the window, his thoughts still not clear on what he should do.

The state of uncertainty puzzled him all the more. It wasn't like him to be scatter minded.

He knew that woman would be trouble.

"Something has happened. What is it, Colin?" Ian asked, propping up on one elbow.

"'Twould seem our guest has left."

"You mean Amelia?"

"Aye." He moved to the window to look out over the island.

"Damn it, man, go after her!"

Crossing his arms firmly over his chest, he said, "Nay." He waggled his head, satisfied that he'd ended his moment of confusion. She would no longer bedevil him. "I grant her safe journey and good riddance."

Ian climbed to his feet and grabbed at the corner bedpost for balance. "You cannot leave her out there on her own. The MacKenzies will kill her on sight."

Colin clenched his jaw at the thought. "She made her choice." If she was careful, she could avoid them. He believed she wasn't whom the MacKenzies truly wanted, not in light of his father's recent injury by their hands.

Ian pushed himself across the room and leaned against the wall by the window, his gaze pinned on Colin. "At least send some men to protect her until she finds safe passage off the island."

"I'll not risk my men on a woman I know nothing about." He clenched his jaw tighter as everything he did know about her flooded his thoughts. Her shapely visage by firelight, her soft soothing voice as she read, the way in which she cocked her head with a lissome quirk of her rosy lips and a sharp remark on her tongue. Her strength, her determination, her courage, and her blasted stubbornness. By the saints, he was actually going to miss the shrew.

"She saved your life, man, and mine," Ian argued. "You simply cannot stand the fact that she isn't cowed by you. That she pulled you from your damned horse." He shuffled to the opposite wall and retrieved his tunic from a peg. "If you refuse to go after her, then I will."

Colin snatched the clothing from his shaking hands and tossed it in a chair. Grabbing his friend by the arm, he directed him back to bed. "You're in no condition tae be going anywhere."

"I will not stand by and let that woman die because she's bruised your bloody pride!" Ian struggled vainly against Colin's grip. "The MacKenzies will assume she's a MacLean. Her life will be forfeit." Ian clamped his eyes closed and grimaced.

"Be still, you damn fool." Colin knew he'd regret what he was about to say, but his friend left him no choice. He'd kill himself going after her. "I'll fetch the she-demon back, but I make no promises. I'm likely tae kill her myself once I lay my hands on her."

Ian's head hit the pillow with a grateful sigh. "I knew you could not be all barbarian, contrary to popular opinion."

Colin shot him a glare. "I must be daft tae go after that woman again."

His friend chuckled a moment before his mouth turned down. "Again?"

He jerked at Ian's covers and tossed them over him. "Aye. She left the night you were deep in your cups. She— she caught two men lurking about in the wood," he grudgingly admitted.

Ian snickered then cleared his throat. "Ah, yes. Her injured wrist."

"She scaled the damned wall! She could've fallen tae her death. I tell you the lass is mad."

"Mad or not, you must find her. Take several men with you and mind your back. The MacKenzies—"

"Shut your yap, you Sassenach. I know what I'm about."

"I wonder, at times. I truly do," Ian said with a theatrical sigh.

"You know how tae try a mon's patience."

Ian chuckled roughly. "Just find her, Colin. There's something about that woman, I feel it."

"Aye, you're in love. Again."

"Is that jealousy I hear, old boy? Have you finally succumbed to the power of love?"

His teeth would be dust if he didn't take his leave soon and find the wretched female. "You're off in the head. That woman is a pain in the—"

"Ah, but what a lovely pain she is. Find her, Colin.

Whatever she is to you, she does not deserve to die at the hands of a band of ambushing demons."

He sighed heavily. "Nay. That she doesna." He moved toward the door muttering beneath his breath. "If the woman would only do as she was told, if she would behave as a woman ought, I wouldna be in this mess."

"True. However, you would be dead, more's the pity."

Ignoring that remark, Colin asked, "Did she tell you anything that would be of help?"

Ian glanced to the window, his eyes narrowing as he thought. "Not exactly. She said she was from the U.S., wherever that is, and that she learned to fight in some army."

A laugh burst through his lips, then halted. "You are serious. And you believe her?"

"Yes," Ian said with a stern frown. "I know nothing about her land of origin, but I saw her fight, my friend, while you were otherwise occupied." He rubbed his shoulder. "She is quite skilled. How many men do you know who could successfully get past your guards, day or night, capture two men, and have only a slight wrist injury from their endeavors?"

Colin let out a long, suffering breath, recalling her comments about taking command. Could it be true? "I dinnae have time tae debate you. Did she say anything else?"

Ian nodded. "Yes, she said something odd before she left my chamber."

"Well, tell me, mon, so I can get on with this daft business!"

The corner of his mouth twitched. "So much alike."

Colin growled.

"She said something about doing her job," Ian said quickly.

"What the devil does that mean?"

His friend shrugged slightly. "I suppose you shall have to ask her when you find her. And you must find her."

"Aye, I'll find her and when I do..." He strode purposefully from the room. If one of his men received so much as a scratch because of that woman, he'd gladly take her over his knee and paddle the sass out of her.

He swallowed hard at the image that thought invoked. Her perfectly shaped backside pointed to the rafters, her breasts pressed against his thigh as he held her across his lap.

"I'm the one who's daft," he grumbled, and hurried out of the keep.

Jo Barrett

Chapter Twelve

By searching the immediate perimeter around the field, Tuck was certain she'd found the water source that fed the fountain. Situated in a small clearing with moss and fern growing in abundance along the banks, it looked almost ethereal, like a fairyland. It had to be the one.

"Well, here goes," she said with a sigh and pulled her knife. She wasn't sure where this little trip would land her, but she was determined to be ready for anything.

Taking a deep breath, her knife clutched tightly in her fist, she lifted her foot and paused, letting her boot hover over the water. If this worked, she'd never see Elspeth or the others again. She'd never see MacLean again.

"It doesn't matter. They're already dead." But it did matter, and it bugged the hell out of her.

"Damn it, I've got a job to do." She nodded firmly and stepped into the spring before she could change her mind.

She waited, her feet and ankles getting colder by the second, but nothing happened. Her shoulders sagged with part relief and part disappointment as she trudged back onto the bank. She was either stuck in the past or there was a piece of the puzzle missing. She'd found the spring, or so she assumed, but she wasn't a water sprite. Not as if she could do anything about that part. There had to be something else. Something she was supposed to do, or say, but what?

An idea popped into her head, although it was crazy. "Huh, like sitting here expecting this stupid spring to take me back to my own time isn't crazy?"

She dug into her pocket and pulled out a penny. Clutching it tightly in her fist, she wished she was back with Jenny. The "kerplunk" was muffled by the trickle of the water.

Pushing thoughts of the people she was leaving behind from her mind, one in particular, she jumped in

112

with both feet.

After several seconds she opened one eye, then the other, warily looking around.

"Damn. Still in the past," she said with a weighty sigh.

Thoroughly disgusted, she tromped out of the spring and through the wood toward the shoreline, nibbling on a pineapple flavored Gummy Bear, savoring it for as long as she could. She had to ration them since it looked like she was stuck in the wrong century. Her favorite vice wouldn't be invented for a very long time.

Tuck walked along the shoreline, kicking stones as she went. She may as well stick it out back at the castle until she could come up with another plan. Without any real provisions, she couldn't rough it outside for any length of time.

Her hands shoved deep in pockets, her cold feet shuffling along the sand and stone, she rounded a small point. Children's laughter caught her attention, and she raised her head.

The fortress loomed above the small group doing what children tend to do at times. Single out one of the smaller kids and torment him. She'd been there many times, yet being bigger than most, she'd suffered the taunts and jeers from behind her back. But they were no less painful than the ones to her face.

At first she was only going to make her presence known to the kids, figuring they'd let up once they realized an adult was around, but the moment the little boy was shoved to the ground, she'd seen all she cared to see. She had to get involved.

"That's enough," she ordered, moving closer.

Their faces paled as they scurried back. She heard mumblings of witch, but ignored it. Maighread's little storytelling would take some time to kill. Something she should probably see to when she got back to the castle since she was stuck here for a while.

She looked at the boy on the ground. He didn't look more than eight or so, and a scrawny eight, at that. Her gaze flickered over the crude crutch by his side. Not only was he smaller than the others, he was crippled as well.

Reining in her anger, she asked, "You okay, kid?"

113

His dark eyes wide, he warily nodded.

She picked up his crutch, then leaned over and stuck out her hand. He didn't move a muscle.

"Look, I'm not going to hurt you, regardless of what you've heard." She waited patiently, testing that slim virtue. "Look at it this way. You take my hand, and they'll think you're the bravest little Highlander of all," she whispered with a wink.

He cocked his head to the side as he considered what she said. His gaze darted to the others, then back to her. He swallowed and slowly reached for her hand.

His filthy, quivering fingers slid into hers, and a load of relief relaxed her tense neck muscles. Scaring the bad guys was part of the job, not innocent little kids. She helped him to his feet to the sound of gasps and set him right with his crutch.

Satisfied the boy was okay, Tuck turned to the other children. "This won't happen again. Will it," she said flatly, making certain they knew it was not a question.

They shook their heads as they stumbled backward, then spun around and broke off in a dead run down the beach.

"Ye aren't really a-a-a witch, are ye?" the boy asked, his eyes still wide.

Tuck shook her head. "Not the last time I looked, no."

His face fell and he dropped his chin to his chest. "Oh." Struggling across the rocky terrain, he turned toward a path up the side of the hill to the keep.

Not that she expected much, but a "thanks" would've been nice. She walked alongside him, curious as to why he seemed disappointed when he'd been so scared of her.

"You don't seem too happy about that. Care to tell me why?"

"I thought if ye were a kind witch, kind enough tae tend Master Southernland, then ye might fix me leg," he muttered at the ground.

"I see." She cupped his bony shoulder. He tensed slightly, but didn't pull away.

From what she could tell with a quick glance, he'd been born with a clubfoot. She'd heard of braces and casts on babies to fix the abnormality, but in the boy's case, surgery was likely what he needed. That was something she couldn't do.

"You got a name, kid?"

"Robby."

"Well, Robby, I can't heal you, but I can help you," she said.

He stopped and peered up at her. "How?"

"Oh, a few little maneuvers, some strengthening of your muscles. Basic stuff really."

"I'll never be strong." He dropped his chin.

"Look, you're tired of getting picked on, right? And you'd like to be able to take care of yourself?" His puzzled expression pulled at her lips and she grinned. "I could teach you how to fight."

His dirt smudged brow furrowed. "But ye're a woman."

Tuck rolled her eyes heavenward. "God, they brainwash them young around here." She looked down at the boy with a heavy sigh. "Do you want to learn or not? The only thing wrong with you, other than lack of faith, is a bad foot. The rest of you seems to be in perfect working order." She poked and prodded at his muscles, winning a faint giggle from him.

"But my da says I'll always be sickly. That I'll never be—be worth anythin'," he ended softly.

Familiar pains pierced her armored heart. "Your father is wrong, Robby. Dead wrong. Now, come on down here where the ground isn't as rocky and let's get started," she said with a jerk of her head.

He hesitated, not convinced in the least. The spark of hope in his dark eyes overshadowed years of pain and rejection.

"Hey. It can't hurt to try, can it?" she asked.

Slowly, he moved back down the path, closer to the water.

A glowing warmth spread across her chest, and she welcomed it. She'd never been this mixed up in other people's lives without a paycheck being involved before. Maybe falling through that hole in time wasn't such a bad thing after all.

As long as Jenny was okay.

****

"What is that woman doing?" Colin asked no one in

115

particular. Her odd movements which she had Robby mirror were strange and slow.

He looked to his side and took note of the distinct fear on his men's faces. If one more man crossed himself...he rubbed his hand down his face. "Stop behaving like a passel of frightened women. She's no witch."

"Even if she be one, she be a kind one, lad," William said. One of the last of his father's guard, he was the only one who didn't seem as concerned about her. Only cautious. "Look you, what she did fer Robby. The lad was gettin' a sore teasin', he was."

That was better than what Colin had heard since they'd started after her. Perhaps they were making some progress. But he didn't mistake the fear in some of their eyes as she continued her odd movements at the edge of the water.

"Go back tae the keep, the lot of you," he said with a sigh. "I'll be along shortly."

"Are you sure?" Michael swallowed, his eyes wide and black rimmed.

She'd broken his nose but good. So much for Elspeth's opinion on how little the lass would hurt him. Colin almost chuckled.

"Aye. Get back tae the castle. I've had all I care of your blathering about witches and such. I'll tend tae the woman. It seems she was headed there as well until she met with Robby." He dismounted and handed the reins to Michael.

"Mind you be careful, lad," William said.

Colin nodded and waved them off. They rode away casting concerned glances over their shoulders. What a sorry bunch they were.

He looked to the woman by the water and the lad she'd aided. Why was she returning after spouting about nothing but how badly she wanted to leave? And her strange behavior by the spring could not be believed.

A sick ball formed in the pit of his stomach. Had she intended to meet with an accomplice in the wood, but knew she'd been followed? Was she the true spy? As much as he hated to believe it, the possibility couldn't be ignored. Yet she'd saved Ian and aided Robby. Fiona thought she was nice, of all things, as did his aunt. Why would she be good to his friend and his clan if she were out to destroy them?

She ceased her odd movements and handed something to the lad. He hesitantly placed it in his mouth. Barely a moment passed before he was smiling and chattering away.

The pair started up the path to the castle, her hand on the boy's shoulder.

Colin grinned. He couldn't remember ever seeing Robby smile quite so brightly before. Whoever she was, whatever her purpose for being there, he couldn't discount her kindness. Perhaps she was merely caught up in something she didn't know how to get out of.

Rubbing his throbbing brow, his heavy feet carried him back through the wood where he met with the path several yards behind them. He would watch and wait, it was his only recourse. He wanted to trust her, but he needed more proof of where her loyalties lay.

Shouts and screams lifted his head from his perusal of the ground as he passed through the gate into the bailey.

"Please, Tuck. Dinnae hurt him," Robby cried.

"Hurt him? I'd like to kill him!"

"Nay," wailed the lad's mother.

William, Michael and several others joined Colin as he rushed across the courtyard to the blacksmith's cottage.

Standing before the entrance to the forge, Tuck had Malcolm by the throat with one of his beefy arms twisted behind his back.

"Leave off, ye witch," Malcolm snarled roughly, struggling for breath.

Colin couldn't believe his eyes, but there she stood, grappling with a man more than twice her size.

And she was winning.

Trying to urge the lad to stand aside while she wrestled with Malcolm, she didn't see his meaty fist reach out and snag an iron hanging on a nearby post. She wouldn't be winning for long.

Colin stepped in front of Malcolm, instantly noting the sickly sweet smell of drink and plucked the rod from

117

his hand. "Release him," he ordered.

"Like hell," she snarled.

"Do as I say, woman!"

With a feral growl, she shoved the man to the ground, and placed her foot firmly on his crotch. "You so much as flick your little finger at your wife or son again, so help me I'll kill you." Her tone as icy as a fierce north wind, there was no doubt she meant what she said.

Malcolm stilled, his gaze narrowing menacingly, but there was a distinct flicker of fear in his eyes.

No one moved for several heartbeats until she removed her foot and stepped aside, but she didn't go far. Crossing her arms firmly, her feet squarely planted, she turned her heated gaze on Colin. No doubt waiting to see what he would do.

He glanced at the boy, his face wet with tears, then at his mother, her face wet as well. The imprint of a hand burned brightly on her cheek.

Clenching his jaw, Colin motioned for a pair of his men to lift Malcolm to his feet.

He stared hard at his blacksmith. "What do you have tae say for yourself, mon?"

"That she-demon came out of nowhere with her claws. I was protectin' me family," he sputtered fiercely.

Tuck lurched forward. "You lying son-of-a-"

Colin shot her a look.

William braved her wrath by gripping her shoulder. "Patience, lass," he murmured, and she magically fell silent and still.

Colin looked back to Malcolm. A man whose size rivaled his own. "You're saying 'tis her hand that left a mark on Mary's cheek."

Malcolm shifted uneasily, his gaze darting to his wife's homely face. His lips twitched nervously before he spoke. "She had no right tae interfere! What I do in me own home isna her business."

"Nay, it isna," Colin said.

A small smile of relief eased over his blacksmith's burly face, while Tuck turned a furious shade of red.

Colin leaned in closer to him, ignoring the foul stench of the man. "But 'tis mine. If you ever lift a hand against her or Robby again, you'll answer tae me."

Malcolm swallowed hard. "Aye."

Colin nodded to his men. "Help Malcolm clear his head, lads."

"Aye, with pleasure," Michael said, and escorted him to the trough. Several of them happily dunked his head in the water and held it there for a very long time.

Turning to Mary and her son, Colin said, "Come tae me, if you have a need."

Tearfully, she nodded, while Robby swiped his face dry. "Soon I'll be able tae protect her," the boy swore, his watery gaze cutting to Tuck.

Placing his hand on the boy's shoulder, Colin said, "Aye, that you will. A braw lad you'll be when you're grown, but until that time, you come tae me, you ken?"

Robby sniffled with a nod.

Turning, Colin tossed aside the iron and snatched Tuck by the arm, ignoring her squeak of surprise. He started off across the courtyard toward the keep, dragging her behind him. Storming into the lass's bedchamber, he flung her across the room.

"Have you lost what little wits you have left, woman?" he bellowed and slammed the door behind him.

Tuck quickly regained her balance. "I knew exactly what I was doing."

Red-hot talons of fury gripped him fiercely as he imagined what Malcolm could have done to her. "You could've been killed!"

"For the love of—" She snatched his dirk from his belt before he could blink and waved it beneath his nose. "You see this? I've killed with something much more lethal," she said coldly. "I've lived in places so hard, so filthy, they make your dungeon look like a palace."

She let the blade fly, impaling it into the door. "I was trained to fight, MacLean. Not to play nursemaid to some man. One who cares about nothing but his stomach or whether or not his shirts are clean. A man who'd rather get drunk and slap his daughter around, than face a single day sober." Her breath quickened and her eyes became glassy. "A man who doesn't give a shit about anything but himself."

She swallowed hard while blinking away her burgeoning tears. "You either accept me for what I am or

119

leave me the hell alone," she hissed and spun away.

He stood silent for several minutes, hating the sharp twinge in his chest. Facing Malcolm had brought a flood of painful memories to the surface for the lass. Things he wished he could undo.

Blast her! Why couldn't she be like other women? Why did she have to reach inside him to places he strived to ignore? Why did he have to want her so much?

He paced and growled, fighting the urge to pull her into his arms, but he knew it would not remain a solace act for long. His desire for her was too strong.

Pausing in his fury, he asked, "Why did you come back? And I'll have the truth."

"Because I felt like it."

He gripped her firmly by the shoulders. "Damn it, woman! You traipsed around the wood for hours. Did your plans tae secretly meet fail because you knew I was following?"

She growled low, the deep pain he'd seen in her eyes and heard in her voice were gone. "It's the same old song with you. You're just too stubborn to admit you're wrong."

Swiftly rotating her arms, she knocked his hands free of her shoulders. "And don't think that because I let you drag me in here like some conquering warlord, that I'm afraid of you. I could put you on your back without stirring a breeze."

He leaned closer. "No *woman* could put me on my back unless that was where I wished tae be with her riding astride," he said lowly.

Her eyes widened and her cheeks colored. So her armor was not so thick after all. The lass had a soft underbelly, but he truly wished he hadn't spoken of such things. The words brought to life too many tantalizing images.

"No woman would want you," she spat, and turned away.

He snagged her by the arm and spun her around. She countered by grabbing his wrist and pulled, attempting to throw him off balance so she could jerk free, but he was too quick for her. Snatching her good wrist, he shoved her hand behind her back and leaned against her, imprisoning her in his arms. The moment he felt her toned shapely body pressed against him, he was lost. He could think of nothing, but how much he wanted to taste her.

His lips met hers—hard. He wildly feasted on her mouth as a low growl rumbled in the back of his throat. She answered the call, pressing against him with just as much force, just as much hunger. It stirred his blood to know that she too suffered the same pains as he, the same yearnings.

His hand slid down her back to the odd trews she wore, relishing the way they molded to her firm, round bottom. Cupping her sculpted flesh, he pressed her firmly against his aching shaft. He had to have her. *Now.*

The sound of metal clashing against metal drifted in through the open window. His responsibilities, his duty came rushing back to him. He jerked his head up, away from the sweetest nectar he'd ever tasted, and released her.

She stumbled backward, her eyes wide, her lips red and swollen from his kiss.

The woman had driven him completely mad! How could he have allowed it? The clan needed him. He had his duty to see to, and it had nothing to do with this woman. This woman who made him lose control. She was dangerous.

He stormed across the chamber and yanked the blade from the door. "Dinnae venture beyond the walls again." He slammed out of the room before he tested what remained of his strength.

Tuck lifted trembling fingers to her lips as she teetered back against the wall. She blinked several times, but the sensation of being zapped with a stun gun wouldn't go away. Never had a kiss been so potent.

His tongue had speared her mouth, and she tasted his strength, his power, his passion. An eruption of sensations, the likes of which she'd never known, had exploded inside her. It was all she could do not to collapse against him in ecstasy.

For the first time in her life she wondered what it would be like to surrender.

Chapter Thirteen

Picking up the book of poetry, Tuck began to read to Elspeth, as was becoming their habit. MacLean always seemed to know when to appear and take his seat across from her.

They'd avoided any and all conversation since the kiss several days before, and often managed to stay out of each other's way for the majority of the day. But he always came to the solar in the evenings. At least he managed to show up without Maighread following on his heels like a puppy.

Tuck would read from the book of poems, and he would close his eyes and drift off to sleep. She enjoyed watching him then, relishing the freedom of just looking at him. She often wondered if it was the only time he knew any peace.

Her instincts had been right about him. He cared for each and every one of the people on MacLean land; his words to Robby and his mother were proof of that. She suspected he would stand up for anyone anywhere unjustly accused as well. He was the sort of a man a woman could depend on—one she could trust. A concept foreign to her until now.

She closed the book of poems, wishing there were more books in English to keep her mind off of Colin.

"Thank you, dear," Elspeth said, and rose.

Tuck gently set the book aside, and followed as she did every night.

She sucked in a breath at the feel of MacLean's hand on her arm as she passed him.

"Stay," he said lowly.

"I'll go see tae Douglas," Elspeth said, and slipped from the room leaving her alone with him.

She looked down at his hand and followed the tan skin up his arm to his face. His eyes were mere slits, but they saw everything.

Confused by her feelings for this man, which seemed to be growing and changing with every passing day, she wasn't sure that spending time alone with him was wise.

He lifted his lids, catching her in his steady gaze. "Please."

Twice, he'd said please, not something he did on a regular basis, she was certain. With a nod, she returned to her chair. There was something different about him since that kiss. Or perhaps she'd been the one to change.

"Thank you for reading tae Elspeth. I know she takes great pleasure in it," he said.

"I enjoy doing it for her."

He nodded and looked into the fire. "Do you write as well?"

"Yes. I can write, read, add, subtract—a great many things you'd think were uncommon or impossible for a woman."

His lips curled up at one corner. "Somehow, I dinnae doubt what you say. For the most part."

She relaxed back into her chair, confused by his partial admission. He must have finally resolved himself to her at least being different.

He returned his gaze to the fire. "I've had the same thoughts as you, regarding the men below and their purpose here. There is more going on, as you say, than the obvious." He paused a moment, seemingly collecting his thoughts before continuing. "I believe someone is trying tae start a war between the MacLeans and the MacKenzies tae weaken our numbers."

He agreed with her suspicions. She felt honored by it in some way. "You think they want to take over the island, is that it?" she asked.

"Aye. Arreyder stands on the crag overlooking the Sound of Mull where Loch Linne and the Firth of Lorne meet. 'Tis a most strategic position."

She nodded, clearly understanding the strategy. "No clue as to who they are?"

He stood and paced to the window. "Nay. We have lived a good many years in peace on the isle. But the men who ambushed us were MacKenzies. So I must assume they are working together." He looked at her over his shoulder, his arms folded.

123

"But what you don't know is whether or not I'm working with them," she said.

He nodded solemnly.

She moved closer and rested one hand on the back of the chair he'd been sitting in. "I'm no threat to you or the clan. I honestly didn't ask to be here. It just sort of happened," she said with a shrug. "Let me go, MacLean. I'm not the enemy." Although, she didn't have a clue how to get back to Jenny, she at least wanted to know she could leave when she wanted without any trouble.

He slowly dropped his hands. "I would like tae believe you, lass, but I canna chance it. If you aren't the enemy, then you must remain here until 'tis safe for you tae leave."

"I can take perfectly good care of myself."

He eyed her wrist, and she decided it would be best to keep quiet on that point. It didn't hurt nearly as much as before, but she hadn't done it any good wrestling with Robby's father.

Crossing the room, he stopped before her. "Be you a friend or foe, I'm responsible for your life, just as I'm responsible for every man, woman, and child on MacLean land."

"You don't want me here, you don't trust me, and I didn't ask to be anyone's responsibility."

"I only wish tae keep you safe." He brushed the backs of his fingers across her cheek. "I'll not find you in the wood with your pretty throat slit."

His touch was like electricity licking her skin, traveling over the most sensitive parts of her body. She wanted him to kiss her and oh so much more, although she knew it was dangerous stuff. They weren't meant for one another. She was from a different time and place, one he could never begin to understand. But that didn't stop her ever-increasing heartbeat or the flush of heat between her legs.

His gaze held hers, and she knew he felt the same pull, the overwhelming desire to lose themselves in one another. He opened his hand and slipped his callused fingers into her hair at the base of her neck. Leaning into his caress, she relished the unexpected tenderness of his touch.

Then he pulled away, his fingers curled into a fist. "You may have freedom tae move about the keep, but remain inside the walls. A guard will be with you at all times."

He turned and crossed to the door. "And put on some proper clothes," he tossed back over his shoulder.

Her mouth snapped closed with that last order. "Tyrant," she grumbled, and turned toward the darkness out the window. She caught her reflection in the watery glass and tentatively touched her cheek, then her lips, remembering the exquisite feel of him.

"One of us has to be crazy."

The next morning, a smiling Fiona arrived after breakfast, hoping for another Tai Chi lesson. But this one was going to cost her a favor. Tuck took a few minutes to explain what she needed to the giggling girl then proceeded to demonstrate her latest lesson.

Fiona caught on quickly, but she had a bit of a temper. She was so frustrated with her skirts getting in the way of her exercises, she nearly ripped them to shreds while cursing a blue streak in a mix of Gaelic and English. Poor Michael had his hands full with this one.

She managed to save the girl's clothes by suggesting she knot them at her waist so she could move more freely. The tight bodice, however, was a different story. It had to go. Once she was set, they began again. She envied Fiona for her petite beauty and natural grace.

A choked gasp brought their heads around as they performed a slow turn, crossing one foot in front of the other.

"Just a minute, Elspeth. She's almost got it," Tuck said, as they completed the last step. "There, perfect. You're a natural, Fiona."

"I'm hopin' that means what I'm thinkin'."

Tuck chuckled. "It does."

"What are you—why is she—explain yourself," Elspeth sputtered, her hands splayed on her hips.

"I'm teaching Fiona a few exercises."

"Whatever for? She gets enough work as 'tis."

"Oh, well, uh, it's a way to relax. To unwind."

Fiona sighed as she untied her skirts and laced up her bodice. "'Tis no use, Tuck. She knows things, she has

Jo Barrett

the sight. We might as well tell her."

"Look, Elspeth." Tuck draped her long arm over her shoulder. "I'm just teaching her a few moves in case she ever needs to defend herself."

"Fighting is for the men," Elsepth said, puffed up like a mother hen.

"Yeah, well, I won't argue that one. Even though you're wrong," Tuck said. "But it's a rough life here. It doesn't hurt to be prepared. You never know what might happen. You're not going to squeal on us are you?"

"I dinnae know. It doesna seem proper, a young lass learning such things."

Tuck ignored the unintended dig. Elspeth wouldn't hurt a soul, but the fact remained she was a lass, and she knew how to fight. Did that make her less of a woman to these people? To MacLean? Was that why he didn't want to kiss her again?

Geez, when would she make up her mind? First she wanted him to see her as a soldier, now as a woman.

Shaking off her annoying waffling, she said, "I tell you what, Elspeth. Why don't you come back for her next lesson tomorrow morning and watch? If I do something or show her something you think isn't proper, you can shout out. Okay?"

The older woman pondered it a bit, her brow crinkling. "Verra well. I'll watch, but I'll not be having any of your nonsense. You'll stop when I say stop," she said, wagging her finger in Tuck's face.

She snapped to attention and saluted. "Yes, Ma'am."

Elspeth grinned wryly. "Off with you, Fiona. 'Tis time tae tend your duties."

With a wave and a wink that she'd return shortly, Fiona was gone.

"I know you care for the girl, dear," Elspeth said as she turned to her. "But mind you, be careful. I wouldna want any trouble between her and Michael, you ken?"

Tuck held up her hand, and vowed, "I promise."

"Good," Elspeth said, patting her cheek.

She giggled softly at Elspeth's mothering, welcoming the sensation, having never felt it before. Or at least none worth remembering. Those memories always brought back the pain.

126

"Now I've come tae ask a favor. I hope you dinnae mind," Elspeth said.

There wasn't much she wouldn't do for Elspeth. "Whatever you want, I'll see what I can do."

"'Tis the laird." Her usually bright face fell with her words. "Maighread was called away last eve tae a cottage some distance from here. She'll not be returning anytime soon, and I need help tending tae Douglas. He doesna take his healing drafts well and with you being such a big bonny lass and ye have the skill, I thought...you see, he minds Maighread, but doesna take kindly tae others."

Tuck nodded. "Of course I'll help." She may as well make herself useful until she could figure out how to get back to her own time. A time without incredibly sexy Highlanders whose kisses were more passionate than anything she'd ever imagined.

But whose ogre-like tendencies drove her insane, she added to that thought, chiding herself for getting caught up in her stupid fantasies again.

"Thank you, lass. I'll come and fetch you after the midday meal." Elspeth toddled out, her smile once again gracing her round face.

Tuck readied herself for Fiona's return, eager to play her next card in the battle of wills between her and MacLean.

****

Colin sat down at the long table in the great hall, his mind not on his meal. He should be well and tired, his body fatigued from training with the men, but he still felt restless.

It was that blasted woman and that unforgettable kiss. She was seeping into his blood like a sickness. No matter how many hours he trained, no matter how cold the wind atop the battlements, he could not drive her from his mind.

He absently sipped from his cup, relishing the lack of herbs and the pestering of his cousin. Glad he was she'd been called away to a birthing.

An unnatural silence fell on the hall. He lifted his head and followed the gazes of his men. All eyes were on Amelia.

His mouth fell open as his anger boiled. What in

bleedin' hell was she doing wearing a kilt?

She strode across the room to her place at the table with a slightly pale Michael trailing behind her. The only sounds were her heavy footsteps from her odd boots as she crossed the stone floor.

"You," he said lowly. "Come here."

She paused and considered the matter, then casually strolled toward him, and stopped by his side. "Did you want something?"

"Sit."

Her gaze darted to the bench beside him. She lifted her foot to slide in, showing a goodly amount of bare thigh before she sat. He gripped his cup tightly, holding in his groan.

She turned her head, her chin at a jaunty angle, and grinned cockily. "Happy now?"

He narrowed his eyes. "What are you about?"

"I'm about to have lunch."

He snarled at her comment and the growing pain in his head. "Your clothes, you taupie," he snapped.

She set down her cup and glanced around the hall, taking her time to respond. "I put on some *proper* clothes."

A faint snicker or two reached his ears. He turned to see the entire room either gawking or laughing behind their hands.

"Go about your business," he ordered.

The sounds in the great hall returned to normal, albeit much more subdued. He'd wager every ear was turned to his discussion with this arrogant female beside him.

"You know what I meant," he grumbled. "You were tae put on woman's clothes."

"But that's not what you said. You said proper clothes. These are the proper clothes for a soldier. Which is what I am."

He leaned in close to her ear, hating himself for noticing her tantalizing scent. "You sit here only because I wish tae save you the embarrassment of displaying your backside tae every eye in the room. Else I'd throw you over my shoulder and toss you back intae your chamber and leave you tae starve."

"Huh, like you could. But even though I am a soldier,

I'm not quite as free beneath my kilt as you," she said, and stuffed a piece of bread into her mouth.

He ignored her continued bletherin' about being a soldier, determined to gain the upper hand, and leaned closer, nearly touching her ear with his lips. "Mayhap I should help you tae your chamber and find out for myself," he murmured, his voice laden with suggestion.

She choked and frantically reached for her cup, her cheeks burning brightly. He smacked her on the back a time or two, more than pleased.

Quickly regaining her composure, she shot him a glare. "You try it and you can forget about ever having any heirs."

"Blast you, woman," he said, irritated with her quick footedness. "Go back tae your chamber and change. Wear whatever the devil you like, but doona e'er show yourself in a mon's kilt again or I will rip it from you no matter the audience."

She swallowed another bite of her meal, took a slow sip from her cup then quietly left the great hall. He'd lost this battle, but the lass would not be so lucky the next time.

****

Happily back in her comfy jeans, Tuck followed Elspeth down the hall toward the laird's room. She shuddered as the image of MacLean throwing her over his shoulder and carrying her to her bed repeatedly flashed through her mind. It was definitely the stuff dreams were made of, or scathingly erotic fantasies. Either way, she was having one serious sexual meltdown, but how would it end? With a bang or a fizzle?

Elspeth paused at the chamber door, putting a halt to the irritating questions and the disturbing changes happening inside her. She had a task to perform, and she refused to let Elspeth down.

"Mind you, he can be verra stubborn, although he's weak," Elspeth said.

"Not a problem. I've dealt with plenty of stubborn men in my time."

Her eyes twinkled with her grin. "Aye, that you have." She turned and led Tuck into the room.

The first thing Tuck noticed was the gloom. The

heavy tapestry drapes were pulled together, shutting out the sun. Eerie shadows cast by the fire flickered over the bed where the MacLean Laird lay. She'd expected a sickroom odor, but found none. Only stale air, and an odd smell she couldn't place.

Her eyes caught sight of a small brazier on the floor by the bed. A thin trail of smoke snaked into the air. Herbs of some sort, she guessed.

Elspeth moved to a table across the room littered with various bowls and jugs. Tuck stepped up beside her as Elspeth took carefully measured spoons of the herbs and powders and combined them in a large cup.

"What's wrong with him?" she asked, trying to ascertain why he'd need so many drugs.

"He hasna been well since he was clouted over the head." She added ale to the mix and stirred. "He canna think clearly any longer and has no want for food. We can only make him comfortable." She cleared her throat softly. "I'll need your help in propping him up tae take his tonic. I didna wish tae ask Colin. It grieves him so tae see his da like this."

"I, um, understand." But she didn't, never having felt much of anything for own father other than contempt. "So what's in this thing?"

"I dinnae know all the names. 'Tis Maighread's brew. It helps him rest." Elspeth turned toward the bed and moved to the laird's side.

Tuck hesitated by the table, more than her curiosity peaked. Having never been left to her own resources in the bush for longer than her rations lasted, she'd never needed to rely on her knowledge of the various plants, both edible and medicinal. Now she found herself putting that information to the test.

She took a pinch of one of the powders and carefully tasted it. Ground heather, not dangerous, but not very helpful. She moved to another container and lifted the bowl. She gingerly sniffed, but couldn't place the plant. Although it smelled of apples, it was distinctively different.

"Mandrake," she hissed, her memory kicking in. The plant was commonly used in medicines over the ages, but could be poisonous. The amount Elspeth had placed in the cup wasn't overly much, but still, what good would it do the man?

She moved to another, recognizing it as scotch broom, harmless, then continued until she'd identified each powder. There didn't seem to be any great threat from the many herbs as long as they were carefully administered. But all at once and mixed with ale?

Her internal alarms blaring, she dropped the last bowl on the table, rushed across the room to Elspeth, and snatched the cup from her hands.

"What are you doing, lass?" she gasped.

She turned to the chamber pot sitting beside the bed and emptied the cup into it. "This stuff is killing him."

"But Maighread—"

"Doesn't know squat about medicine. All those herbs mixed together with ale is only making him sick."

"But the draft soothes him. It lets him rest."

Tuck snorted. "Oh, he'll rest all right. In peace."

She set the cup on the table and went to the bedside and touched his brow. He felt unusually cold, but at least there was no fever. Sliding his limp hand from beneath the covers, she felt his pulse. Weak, way too weak. She looked over the wound at his temple. It had scabbed over, but the coloring around it was still too purple for the amount of time that he'd been laid up. It wasn't healing.

"What have you been feeding him?" she asked.

"Broth, when he would take it. With some of the herbs mixed in."

That explained it. Not only were they mixing all sorts of potentially poisonous plants with alcohol, a dangerous combination, they were giving him too much. He was over drugged.

An odd thought crossed her mind. If Maighread was such a great healer, why didn't she realize she was killing the man? She'd been taking care of him for weeks.

She shook off her suspicions for the moment. The laird needed medical care. "No more drafts," Tuck commanded.

"But he needs them. Tae ease his mind, his pain."

She sighed heavily. This wasn't going to be easy. "What he needs is to be left alone. Those drafts are sucking the life out of him." She ran a hand through her hair at the look of consternation on Elspeth's face. It would be difficult for her to turn her trust from Maighread to her, but she had to if the laird was to live.

She grasped the older woman gently by the shoulders. "I'll try to explain this to you as best I can. Mixing all those herbs together with ale and putting them in his food has made him weak. His body doesn't have the strength to heal."

Elspeth shook her head slightly, her round face pinched with worry. "I dinnae understand."

"Have you ever heard the saying too much of a good thing is bad for you?"

She looked at the man lying listlessly in the bed. "You mean tae tell me, I've been—I've been hurting him?" Her hand flew to her mouth with a choked cry.

"It's not your fault. You didn't know. Now, here's what we're going to do. First we get rid of Maighread's potions." Tuck marched to the table and snatched up the containers, then promptly dumped them in the chamber pot.

"And as for this," she lifted the lid to the brazier, and instantly felt dizzy as a waft of smoke encircled her head.

It wasn't opium, but she suspected it caused a distinctive effect on the nervous system. Shaking her head, she snatched the basin of water by the bed and dumped it onto the smoldering weeds.

"We need to fill this room with fresh air and the laird with good food, but not solids. We need to build up his strength first. Weak ale at best, no whiskey, and plenty of broth—without any of Maighread's herbs."

"And the leeches?" Elspeth asked tentatively.

"Good God, that too? No wonder he's half dead." She grumbled an apology at her choice of words. "But keep those things away from him. Don't use them. Ever. On anyone again. Do you understand?"

"But why? They take the bad humors from the body. How can a person heal with bad humors?"

"You're just going to have to trust me, Elspeth. All those slimy things are good for is getting rid of a bruise."

She repressed a shudder. Leeches were one of her pet peeves. The nasty little buggers found their way into her fatigues on more than one occasion while she waded through shallow waters in the army.

"Now you go down and get a very big bowl of broth," she said. "We've got to flush all that stuff out of his system so his body can begin to heal itself."

Elspeth scurried out of the room, muttering "oh dear" beneath her breath several times.

"Don't worry, sir. We'll have you back on your feet in no time." Tuck hoped.

She moved to the window, threw open the curtains and let the sunshine in. Her stomach roiling with all the chemicals she'd inhaled, she opened the window to air out the place.

Chapter Fourteen

Colin paced the battlements, irritated with the constant thought of her. He tried to cast her from his mind, but repeatedly found himself thinking of her, watching her, and listening to her read.

In an effort to drive her from his mind, he spent long grueling days pouring his energies into training the men, then making quiet, fairly safe raids on MacKenzie farms.

Years of peace had weakened his clan's skills and he refused to risk their lives until absolutely necessary, but they were good lads and eager to strike back at the MacKenzies. He could not hold them back, so he appeased them with reiving. Yet were the MacKenzies the true enemy? Was someone trying to tear the island apart by pitting the clans against one another?

"Damn puzzles," he growled.

A war was at hand, and he could think of nothing but a stubborn female with lips like the sweetest heaven, a voice that spoke to his soul, when she chose to use it, and wearing trews. If he didn't regain control soon, his clan would pay for his weakness.

Time and again his mind replayed the way she'd strode into the great hall in a kilt, her long firm limbs plainly visible for the world to see. He wanted to throw her over his shoulder, storm back to her chamber, and explore every inch of her skin with his hands and lips. Madness, it was!

A light mist began to fall and he retreated inside, his determination firmly embraced. His fate was before him. He had to accept it, although he was not happy with the direction his life would take. Why had his expectations changed? Why did he find himself wishing he was not the man he was? He'd always known he would be laird one day. Why did he feel so differently about it now?

He hoped beyond hope that the answer would not have anything to do with Amelia. Aye, he could no longer think of her as Tuck, and never truly had, not when he whispered her name over and over in his dreams.

A shrewish voice echoed in the corridor answered by a deeper menacing one. He strode firmly onward, beyond his bedchamber and came to a stumbling halt before his father's open door.

"Why don't you find your broom and take flight," Amelia snarled.

Maighread raised her hand to strike her across the face, but Amelia quickly snatched her arm before she could deliver the blow and spun her around. She shoved his cousin across the room straight into his arms.

Wearing a wounded look upon her face, Maighread said, "Colin, did you not see what she's done? She tried tae kill me so she can get tae your da. I tried tae stop her, I did."

Why Maighread ever thought she could defeat Amelia was one of those female mysteries he'd yet to decipher. Not only was she a half foot taller than his cousin, she was faster and stronger. But what was she doing in his father's bedchamber?

He shoved Maighread to the side and entered the room, stopping before the woman who plagued his every waking thought.

"What are you doing in here?" he demanded. He gave only passing consideration to Maighread's words, but couldn't ignore the fact that the woman was where she didn't belong.

Amelia propped her hands on her hips and shook her head. "You still don't trust me. After everything that's happened. Ian, Robby, those jerks in the dungeon. You can actually stand there and think I'd do something to hurt your father or this clan."

He clenched his teeth against the hint of hurt in her voice, but she was right. He'd mistrusted her from the beginning, as he should, and yet over and over, she'd proven herself honorable.

He'd watched her many times from the parapet as she worked to teach Robby her odd dance amid the gardens beside the keep. The lad seemed stronger, not in muscle but in heart. He held his head high as he went about his chores, and the other children had ceased their teasing. Much could be said for her way with the lad and others who had accepted her. Nay, she was not a threat to his people.

Only to him.

"That still doesna explain why you're in my father's chamber," he snarled, unable to contain his anger with himself. He wanted to snatch her up, feel her sweet firm body pressed against his as he devoured her mouth.

Her eyes narrowed and her lips pulled into a tight line. "I happen to be helping Elspeth, who happens to trust me."

"I am the healer," Maighread shrilled as she rushed to his side. "You have no right tae be here."

"Be still, cousin."

She clawed at his arm. "She is evil, I tell you. She means tae harm your da."

Amelia poked him hard in the chest. "You let her in here to screw up the progress we've made, and I swear I'll deck you," she growled through clenched teeth then looked at Maighread. "Right after I sweep the floor with her."

He opened his mouth, but was at a loss for words as the two women prowled around him like mad cats. How had he come to be in the middle of this feud? And how was he to bring it to an end?

His cousin shrieked, piercing his ears. "She casts her spell! Beware, Colin."

"I'll cast something, but it won't be a spell," Tuck said, reaching for Maighread.

"Leave off, the lot of you! You're ruining my first good meal in an age."

Colin's heart jumped to his throat, his jaw fell lax. He'd been so distracted by the women, he'd failed to notice his father sitting up in bed eating his supper.

Slowly, he turned to where the voice, the tone, the strength he thought he'd never hear again had bellowed heartily.

"I taste your hand in this wonderful stew, Ellie," his father said then winked at his aunt who promptly blushed. "'Tis the finest I've ever tasted."

Colin cast a quick glance back to Amelia. Her arms folded and her lips pulled up in a cocky grin. She had done this. This woman who tormented him at every turn had brought his father back from the dead.

Unable to contain his joy, he plucked her off the floor, and kissed her soundly. She squeaked at the sudden connection, and he took full advantage, slipping his tongue into her mouth. She tasted better than he remembered.

"'Tis her witchcraft. She's spelled him, she has," Maighread cried shrilly.

Stunned by what he'd done, he carefully returned her to the floor. His hands glided up her arms, along her throat to her cheeks, relishing the simple pleasure in touching her. Gently cradling her face, he smiled at her dazed expression. It was one of those rare moments in which her mask fell away and all her thoughts and emotions were bared to the world. She'd enjoyed the unexpected kiss as much as he.

"You must resist her, Colin. Dinnae let her bewitch you," Maighread demanded, tugging on his arm.

His thumbs danced lightly across her damp lips then he pulled away. Setting his teeth, he glared down at his cousin. "I've heard enough of your talk. Be off with you."

"But Colin—"

"Out!" He shoved her toward the door, wishing he were shoving her out of the castle once and for all, but she was family. She'd tried to heal his father, and though he would not fault her in failing, he couldn't bear to hear her disparage Amelia's success.

Maighread ran into the corridor, her face red with rage. Perhaps if he was lucky, she would leave him be for a time.

His eyes lit on Amelia for the span of a heartbeat then he quickly stepped to his father's bedside. "I'm pleased tae see you so well, Da," he said. Hating the slightly tearful tone of his voice, he roughly cleared his throat.

His father looked at him with a solemn smile and clear eyes that held a bit of teasing sparkle. "I'm glad tae see you, lad. Sit and speak with me a while."

With a nod, Colin retrieved a chair from across the room. Elspeth took Amelia by the arm and guided her to the door.

"Wait," Colin said.

Amelia paused at the threshold and looked back at him, her mask quickly falling into place.

"Thank you," he said with a small smile.

She nodded faintly and left.

He jerked his gaze away from where she'd disappeared, determined to put her from his mind. He had to be strong for his father and for the clan. Amelia Tucker was not a woman he could bed and easily walk away from. And he would have to, if his father still intended for him to wed Aileen.

Chapter Fifteen

Staring up at the canopy over her bed, Tuck tried to shove thoughts of MacLean and his kisses aside. It didn't do any good to think about him, to want him. But she couldn't stop herself.

She bolted up from the bed and paced furiously, ticking the events off on her fingers. The first kiss was a control thing. It was the only answer she could come up with. The man could barely tolerate her. She'd been in similar struggles before. This wasn't anything new.

She paused in mid-pace. Those old power plays in the army never included kisses that made her see things in triplicate, all hazy with stars around them. He'd seemed to genuinely enjoy it as well.

A delicious shudder ran through her with the memory. "Damn, I'm a mess," she said, slapping her hands against the far wall. She rested her forehead against her arm and absently noticed her wrist didn't hurt any longer.

How could he want her, of all people? *Why* would he want her? She shook her head. Nope, it wasn't possible. She was just trying to rationalize his kiss, make it into what she wanted.

She paused, leaning back against the cool stone. "But there was that second kiss," she murmured, as she unwrapped her bandage.

"No, that was in thanks." She sighed, tossing the wrappings into a chair. He was overcome with joy. Who wouldn't be? She'd pretty much saved his father's life. Nothing wrong with a kiss. People often hugged and kissed their doctors when there was what seemed to them to be a miracle.

Tuck pushed off from the wall and paced back to the bed. "Okay, so a thank you kiss doesn't usually include tongue action." But she hadn't minded. Heck, she'd participated!

Flopping down onto the bed, she resumed her perusal of the canopy. No use in denying it, she had it bad for Colin MacLean, a man who believed women should be soft and yielding, and do what they were told. A couple of stolen kisses, a brush of his fingers against her cheek, were nothing in the scheme of things. Even if he did want her the tiniest bit, she wasn't a highborn lady with all the proper manners and whatnot, and she absolutely refused to give him the kind of power men demanded. She would retain control of her life, her future, and her body, handsome Highlander be damned.

There was a knock at the door.

Climbing to her feet, she called, "Come in."

"Good afternoon, dear heart," Ian said, strolling into the room.

Tuck planted her fists on her hips. "So, you've finally decided to get out of bed."

"I am much improved, thanks to your skillful hand. And since you refuse to fuss over me any longer, what choice did I have?"

She chuckled and shook her head. He'd been able to get out of bed for some time, but refused to do so. It wasn't long before she realized Ian was using her daily visits to his room to try and convince her to train the men. And she, sadly, had been using them as an excuse to get a closer look at Colin while he worked in the lists from Ian's window. Oh, she was definitely in deep.

"But more importantly," Ian continued. "I've come to inform you that you are no longer under guard."

Crossing her arms, she smirked. "The ogre has decided to let me off my leash? Why do I find that hard to believe?"

He smiled, his eyes bright with a roguish gleam. "Our illustrious host has had, shall we say, a change of heart."

"Want to tell me how you pulled that one off?"

"I did not, my lady. You did by saving his father's life. He is in your debt, as am I," he said with a graceful bow.

Her arms fell limply by her sides. MacLean trusted her. A smile, a really big smile, built up inside her, struggling to get past the muck and mire she'd known her entire life. It blossomed slowly, and not quite fully, but it warmed her from the tips of her hiking boots to the top of her curly hair.

It wasn't much in the way of what her heart and body kept whispering, but it was one of the best things to happen to her in a long time. Silly as it sounded, she wanted his trust and respect as much as she wanted the man. Perhaps there was a chance to have it all, to have him, without giving up control. Was it possible? Could she tone down her rather loud and often forceful opinions?

Her gaze strayed to the trunk where Elspeth had neatly folded her one and only borrowed dress. Could she be like other women he knew, be a woman he could really want?

"I see your wrist has healed," Ian said, taking her hand.

She held her surge of hope and excitement inside as she pulled from Ian's gentle grasp. "My wrist is fine, thank you."

"Then shall we go for a stroll before we sup? 'Tis a lovely evening, and I yearn to see your hair catch the sunlight before it sets."

"Give me five and I'll be right with you."

His brow furrowed, but he seemed to get the general idea and backed out of the room, closing the door behind him.

With a smile Tuck rushed to the trunk, stripping along the way. After some serious huffing and puffing, she wriggled into her feminine battle gear. She even set aside her beloved hiking boots for the quaint leather slippers. Her knife, however, she would not go without and strapped it to her thigh.

She practiced walking across the room, and giggled softly. Although her feet were decidedly colder, she felt almost graceful. She ran her hand over her skirt and took a deep breath. Elspeth and Fiona were going to drop their jaws on the spot, but what would MacLean think?

Only one way to find out. She flung open the door to go in search of her handsome escort, but didn't get far. He was patiently waiting, leaning against the wall across from her chamber door.

Ian straightened, grinning broadly. "You are the most fetching creature on the earth. I shall be most envied this eve."

Laughing, she took his proffered arm, realizing she'd never done anything like it before. Then she'd never been treated like a woman before on such a grand scale.

"You never give up, do you? Always the ladies' man," she teased, but thoroughly enjoyed his comments.

"I cannot change who I am, my dear."

Her heart headed south on an icy slide. "No. You can't, can you?"

She kept her mouth from turning down into a scowl as they walked the battlements. A pretty dress wasn't going to change who she was on the inside, a hardened soldier. Not a woman of the soft and yielding variety, the sort who never thought for herself. She would never be like that.

The sunset was magnificent, but neither it, nor Ian's continued flattery, although sweet and genuine, could bring back the buoyancy she'd had. She wasn't right for Colin MacLean. She wasn't right for anyone.

Elspeth bustled up beside her as they stepped off the stairs into the great hall. "There you are, lass. I was beginning tae worry over you." She patted Tuck's hand and winked. "You look lovely, dear."

Tuck never turned away from a challenge, not when she'd set her sights on a goal, no matter how badly the odds were against her, but she fervently wished she'd gone back to her room and changed. Losing tasted bad enough without having her strategy exposed like a freshly filleted salmon.

Elspeth took her place near MacLean while Tuck and Ian followed. She lifted her gaze and found Colin watching her, appraising her, and apparently not finding her lacking. Or had he ascertained her stupid plans as well?

Tuck tilted her head and returned his intense perusal, determined not to let him see how embarrassed she was by her foolishness. As Colin's gaze roamed over her body, thoughts of plans, strategies, and failures fled from her mind. A wonderful tingling sensation ran across her skin, and her imagination quickly slid into gear, conjuring up the feel of his rough hands and the unexpected gentleness of his touch.

Maighread stepped between them, breaking the

heated connection. Tuck quickly took her seat, hoping no one had noticed her making an ass of herself. Somehow, she had to get a grip on these crazy urges. Her little war was over, she'd lost before she had a chance to really begin. It was time to move on.

An irritating whine crawled up her back like a spider. Maighread was doing her best to get back into MacLean's good graces. Tuck could barely stomach all the purring and obvious sexual promises the woman was making. Never in her life had she indulged in a fight over a man, but she yearned to tear into the little witch. Her fingers clutched her skirts tightly beneath the table, her silent lecture on giving up quickly forgotten.

Ian cleared his throat, pulling her attention away from Maighread. His gaze was fixed on her thigh where she fondled her knife. A slightly lascivious gleam sparkled in his eye. She hadn't realized she'd hiked her skirt high enough so she could pull it out in case she needed to use it—or wanted to use it. God, she was pathetic.

Tuck moved her hand to her hip and cocked her head at Ian as he continued to stare at her leg, doing her best to forget about MacLean and Maighread.

Ian cleared his throat and blinked a time or two. "My apologies, dear heart. Your, um, weapon and the way in which you, uh, wear it, is most fascinating."

She grinned as he fidgeted in his seat. "I can't believe it. You're blushing." Ian Southernland, rogue extraordinaire, was blushing from catching a glimpse of her thigh.

"Nonsense," he sputtered. "I have had too much excitement so soon after my injury. Yes. Yes, of course. I've over extended myself this evening."

Leaning toward him, she peered at his face closely. "Nope." With a chuckle, she poked his cheek with the tip of her finger. "That's a blush if I ever saw one."

He leaned away from her, but she wasn't letting him off the hook that easily. Because of him, she'd experienced one of the most wonderful sensations in her life. She felt attractive, pretty...wanted, on a small but significant scale.

She kissed him on the cheek. "Thank you, Ian. That's probably the nicest compliment I've ever had."

143

He looked at her solemnly. "You are most welcome." A slow smile spread across his face. "But if you wish for me to retain my head, I suggest you not bestow your thanks on me in such a manner again." He motioned with his head across the table.

Confused, she turned and found MacLean glaring at them. The fire in his eyes burned hot enough to warm her cheeks and every other part of her anatomy. But what did it mean?

Colin growled softly and lowered his gaze. She was free to kiss whomever she pleased. It was none of his affair. He was betrothed, or would be once his father received word from the MacKenzie. Aileen was said to be quite fair. Some rumored she was part fey, which he dismissed off hand, but a pleasing face was not too much to ask.

He glanced at Amelia from beneath his brows. Her red ringlets danced around her face as she shook her head with a winsome smile at something Ian said. It was enough to sour his stomach.

"Is your supper not tae your liking, dear?" Elspeth asked.

He grunted and shoveled a bit of meat into his mouth.

Women. Why did he have to be plagued by women? Elspeth, Maighread, and *her*.

He missed the simplicity his life once had. He knew who he was, what his future would hold, and had no qualms about it. Now, however, he no longer found comfort in the thought.

Amelia's throaty chuckle mixed with Ian's hearty laugh gripped him fiercely. What did they have to be so bleedin' happy about?

He rose abruptly and made his way to the solar. Slamming through the door, he strode to the large window overlooking the sound and firmly crossed his arms.

Ian had managed to win a semblance of a smile from her, a real one, damn him. Not one of those smug grins she often gave him, or that look she had when she called him odd names. She'd kissed the man, too, albeit chastely on the cheek.

Had she also blessed his friend with the same passionate exchange they'd shared? Not time nor barrels of well-aged whiskey could wipe the taste of her from his mouth. Kissing her again had only increased his appetite for what he could not have.

"My, what a fine e'en," Elspeth said, as she stole into the room.

He grunted a response, too weary for words, as she took her customary place near the fire and retrieved her stitchery. Perhaps he would find some peace this night. Perhaps he could contain his lust for the woman, for that was all it was. He could not care for her. He could not care for any woman.

Laughter shattered the silence.

They strolled into the solar without a care. He despised the warm glow filling Amelia's cheeks, yet Ian had not been the one to put it there.

Elspeth leapt from her chair. "Douglas, what are you doing out of bed?"

Grinning, he patted Amelia's hand resting in the crook of his arm. "I needed—" He looked to her, his weathered brow furrowed.

"A change of scenery," Amelia supplied with one of her small grins.

He nodded. "Aye, a change of scenery."

She slipped from his grasp and guided him to a chair by the fire. Elspeth sat down beside him, her eyes overly bright.

"You still need a lot of rest, but a few minutes out of your room will probably do you some good," Amelia said.

"Aye, that it will. A man canna help but get well with such lovely lassies tae tend him," he said with a broad smile and a wink for Elspeth.

Ian snagged her hand and pulled her toward the chess table. "Come, my sweet. I challenged you to a game, remember?"

"Women dinnae play chess," Maighread said, gliding into the room.

Colin held in his groan as she made her way directly toward him. With a sigh, he took the cup she offered and sipped the whiskey, letting it release the tension from his body.

Jo Barrett

"Well this girl does," Amelia said. She rubbed her hands together greedily. "I plan to stomp you into the ground, hotshot. I hope you can take being beaten by a mere female."

Ian chuckled. "Only by you, my sweet."

Colin tossed back the remainder of his drink and slapped the cup down on a nearby table. Maighread rushed to fetch him more.

He'd been the one to demand she put on skirts, and now he sorely wished he had not. The soft swell of her breasts, visible to all, was as torturous as her long firm limbs encased in those bedeviling blue trews of hers.

He ran a hand down his face then sipped at his refilled cup while they began their game. Watching, feigning idle curiosity, he was stupefied to find her so skilled.

Over the course of an hour or so, he settled in a chair nearby with Maighread buzzing around him. He barely took notice of her or his father's unusually quiet discussion with his aunt, as the game held him enthralled. He no longer cared if they noted his steady attention.

Ian chuckled, shaking his head. "I do believe you have just placed me in check."

The woman grinned. "Uh-uh. Checkmate."

She was absolutely marvelous, Colin thought with a subtle shake of his head. Before him sat a woman who could read, knew ways in healing that had brought his father back to him, had the courage to take on a man twice her size, and could play damn good chess. He'd never met anyone like her, and knew he never would again.

"Congratulations, my sweet. You're a fine player," Ian said, taking her hand and kissing it.

"You're wounded and fatigued. 'Tis no wonder she beat you," Colin groused, knowing he spoke utter nonsense. But blast it! He couldn't stand the sight of Ian slobbering all over her hand, and her bestowing the slightest smile on the prancing peacock.

"Bosh," Ian said as he stood. "I find it fascinating that a woman could possess so many marvelous traits. Intelligence, agility, strength, and beauty. Quite the

146

combination."

Tuck's eyes flashed with a mix of humor and perhaps sorrow, but he couldn't be certain.

She cleared her throat. "Thank you." Shifting her gaze, her emotions expertly hidden, she focused on Colin. "Being a mere female, I suppose I couldn't possibly beat you," she said, one brow quirked.

Colin's gaze narrowed as he jumped up from his chair, shoved his friend out of the way, and sat opposite her at the table.

The silence returned to the room as their game began. Maighread slid up beside him, splaying her fingers across his shoulders and started to rub.

"Off with you, cousin," he grunted, his eyes intent on the board.

With a huff, she stormed across the room. No doubt to pout for a while before turning her disquieting smile on him again, but he could not think of her now. He faced a worthy opponent, one he was determined to beat. One he was beginning to admire more than he ever thought possible.

His elbows on the table, his fists clasped at his chin, he observed her slender finger tap the top of her queen as she considered her next move.

He'd touched those hands. They were not soft nor were they weak, as some ladies he'd known. They were the hands of a woman who'd lived a hard life, and yet he wondered how they would feel against his skin. He absently noticed William stride through the room to his father's side.

"Colin, I've received a response," his father said.

He grunted, his gaze still held fast to Amelia's hands, not listening as closely as he aught.

"MacKenzie has agreed."

His jaw clenched as the muscles stiffened at the back of his neck. Raising his head, he looked to his father.

"He has promised Aileen's hand," his sire said. "You will be wed as soon as may be. Then this reiving business will be done." He fingered the mark at his brow. "And no more friends will be lost," he muttered sorrowfully.

A coldness slipped over Colin as he turned his gaze from the stunned faces around him to his opponent. No one knew of his father's plans except him.

Maighread had dropped something while Elspeth had gasped softly. Ian continued coughing and sputtering on a sip of whiskey, but Amelia had fallen perfectly still. Her head bowed as she seemingly continued concentrating on her next move. He looked to her hand and noted a faint quiver and wondered if his upcoming nuptials disturbed her as much as they did him.

She lifted her hand from the piece, letting it hover for a moment then moved it across the board. "Checkmate," she said, breaking the odd stillness in the room.

Ian applauded. "Well, done, my dear. Well, done."

"She cheated. 'Tis the only way she could've beaten him," Maighread fumed.

Lifting her head, Amelia met his gaze. Colin peered deeply into the emerald depths, searching and finding the bittersweet memory of kisses he'd had no right to take and the soulful yearning for more. His chest tightened, as did his throat.

"She did not cheat," Ian said.

Maighread marched across the room and placed a hand on Colin's shoulder. "Then he let her win." She patted him like a dog. "A gentleman, you are, Colin, tae throw the match."

He swallowed hard, still ensnared by Amelia's steady gaze. "Nay, she won fairly."

"Ah-ha! You see? She is most definitely a talented player," Ian said.

Maighread huffed. "I say she used witchcraft."

Colin blocked out their continued arguing, his attention solely on Amelia. Perhaps she had bewitched him after all.

Unable to bear her presence any longer, and recognizing the same desires in her eyes that he struggled with daily, Colin silently left the room. The puzzle of Amelia Tucker weighed heavily on his mind, and, he was afraid, his heart as well.

His cool departure left Tuck feeling sick inside. She pressed her hand to her quivering stomach.

"I shall not argue with you any longer, Maighread. The truth speaks for itself. Now, if you ladies will excuse me, I am greatly fatigued," Ian said with a bow.

"I'll walk with you, Ian. I'm worn thin meself," Douglas said. "Coming, Ellie?" He held out his arm and escorted her from the room.

Great. Even her quasi-date was running out on her, but he had a good excuse. He wasn't completely healed. MacLean, however, was another story entirely.

She couldn't help it if she bruised his pride. She refused to lose just to save face. Could she help it if she was a good player? If she were a man, he wouldn't want her to let him win. He'd be slapping her on the back and congratulating her on a great play. But nooo. She was a woman, and women didn't play chess, women didn't fight, women didn't have a brain! Silently fuming, Tuck slapped the pieces in their appropriate places on the board.

Her movements slowed considerably as the truth filtered to the surface. She wasn't mad because he walked out, she was mad at herself for believing he'd want her. Too tall, too freckled, Amelia Tucker. What had passed between them across the chessboard was powerful, but he didn't want anything to do with it—with her.

"You canna have him," Maighread hissed. "Dinnae think that because you can make him look at you, that he is yours." She puffed up her chest and looked down her nose. "You're naught but a freak." She threw out her hand, scattering the chess pieces across the table and floor, then rushed from the room.

"What is that woman on?" Tuck muttered.

Shaking her head, she cleaned up the game pieces. Loony or not, however, Maighread had a point. Colin was marrying Aileen somebody. Not her.

It was just as well. Her feet were cold wearing the dumb slippers, and the bodice was starting to bind and itch. In the morning she'd go back to wearing her own clothes. She was who she was, and if that wasn't good enough, too bad.

Making her way to her room, she refused to credit the subtle slump of her shoulders to anything but fatigue. She slipped out of the dress and curled up in front of the fire in her shift. Bed didn't sound very appealing. She knew he'd be there in her dreams.

There was a soft knock at the door.

"Who is it?" she called, not really in the mood for

company.

"'Tis Fiona."

With a sigh, she crossed to the door and let her in. Maybe a workout was what she needed. It was a damn sight better than thinking...or dreaming.

"Did you hear the news?" Fiona said, as she danced through the doorway.

"What news?" She shuffled back to her chair and flopped down, not really giving a rat's ass about the latest scuttlebutt.

Her smile ridiculously wide, Fiona said, "Colin is tae marry."

You'd think she was the one getting hitched. "Yeah, I heard. He's marrying the MacKenzie chick."

Fiona perched on the edge of the chair opposite her. "'Tis said she is part fey," she whispered.

Naturally. Well, what did I expect? MacLean was a virile, sexy Highlander, who was in line to be the next laird of the clan MacLean. Of course she'd be beautiful, and he'd have no problems whatsoever getting her to keep to her place. Independent, freckled female soldiers weren't his type. She wasn't anyone's type. Her father had drilled that into her head often enough.

Tuck rubbed her hip then wrapped her arms around herself, her gaze lost in the flickering flames as memories played out in her mind.

"What are you wearing?" her father had asked hotly, his words slurred.

"A-a dress. I have a date," she replied.

He laughed harshly. "Who'd go out with a pitiful excuse of a girl like you?" He staggered closer and flicked one of her curls. "Don't know where you got that head of hair," he said with a sneer. "God-awful to look at. Just like the rest of you. Worthless piece of—"

He tipped back the bottle, draining its contents. With a growl he threw it down, shattering it against the scarred wood flooring.

She sat perfectly still on the couch, terrified of what he'd do next. The more he drank, the meaner he became.

"Go get me another bottle," he shouted, waving toward the cabinet across the room.

"There isn't anymore." She'd poured most of it down

the drain and hid the bottles in the garbage, hoping he would think he'd drank it all.

His hand flew out, striking her across the cheek. "You lying bitch! I said get me some more!"

She bit back her tears. "There isn't any!"

He grabbed her by her hair and pulled her from the couch. Dragging her behind his stumbling feet, he crossed to the cabinet and tossed her to the floor. "Open it!"

She quickly yanked open the doors so he could see there was nothing left. A frightening stillness engulfed the room. She peered up at him from beneath her damp lashes.

"What did you do with it?" he snarled.

She didn't answer. He grabbed her up by the front of her dress, tearing it. When he shoved his face into hers, she gagged on his horrid breath.

"Where is it?" He shook her hard, over and over. "Where, damn it!"

"It's all gone," she cried.

With a roar, he shoved her across the room. She caught herself on the edge of the couch.

He waved his hand in the air as he swayed. "Get out of my sight."

"But my date—"

"Get out, so I don't have to look at your ugly face!"

When she didn't move, he shoved her toward the hall. Her foot caught on the edge of the coffee table, and she fell on the broken bottle. The glass dug painfully into her chest and hip.

"I said, get out!"

Afraid he'd kick her and crack a rib, as he'd done before, she scrambled to her feet. Although her vision blurred with tears, she clearly saw the red stain blossoming like a flower across her chest and side. Her soft yellow dress grew damp and stuck to her skin.

She stumbled to the bathroom and carefully picked the glass from her breast and hip, nearly fainting from the intense pain. Pressing towels against her body to stop the bleeding, she grew dizzier with each passing second.

The doorbell rang, or so she thought, she couldn't be sure, her head spun wildly, but she heard her father yelling at someone. She staggered into the small living room, clutching the towel to her breast while holding onto the meager array of furniture as she went.

"Hospital," she breathed.

She heard a gasp and a curse as she felt the floor come up to greet her, then total silence.

Her date had saved her life, but he'd never asked her out again. No one did. But then he hadn't really asked her out in the first place. She practically blackmailed him into it with one major guilt trip after she helped him with his algebra.

Why should now be any different? Ian was only being kind because she'd saved his life, and MacLean's kisses were nothing more than a way to control her, to put her in her place. She was still the ugly redheaded Amazon nobody wanted.

Tuck huddled deeper into the chair, wishing the painful truths would go away instead of hovering around her like the annoying pests they were.

"Do you not see? This means that Michael and I can be wed," Fiona said, bouncing like a child in the chair, pulling Tuck from her agonizing thoughts.

Forcing a small smile to her lips, Tuck said, "I'm happy for you, Fiona. Really." She rose from her chair and went to the bed. "I'm pretty bushed. Mind if we skip our session tonight?"

"Are you not well, Tuck? You dinnae seem tae be yourself this eve."

"No, no. I'm fine. Just tired." She faked a big yawn and turned down the covers.

"Verra well. I bid you good rest."

Tuck nodded as she left, then slid between the covers. A faint sniffle slipped out, and she flipped over and buried her face in her pillow.

"I hate weddings," she muttered roughly as her pillow grew damp.

Chapter Sixteen

The sun cut across Colin's cheeks and open eyes as it had done every morning for weeks. Mostly he spent a good deal of the night staring at the canopy above his bed, obsessed by a woman like none he'd ever known. She'd saved his father, his friend, and his own life, although he never admitted it openly. He admired her spirit, her bravery, and she drove him to near madness. Try as he might, he could not stop thinking of her.

He avoided all contact with Amelia. Had gone so far as to eat at odd hours so he wouldn't have to see her on Ian's arm, hoping to drive her from his thoughts. But every night she hounded him in his sleep, the vision of her scantily clad body, the swipe of her tongue across her lips, the very scent of the woman would find its way into his dreams, into his senses. He ached to hold her, kiss her, but he could not. He was betrothed and would soon wed.

He'd grown weary of waiting on Aileen's arrival these last weeks. Why would MacKenzie not make haste so he could get on with his damn wedding? Then, perhaps, Amelia would leave his thoughts once and for all. But the taste of her—no, that he could not easily forget.

Donning his clothes, he idly wondered if Aileen could play chess or read. He ascended the stairs to the battlements, turning his thoughts to his father's increasing good health. His plan to join the clans to end the warring was sound, although he wished fervently there was another way.

His father had yet to regain his full memory, leaving more questions as to this unexpected war. What had happened that fateful night when Fergus had brought him back to the castle? Did it have to do with his own suspicions, that there was someone outside the clans orchestrating everything?

The hole in his sire's thoughts often irritated the old man to the point of being ill. It took Elspeth's sweet voice to calm him. Another interesting turn of events. Colin had known for some time that his aunt had deep feelings for his father, but the man never seemed to notice. Now, the laird's eyes were alight with something new whenever he looked at her.

He shook his pounding head. It wasn't like his father at all, and he wondered if the blow to his head had done more than steal his memory. Had his injury addlepated him as well?

The Laird had yet to see the spies still kept in the dungeons, nor would he listen to any of Colin's theories regarding them. He spoke only of the impending arrival of his betrothed while quietly wooing Elspeth.

The wind wrapped around Colin as he stepped onto the parapet. He inhaled deeply, letting the salty air soothe his weary, confounded brain. Leisurely, he strolled to the opposite side of the castle where the sun was warm and welcoming with the full bloom of spring and paused.

She was there.

He took the opportunity to study her, the woman to whom he owed his gratitude, the woman who haunted him at every turn, before she noted his presence.

Standing in her stocking feet, her extraordinary boots set aside along with her coat, she lifted her arms and legs in the oddest manner. 'Twas a dance of some sort and was hypnotizing with its fluid movements. He'd seen her once or twice with Fiona doing the like, and something similar with Robby, but had never ventured close enough to see her face.

The bite of the wind had turned her cheeks to a soft crimson while her cap of red curls twisted and turned ablaze in the morning sun. The serene smile upon her lips was the most captivating of all. He'd seen her smile at Ian over some jest, but this turn of her lips was different— unique. It came from her soul.

She turned slowly, her arms gracefully gliding through the air, and her gaze met his. Without the faintest hesitation, she continued her dance. He watched her for several more minutes, wondering about her homeland, her people, and why she had traveled so far. Why she was here.

Her eyes closed, and she let out a long exhale while

bringing her arms back to her sides, ending the odd dance. She silently crossed to her shoes and put them on. Once done, she rose and slipped on her waistcoat. He remained silent, not sure what to say.

She turned to face him after closing the odd garment. "Did you want something?" she asked, breaking him from the spell she'd cast over him.

"What is it that you do? Those strange movements you make," he said, motioning with his hand.

"I was doing my exercises. It's called Tai Chi. It's a great stress reliever. It also lends me strength and flexibility in hand-to-hand combat."

"Combat," he scoffed. "Women are not made for such things. They're too soft, too weak."

"You seem to forget, as usual, that this soft, weak female beat the crap out of the MacKenzies, took out two of your guards, handed you two trespassers, and managed to overcome your blacksmith."

He shook his head. "You use surprise and tricks as your weapons. 'Tis not real fighting. I will admit you have some skill, but you are no match against a healthy—sober man, one who is aware of your tactics."

Her jaw clenched. "When are you going to get it, MacLean? I'm a soldier, first, last, and always."

"A woman soldier?" He waved his hand at such a blatant bit of nonsense. Aye, she was skilled, but not a true soldier, she had to see that.

"Fight me and find out," she said, shifting her stance, readying herself as if he was about to attack her. "I dare you."

He snorted. "Daft woman. You're speaking foolishness. I'd crush you in an instant."

She visibly relaxed. "Hmm, just like you crushed me in chess. You're afraid, MacLean. Admit it."

"You're no warrior, damn you! You're a woman." One he wished to God he did not want so fervently.

She tilted up her chin, her eyes narrowed. "You can bellow and bluster all you want, but it doesn't change the facts. You're afraid I'll beat you." Tuck moved past him, her back as straight as his sword. "Again," she tossed back over her shoulder as she trotted down the stairs.

"Afraid, aye," he murmured, leaning against the wall,

his gaze falling to the churning waters below.

Afraid he'd lay his hands on her and not let go. He wished he hadn't seen how graceful she was, how calm and serene. And she'd challenged him without so much as a flicker of fear in her eyes. She was a rare woman whose mere presence spoke to parts of his being he was finding it harder and harder to keep buried. But his duty was to the clan. He could not let these growing feelings rule his actions.

His fate lay down another path with another woman.

****

Furious, Tuck stomped down the stairs and outside to the lists. She wanted, needed a good workout.

She stopped at the edge of the small field and observed the men as they started their daily routine. The sound of steel against steel reverberated in the air. She caught sight of Michael standing to the side talking to Fiona, his heart in his eyes. No man would ever look at her that way. Least of all, the one she wanted.

With a snarl, she stomped toward the lovebirds. "Fiona, you ready to work out or what?" she said gruffly.

Fiona's mouth opened and closed as she blinked.

"What mean you?" Michael asked, his face twisted with confusion as his eyes darted between them.

Tuck ignored him, her gaze firmly on Fiona. "Well?"

"I, uh, I suppose."

"Good," she said with a firm nod. "Then let's work over there."

"In the lists?" she gasped. "Nay, we canna."

"Why not? It's the best place to do it. Plenty of room to move around. Come on." Tuck grabbed her arm and dragged her across to the far corner where the men were few. Michael followed, demanding to know what they were doing.

"You daft females. Do you wish tae get your heads taken off?" he sputtered. "Women dinnae belong in the lists."

"Mayhap we shouldna do this, Tuck," Fiona said meekly.

Tuck puffed out a breath and turned on Michael, her hands fisted on her hips. "Look, I'm teaching her how to defend herself. You got a problem with that?"

He scowled. "She doesna need you tae teach her such things. I'll protect her," he declared, pounding his chest.

Rolling her eyes, she positioned Fiona where she wanted her and began. "I'm going to show you how to get loose if someone grabs you by the wrist."

"Fiona, I forbid you tae do this," Michael barked.

Both women stilled and turned their heads, their faces set in firm scowls.

"You forbid me?" Fiona asked, her hands mimicking Tuck's, fisted and planted firmly on her hips. "You aren't my husband yet, Michael Fraser, and I'll thank you tae be remembering that."

He clenched his jaw as a crowd grew around them. "Husband or no, your da wouldna approve of this. 'Tis not fittin' for a woman tae fight."

"Geez, not that again," Tuck muttered. "Fiona, if you want to do this, let's get on with it."

"Aye." She nodded firmly and turned back to Tuck.

"Good. Now, using your free hand, grab the top of your fist and then pull back against the attacker's grip. Especially against his thumb, it's the weakest link. By pulling back on your own wrist, you're pulling his shoulder forward which can interfere with a punch from his other arm. Also, by sinking back, you can shift your weight, giving you a chance to get in a snap kick. You remember that, right?"

"Aye, but I'll not be able tae do it with my skirts."

"True, they'd get in the way, but this will give you a chance to run for it. Now, let's give it a try."

Tuck acted as the attacker, and they moved in slow motion a time or two to practice. When Tuck felt she was ready, they did it for real.

Michael looked on with his mouth hanging open, apparently stunned that Fiona had disobeyed him. One of the men tossed a wisecrack in their direction, setting his face on fire. Michael squared his shoulders and stepped up beside them.

"Stop this nonsense, Fiona. I'll not have you lookin' the fool," he demanded, slapping his hand on Tuck's wrist where it sat atop Fiona's.

That was a very...big...mistake.

Tuck pulled him forward and kicked him squarely in

the stomach. He fell on his butt, gasping for air.

"How's that for nonsense?" she asked, standing over him. She'd had it with all the women don't do this crap.

Fiona fell to her knees beside him. "Ach, Michael, are you hurt?"

He shook his head, glaring up at Tuck as William and the others laughed at his expense.

"How does it feel tae be beaten by a woman?" one of the men called. "At least she left your nose intact this time, eh Michael?"

"Did she bat her lashes at you before she put you on your arse?" another added. "Or were you struck dumb by her charms?"

Tuck gritted her teeth. That last crack was aimed more at her than Michael, but they'd get their turn, and she'd enjoy every minute of it. But first she had to finish with Fiona's fiancé.

Looking down at him, she asked, "Care to take a shot at me? I kind of owe you one for that sucker punch a while back."

"I'll not fight a woman," he spat, climbing to his feet.

She rolled her eyes heavenward. When would these guys get with the program? Reaching out, she took his arm and flipped him over her back. He landed with a glorious thump at her feet.

Fiona dropped beside him again. "Please, Tuck. Dinnae hurt him."

Michael shoved her aside as he got back on his feet. Fiona's begging had hit a soft spot. She could see it in his eyes. He wanted a piece of her so bad he could taste it.

"How about now?" she taunted, eager to get a real work out. She'd hidden out in her room and various other places since that night she'd heard about MacLean's upcoming wedding. Pouting, of all things. Well not anymore.

Michael's fists clenched by his sides as the men made a circle around them, laughing and joking, yet he still held back.

She grinned at his show of chivalry, admiring how well he was taking the ribbing. But she needed a good fight to get a certain Highlander off her mind, and these guys needed a lesson.

"I tell you what, Michael," she said. "No punches, no biting, no clawing, just a good old fashioned wrestle. Whoever pins the other, wins. Think you can handle that?"

He narrowed his eyes.

"Come on, don't be a chicken."

That did the trick. He lunged at her with a roar, but she sadly put him on his back again.

The men called and cheered. "Dinnae let her beat you, lad! She's just a woman!"

She gave him his lead for a while, letting him think he might win. Humiliating him wasn't on her agenda, but she eventually pinned him, and he grudgingly conceded with a winded grunt.

Feeling invigorated, she rose to her feet, dusted off her jeans and turned to the men laughing their kilt-clad butts off.

"What sort of fankle is this?" MacLean blustered, as he and Ian strode into the list.

"The wee lassie here bested Michael in a wrestling match," William said with a wide grin. Crossing his arms over his broad chest, he said, "And a damn fine job she did too."

Tuck grinned and bowed her head slightly toward the old Highlander who gave her a friendly wink in return.

One down and a few dozen to go, she thought, looking over the rest of the men.

"What rotten luck," Ian said with a broad smile. "I would have liked to have seen that, now that I'm not battling for my life."

"Bloody hell," MacLean groused. Had his entire garrison lost their wits?

"Oh, but the show's not over yet," she said. "Who's next?" The men quieted to a few soft chuckles, but continued grinning like buffoons.

Colin shook his head and pinched the bridge of his nose at his increasing headache. Why had he been plagued with this female?

She spread her feet and planted her hands on her hips. A familiar pose, one he was growing accustomed to.

"What's the matter, afraid to fight a woman?" she asked. "Afraid I'll hurt you?" She waved at a red-faced

159

Michael. "He was brave enough to take me on. I guess that means the rest of you are just a bunch of cowards."

She shot Colin a smirk. "Looks like you've got yourself a bunch of wimps, MacLean."

By the saints, she was insane. They would break every bone in her body to ease their sorry egos.

"I'll be happy tae wrestle you," one man boasted. "Beneath the covers!"

Laughter erupted around them, but Colin gave it little notice as he moved to swipe the smile off of Ronald's face. Although a good warrior, he'd always been an arse. It was time to teach him some manners.

Ian stayed him with a hand on his shoulder. "Let her deal with him," he said softly. "She must finish what she has started. After all, you can always kill him later," he added with a grin.

"Aye," Colin growled. "But they'll tear her apart first."

Ian chuckled with a nod toward Amelia. "I seriously doubt that."

She strolled up to Ronald, a quirky grin on her lips. In a heartbeat his guard was down on the ground struggling to suck in a breath. Her foot had moved so quickly, connecting with his chest, that Colin had barely seen it.

He closed his gaping mouth. The woman could actually fight, and not mere tricks as he'd repeatedly claimed.

"You were saying?" she asked Ronald while he continued his attempts to breathe.

Lifting her head, she eyed the others. "Anyone else care to take a shot at it?"

"Did I not tell you?" Ian asked quietly.

"Aye, that you did, but can she handle all of them? She has yet tae face the worst, and they'd not been prepared for a worthy opponent. Now her skills will truly be tested."

"Perhaps a show is all they require. I suspect Michael did not give his all, afraid he would hurt her." Ian stepped forward. "I should like a go," he called to her.

She turned, shaking her head. "I've nothing to prove to you. They're the ones that need to learn a lesson."

"Be that as it may, I have accepted your challenge. You cannot back out now." He took her hand and bowed over it before placing a quick kiss.

Several men chuckled, while Colin tightened his grip on his folded arms. Why the devil was he always kissing her hand?

"Okay, you're on," she said.

She took off her coat and tossed it to Fiona, whom he noticed was grinning broadly. Just what he needed, he thought with a weighty sigh, more women who wanted to fight.

Ian and Amelia took their places opposite one another.

"I'll do my best not to hurt you," she said.

"I appreciate that, dear heart. And I shall do the same," he replied, and lunged toward her.

Colin jerked, wanting to block his move, but managed to stand his ground. Skilled or no, he doubted the day would ever come that he would be truly comfortable with a woman—with Amelia fighting.

Ian landed squarely on his back. Colin grinned behind his hand.

"Are you okay?" she asked.

"I believe I am well," Ian said, his voice not nearly as congenial as before.

"Fight, Southernland. Dinnae let her beat you, mon!" someone called.

"Ach, she'll beat him, 'tis certain. I'd bet me gold on it," William called.

"As would I," said Michael.

A betting frenzy ensued, leaving his garrison split down the middle as to who would be the victor.

"Ach, he's sweet on the lass. He has tae let her win," someone said.

She helped Ian up, and they took another go at one another, but once again his friend was quickly on his back.

Amazing. He'd never met a woman who could actually fight.

Ian rose slowly, his breath coming in pants, and dusted off his clothes. "I believe I have had all I care to take for one day, dear heart." He took her hand in his and kissed it.

Again with the kissing? "Aye, you're not well enough tae be fighting," Colin grumbled.

Her brow shot up.

"But I'll admit you are quite skilled, lass," he quickly added. She'd proven herself in more ways than one. He wouldn't deny the lady her due.

"Why dinnae you fight her, Colin?" William asked.

She cast him a grin. "Yeah, MacLean. Show me what you've got. I dare you." She tossed her head, making her hair catch the rays of the sun.

Could he fight her, touch her, without taking her? "I find no pleasure in beating a woman."

"Like I said. You're just afraid I'll beat you."

He glanced at his men, noting their smug grins. If he didn't fight her, he'd never hear the end of it. "Verra well. But when I beat you, I'll not have any of your tears, woman."

"Oh, I wouldn't dream of it."

She took her position on the field, and he warily stood opposite her, waiting for the first move. She came at him stealthily and with a flash of movement he hadn't anticipated, brought him cleanly to his knees, then to his belly. The cheers and jeers abounded.

"Care to try again?" she said, leaning near his ear, her voice low and sultry.

He swallowed hard against the torment raging inside him from her nearness. Snaking his arm out, he caught her foot and brought her to the ground beside him, then quickly pinned her in place. He grinned at the stunned expression on her face, but the flash of desire racing through his blood quickly wiped it from his lips.

The sound of cheers and taunts faded, leaving nothing but her rapid breaths echoing in his ears. He let his gaze roam over her features, noting every spot dotting her skin. The pert tip of her nose begged for a kiss, as did her luscious mouth. The deep green eyes, framed with reddish-brown lashes, held a deep-seated yearning that called to his own.

"Colin, get up and greet your bride," his father said.

He blinked, she blinked, then they both turned their heads to see a pair of dainty slippers not five strides away.

He rolled to his back, and Amelia jumped to her feet.

"You're good, MacLean. I'm impressed," she said, dusting off her clothes overmuch. Nervous she was. The hint of a quiver lingered in her voice, but he doubted anyone could hear it but him. He felt connected to her in ways he'd never dreamed of before and wished for more.

Rubbing his forehead, as he lay sprawled on the ground, he couldn't believe he'd nearly ravaged her mouth, and possibly other more tempting parts of her body, in front of his entire garrison. In front of his blasted bride!

A hand appeared before him, and he clasped it firmly. "You had best watch yourself, my friend," Ian said. "You've already one female in the keep who is less than pleased with your attentions toward Amelia. I would not add your future bride to that list."

He snarled at his so-called friend and turned to Aileen. His mouth, once again, fell agape. The girl was beautiful, but barely reached his chest in height and couldn't weigh as much as a bird. How would he ever be able to bed the lass? He'd be too afraid he'd break her in two.

Ian nudged him in the back.

"Uh, welcome to Arreyder, my lady," he said.

She nodded meekly. He resisted the urge to cast his eyes to heaven. Why had his father saddled him with a lass such as this?

Sadly, he knew the answer to that question, although it didn't ease his mind. He looked to her side and nodded to her guard. "Robert."

"Colin," he replied. They'd butted heads a time or two as lads, but over inconsequential things. He'd always liked Robert, and was glad he'd not been among the men who'd ambushed them. He'd hate to have to kill him.

"Ach, my. You're the image of your mother," Elspeth said, toddling up to Aileen's side. "I knew her when we were but a pair of wee lassies." She took her hand and patted it.

"If you'll excuse me, I have, um, things to do," Amelia said, edging toward the keep.

"Nay, lass. You must meet Colin's intended." Elspeth

snagged her arm before she could escape. "Aileen, this is Amelia. She's visiting with us for a time. And this," she said motioning toward Ian, "is Ian Southernland."

The lass nodded to Amelia, then blushed furiously as Ian took her hand and bowed over it.

"Come lads, we'll have a wee drink and you can tell me of MacKenzie, Robert," his father said. "The women will get Aileen settled. They're sure tae go on about the wedding and lace and other such female nonsense for some time."

Amelia's brows rose. Colin braced himself for one of her biting remarks.

William cleared his throat loudly. "Lass—Tuck, might I have a word with you?"

Her eyes brightened. "Certainly. Um, you run along, and I'll catch up later," she said to Elspeth, then immediately strode off with Colin's lead guard toward the far side of the bailey where the men had resumed their training.

Colin and Ian exchanged puzzled glances then followed his father and the others into the keep. But he couldn't resist one last glance over his shoulder at where Amelia stood talking with William. She was so much more than he ever dreamed, and he wanted her with every part of himself. Tearing his gaze away, he looked to his future.

Chapter Seventeen

"Thanks, William. You're a lifesaver," Tuck muttered.
The old Highlander chuckled. "You're welcome, lass. I didna think you were of a mind tae be lookin' at a bunch of female frippery and such."

She snorted. "You've got that right." She stopped at the far side of the training field and propped her hands on her hips with a puff of air. "I guess this means you guys won't be doing anymore heavy training, what with the joining of the clans and all."

William crossed his arms and stroked his chin. "Well, now that you mention it, I was wonderin' if you'd be kind enough tae show me how you put Colin on his belly so easily. War or no, a man likes tae keep up his skills and improve upon them when he has a chance."

Her day, dreary as it seemed in light of the beautiful fragile female she'd just met, brightened. "I'd be happy to."

Michael and a few others gathered around them as she demonstrated. There were a few catcalls, but they didn't last long.

"'Tis an amazing thing," William muttered, helping her to her feet.

"This is nothing. There are a lot of deadlier moves, believe me." She demonstrated a few and was met with awed faces.

Hours later, filthy from her head to her toes but feeling fantastic, she strolled into the keep and up to her room. There wasn't any more talk of witchcraft, thank goodness, and the men actually listened to her. They discussed techniques and traded old war stories. It was great! Maybe she'd be okay in this century after all.

"My heavens. What happened tae you?" Elspeth said, meeting her in the corridor.

"I was showing the guys some moves. You know, fight techniques." Elspeth followed her into her chamber as she tugged off her knit hat. "And it felt great. I haven't had that much fun in months." She splashed water on her face and wiped away some of the grime.

"You mean tae say you've been wrestling with the men? Ach! I'm afraid tae guess what you'll do next."

Tuck dried her face, muffling her chuckle against the cloth.

"Well, you'll not be getting clean with just a bit of water," Elspeth said. "I'll have the kitchen lads bring up a tub."

"Oh, a bath," she sighed. "That would really feel good."

Later, as she eased her sore muscles into the tub, Tuck let the day play over in her mind. She'd waited until she thought she could handle all the emotional highs and lows without an audience. Wrestling MacLean had been an unexpected pleasure, and not because she'd put him on his stomach, but damned if she didn't nearly make a fool of herself. She'd almost grabbed the man by his hair where it fell over his broad shoulders and pulled him down for a kiss. The tips of her breasts pebbled instantly.

With a groan, she sank lower in the tub.

Pinned beneath him, his thick muscle-corded legs laid out along hers, felt too good to ignore. She snorted softly, resting her head against the edge of the tub. She couldn't have ignored him if she'd wanted to. Hiding from him hadn't done any good. She was more than merely attracted to the man. She felt something for him, inside and all over, but he was about to be married to one of the most beautiful women she'd ever seen.

Aileen moved like a ballerina and had a braid of fair hair that hung below her waist. She had yet to hear her utter a single word, but knew the girl's voice would be as soft and delicate as the rest of her. All the things Tuck wasn't.

Slumping beneath the water, she scrubbed her skin till it was raw. At least she'd proven her point once and for all. She may not be pretty like Aileen, and maybe she couldn't do all those female things men expected, and she sure as hell didn't bow down to their false superiority, but she was a damn good fighter. Not only had she gained Colin's trust by helping his father, at the very least, he seemed to respect her talents as well. That was something, although her heart whispered a little too loudly for more.

She climbed out of the tub and dried off, then jerked up her skirt with a curse. Her pants were way too dirty to put back on, dang it, so she struggled with the confounded laces. She quickly gave her jeans a good dunking in the bath water, and laid them out to dry, then headed to supper.

The great hall seemed brighter and gayer than usual. Talk of peace and Colin's impending wedding circulated throughout the room. She held in her groan.

Ian appeared at her side and escorted her to the table. "You look absolutely charming, my dear," he said and kissed her hand.

Her hand would be raw by the time she got back to Jenny, but she enjoyed the attention. Although it didn't mean anything. It was just Ian's way with all women, she realized.

Silently, she took her place beside him and did everything she could not to look at MacLean. She smiled forcefully at the men who'd chosen to sit near her as they spoke of their afternoon in the lists, but didn't engage in the conversation.

"Surely, ye jest," one of Aileen's guardsmen, said. "No woman could best me."

Tuck ignored him. They'd not seen her working with the men in the lists as they'd been taken inside for food and drink after their journey across the island. But she wasn't in the mood to fight that battle again.

"I tell you, mon, she can and she did," William blustered. He turned his gray eyes to her. "Tell the lad what you did, Tuck. Tell him how you put Colin on his arse," he chuckled heartily.

She shook her head with a wry grin.

"Ye see, she admits yer tellin' tales, auld mon," the guardsman said.

William slammed down his cup and narrowed his eyes. "Care tae make a wager on it?"

Oh, boy. She needed to cut this off and quick. The last thing she needed to do was incite more rivalry between the clans. The tense undercurrent in the room was palpable.

"Look, fellas, I'm not exactly dressed for show and tell. Why don't we leave this discussion until another time?"

The guardsman laughed. "Yer champion has deserted ye, auld mon."

"She'll do more than that," Maighread muttered as she poured the guard more wine. "She'll spell you, she will."

Tuck let out an exasperated breath. Not that old story again. She'd just barely won MacLean's men over and already the witch was stirring up more trouble, but this time with the MacKenzies. What was she, insane?

"What mean ye, lass?" the guardsman asked, eyeing Maighread's ample breasts. Of course, how could he miss them when she practically shoved them in his face like she did Colin every night?

"She's a witch. She's spelled the laird. Tricked poor Colin intae thinkin' his da's well when he's not behavin' like himself," she said, her voice low but not unheard by the men surrounding her.

Tuck's hand slid to her skirt. Ian clasped her wrist beneath the table. She shot him a glare, but he shook his head.

"Nonsense," Ian scoffed loudly with a gentle squeeze of her wrist. "This lovely woman saved my life, and I'll not hear a disparaging word about her."

She held her breath, as the entire hall listened in on their conversation.

Maighread decided to use the center spotlight to its fullest. She gasped dramatically. "She's spelled you, she has. 'Tis likely the lady Aileen will take ill with her here." The witch shot her an evil glare. "She'll murder us all in our beds!"

The ensuing silence pretty much capped it for Tuck. No more playing nice. Her knife slid silently from its sheath and thunked ominously into the wooden table directly in front of where Maighread stood.

The collective gasp rang in her ears. "If I wanted to kill someone, I wouldn't need to use witchcraft," she said, rising from her seat to retrieve her knife. "Besides..." She jerked the blade from the wood. "The role of witch is already taken." She prayed she hadn't made a big mistake by letting her only weapon be seen by everyone, but she'd had enough.

Maighread stood perfectly still, but the hate in her eyes was unmistakable.

Hiding her knife in the folds of her skirts, Tuck glanced at MacLean. If he trusted her, really trusted her, he wouldn't try and take her knife, because if he did, someone would get hurt in the process.

A great bellowing laugh burst from him as he threw his head back. The laird, Ian, and the men she'd worked with for long hours in the lists joined him. A few of the women, Elspeth and Fiona included, giggled behind their hands. Maighread's face burned furiously as she stormed from the hall.

"Well met, lass," William bellowed, thumping her on the back. "Well met!"

Her gaze fell on Aileen, her face as pale as snow, her eyes wide in shock. It was obvious the girl had been overly protected, shielded from the world and the harshness of it. She indeed was a fragile innocent flower.

Everything Tuck would never be.

Tuck left the hall and sheathed her knife. Walking the battlements, she watched the sun disappear until it grew too cold in her skirts. She couldn't stick around and watch him marry that girl, it hurt too much.

She stumbled as she entered her chamber, the truth striking her like a blow to the stomach. She'd tried to ignore it, ordered it to go away on more than one occasion, but it was no use. It had found her and it wasn't going to let go. The one thing she'd craved as a child, the one thing she'd avoided as an adult, the one thing that could tear her apart.

Love. She was in love with Colin MacLean.

Yet just as before with her father, she would never be good enough, pretty enough—woman enough. She had to leave. Tossing off her clothes, she paused a moment to caress the dress Elspeth had given her.

"Next thing you know, I'll be crying," she grunted, snatching her hand back, although the backs of her eyes already burned.

Aileen could have him and so could Maighread. She'd

leave at first light and make that stupid spring take her butt back where she belonged. She had a job to do, and it had nothing to do with a Highlander who'd been dead for four hundred years.

"Damn," she grumbled. She pressed the heels of her hands against her eyelids as she sank onto the bed.

****

Walking the battlements as he did every morning, Colin spied Amelia talking to the guard at the gate. He wondered what they were discussing, then grinned. Fighting techniques, no doubt. She was extraordinary, and he'd discounted her at every turn because of her sex. When had he become such a narrow-minded man? And yet, how often did one meet a woman warrior?

They shook hands then she went through the gate, heading for the woods at the end of the road. He didn't know where she was going or why she'd chosen to leave, but he had the distinct feeling she wasn't coming back.

"Damn the woman. Will she never do as she's told?"

As Tuck disappeared around the far turn into the wood, Colin raced down the stairs. She could take care of herself. That she'd proven, but he refused to rely on her skills to keep her safe from the unknown forces striving to rip the island in two. The combining of the clans could very well cause their real enemy to strike a deadlier blow.

He made his way through the wood with William and Michael by his side. Although he wanted to take the entire garrison, every man he had to keep her safe, the clan was still, and would always be his responsibility. It had to be protected.

Spotting her sitting on a log by the same small spring she'd come to before, he motioned for Michael and William to wait near the road. With a nod they turned back.

He moved toward her, noting her shoulders hunched over and her head bowed as she muttered to herself. It wasn't like her to sit in such a way. She looked defeated, and it troubled him.

He was but ten strides away, when she jumped to her feet and spun around, her blade firmly clasped in her hand.

"What do you want?" she demanded, straightening from her crouched fighting position.

170

Her cheeks were wet and her eyes red. What pained her so? Why did she seek out this spot time and again? And why had she been crying? He shoved the questions aside and moved closer. Her problems did not concern him, could not concern him, only her safety.

"I've come tae take you back tae the castle."

"No, thanks. I'm comfortable right here, and I don't need or want any company. So you can just turn around and march right on back." She waved her knife in the air, shooing at him as if he were a child.

He fisted his hands on his hips. "Woman, you've caused me more pains than a man can bear. Why can you not do as you're told?"

She closed her eyes for a moment and took a deep breath. "You and I both agree that I don't belong there. So the sooner I get out of your hair the better." Her color rose steadily as she spoke. "Now, why don't you run along and go—go jump in the bloody loch!"

"I ought tae toss you intae the waves, you taupie. I've told you time and again, you're not tae leave the keep!"

"I'll go where I like, wear what I like, and do what I like! And what the hell is a taupie, anyway?"

"A foolish female with little brain!"

She growled low and long. "Sooner or later, I'm really going to bust you one."

He threw his head back with a laugh, enjoying their banter more than he should. "Ha! I'd like tae see you try, woman. You lost before and you'll lose again."

Her emerald eyes went wide, and she lunged for him. He should've known he could only push her so far, but by the saints, he didn't want to hurt her! He was only having a bit of sport, not liking the tears still clinging to her lashes. He preferred sparring with the she-devil he admired to watching a sniffling female.

Her shoulder slammed into his stomach with the full force of her body. The air rushed from his lungs as they went down together. He supposed he should be grateful she hadn't run him through with her blade, but it did not seem like her to lose control this way. Then he heard it, the sound of a boar crashing through the bush, barely missing them as it thundered past.

Amelia tried to roll free, but he knew there was no

time to run. The boar would turn and be on them in less than a breath. He snatched her blade from her hand and launched it at the beast, striking it between the eyes. Death was imminent, but the animal continued its charge. Colin wrapped his arms around Amelia and rolled, praying the boar's last rush would miss them.

There was a queer silence. Colin let out his trapped breath and lifted his head. The boar lay beside them, dead. He turned his head and looked into Amelia's eyes and realized—regardless of her skill as a fighter—she was afraid.

"I guess that makes us even," she said.

"Aye, lass. 'Twould seem so." The corner of his mouth tipped up in a small grin. "Although you did do the pushing first."

She let out a shaky laugh and took a deep breath. Colin did his best to ignore the feel of her breasts pressing against his chest.

"Yeah, well, I've no experience with boars," she said. "Thank you."

"You're welcome."

"Colin!" William called, as he and Michael burst through the brush. "We heard the boar." Both men looked down at the beast, then to where they lay.

Colin quickly got to his feet and extended a hand to her. She took it then moved to the boar. Without so much as a flinch, she retrieved her blade and made toward the spring.

Motioning toward the carcass, Colin said, "Take it with you, lads. I'll see Tuck back tae the keep."

Michael and William nodded with quirky grins, then disappeared through the trees with the boar.

Colin watched her for several moments as she cleaned her blade. Any other woman would be crying and carrying on, but then Amelia was no ordinary woman. He needed to know more about her, everything about her. "Tell me—tell me of your home, of your people."

She snickered. "If I told you the truth, all of it, you'd either lock me up or have me burned at the stake. Neither of which do I care for." She sat down on a log and dried her blade along her pant leg.

"And if I swear on my honor tae do neither?"

One brow arched sharply as she peered up at him. "You're not going to believe me. Not a word of it."

"I shall try," he said, and sat down beside her.

Shaking her head, she snatched her cap away and her curls sprang free. "Okay, but I warned you." She took a deep breath. "Remember that castle I wanted directions too? Well, that's where I was a few hours before we met. It won't be built for a couple of hundred years yet." She leaned over and cleanly sheathed her knife by her calf.

A sharp pain began behind his eyes, and he shook his head.

She held up her hand. "Oh, wait. There's more. A lot more. The year I was visiting Raghnall Castle, was two thousand and seven. I fell in a fountain, roughly some yards in that direction." She pointed east then shoved her hands in her pockets as she shuffled her large boots against the earth.

"I won't go into the particulars about how that happened at the moment," she continued. "But needless to say, I fell in the stupid fountain and landed here." She cocked her head and looked at him. "How's that for a hair curler, Sasquatch?"

He rubbed at the ache between his brows. "You said you would give me the truth, but if that's what you think is truth, than I'm not tae ever believe a word you say again."

"Oh, there's nothing like the feeling of a good I-told-you-so," she said wearily and moved to rise.

"Wait." He touched her shoulder, and she paused. "You are right," he said with a sigh. "I said I would try. But lass, you canna expect me tae believe such a tale."

She nodded, her lips pursed in thought, distracting him from their conversation for a moment.

"Okay. How about a little proof?" she asked.

She unfastened her coat in a way he'd never seen, but recognized the odd sound from when she'd removed it in her chamber before. He tentatively reached out and touched the small teeth.

She cleared her throat. "Um, that's not the proof. Not the really good stuff, anyway."

He lowered his hand, curious to what more she would produce.

"This is my wallet. My ID." She opened a small purse that made a horrendous tearing sound. "This is my driver's license, a few bucks, a couple of credit cards, and my bodyguard ID. Note the dates."

He gingerly took the odd pieces and felt their strange texture and deciphered some of the writings. "Bodyguard?" The term must mean what he thought, but a woman as a guard?

"Yep. I'm a professional bodyguard. People hire me to keep them safe, and keep the wackos away. But that's not the best part." She reached into her coat and pulled out another item. "This is my cell phone. It won't work here, but you can see all the gadgets and games on it."

She pressed her finger against it and the thing came to life. He leaned back, resisting the urge to leap away, as it beeped and sang an irritating tune.

"It's okay," she said quickly. "It's a communication device. Um, think of it as a really fancy way to talk to someone else that's far away. Like a carrier pigeon. You've got those, right?"

He nodded, the blood pounding fiercely in his head.

"Think about this. You've got a phone." She held up her device. "And the guy you want to talk to has one too. You simply punch in some numbers and his phone rings. He picks it up and opens it, and voila, you two can speak to one another."

She looked at him expectantly, but he couldn't begin to fathom such a wondrous thing.

"I can see without a live demo this isn't getting through. But you see now, don't you? That I'm not from here, from anywhere around here, from this time. Oh, hey, that's another thing."

She stuck out her arm and pulled up her sleeve. "This is my watch. I'm sure you've seen timepieces before. Well maybe, I'm not sure how common they are yet, but I know you've never seen anything like this baby."

He marveled at the piece, comprehending its function, but the future? "'Tis still more than I can believe. I'm sorry, lass. These—things of yours are wondrous, aye, but that doesna mean you come from the future."

She let out a heavy breath. "Yeah, well, I tried. I said

you wouldn't believe me."

"I believe that you're a lass with unusual skills and unusual treasures, who needs safe passage back tae her homeland. I canna provide it now, but I can offer you food and shelter for the time being."

She narrowed her eyes. "Why? You've seen that I can take care of myself. Why bother housing me?"

He rested his arms on his knees and plucked a twig from the ground. "You've been good to my kin, and—saved my life. I'm grateful," he grudgingly admitted.

"You're welcome."

He nodded, uncomfortable with the topic and her closeness. "I ask that you dinnae show your possessions tae anyone else while you're here. I'd rather not see you burned at the stake." He shot her a grin to lighten the mood. "No matter how irritating you can be."

"Oh, you're a riot," she said with a hint of a smile. "But it's a deal. I need to earn my keep though. If I'm stuck here for a while I might as well look around. I'll need money for that."

His heart twisted with the thought of her leaving him for good. He cleared his throat, silently repeating his duty to himself. He was to be married and naught could change that. "I will give you what you need when you're ready tae go," he said, although it nearly choked him.

"Thanks."

He stood and held out his hand. "Come. It grows late."

She looked at his roughened palm before slipping her hand into his. The connection created a wave of heat and longing so powerful it took all his strength not to pull her into his arms.

Once on her feet, he dropped her hand, unable to bear the feel of her skin against his any longer and turned toward home. Perhaps he should see her on her way soon, before he broke his vow to his clan and to his future bride.

"Your knife is a most unusual weapon," he said, looking for something to say as she silently fell in step beside him. "That too, you should keep hidden, although many have seen it."

She leaned down, pulled it from the sheath, and handed it to him. "I can see you drooling. Go ahead and

175

take a look. You've earned that at least."

He grinned and took the knife. Examining her blade, his thoughts cooled considerably as his curiosity peaked. "How did you make the metal this odd shade? And what is the hilt made of?"

"The hilt is made of a plastic compound, something you don't have here. I don't know how they blacken the steel, but it's to keep it from reflecting light at night. Here, the handle opens too." She twisted off the end just below the compass and a thick line as well as other items fell into his hand.

"Amazing," he said softly.

"Sweet, isn't it?"

He sniffed. "Leave a woman tae call a blade sweet."

"Hey, you guys refer to your claymores as she. I've heard you."

"'Tis not the same."

"Yeah, yeah. So, I let you play with my knife. Do I get to play with your claymore?"

He nearly stumbled from the heated thoughts flashing through his mind. Why could he not have a normal conversation with the woman without every word she uttered, every move she made have him thinking of bedding her?

"Uh, I mean, I—oh, you know what I meant," she grumbled.

He cast her a quick glance and found her face alight with flame, apparently fully aware of how her comment had struck him. He tried to hold it back, but couldn't. Laughter exploded from his chest like thunder. Never had he enjoyed a woman so much. Her wit, her uncanny remarks. She met him challenge for challenge. Exasperating as she was, damned if he could keep himself from liking her. And more.

Handing her back the blade with a remnant chuckle, he said, "You couldna lift my claymore, much less wield it."

She tilted her face in that defiant way she had. "You'd be surprised what I can do. You're just afraid I'll show you up. Afraid of what I can do."

"Aye, lass, you just might be right," he said, his mirth fading rapidly with the dangerous truth in her words. "You just might be right."

She sheathed her blade then shoved her hands into her pockets. "Care to try a little future snack?" Taking his wrist, she placed an odd-shaped yellow morsel in his hand. "That's a lemon flavored one."

He narrowed his gaze at her, then at the strange glob lying in his palm.

"Go ahead, try it." She grinned cockily. "I dare you." She popped one of another color into her mouth.

Tentatively, he mirrored her action. He stopped on the road in mid-stride as sweetened lemons bathed his tongue. Chewing slowly, savoring the flavor, he smiled.

"Good, huh?" she asked.

He nodded and held out his hand for another.

"Hmm, well, don't get hooked. They won't be invented for a long time yet. My stash is only so big, you know."

Ignoring her repeated reference to the future, he slipped another piece of the delicious treat into his mouth, stunned to discover the taste of cherries.

"I, um, want to thank you for trusting me," she said, her voice decidedly softer. "It can't be easy with everything that's going on." She bobbled her head. "And with my wacko story and all. It's nice to have someplace to stay. I appreciate it."

He glanced at her, taken aback by her sincerity. He wondered when she last had a sense of security in her life. Her unusual profession sounded much like that of a mercenary, never staying in any one place for long, never getting close to people. It was a hard life for a woman. A hard life for a man.

"You will always be welcome at Arreyder Castle," he said, looking at her more closely.

She held his gaze for a long moment, then nodded and looked back to the road. There was so much more he wanted to know about her, and yet he didn't dare pursue such knowledge. He was certain it would only serve to embed her in his heart, if she was not already there.

They made the rest of the journey in silence.

Chapter Eighteen

The boar was roasted for dinner and was delicious. So was the wine, of which Tuck had too much. She never drank, not after life with her father, but the water wasn't exactly fit to consume, so she had little choice, and tonight she wanted to celebrate. Silently, of course. She and Colin had come to an agreement, a truce of sorts. It was more than she'd expected.

She stole secretive glances at him all through the night. He was glorious to look at. His broad shoulders, his long tan fingers, his lion-like eyes. The man was amazing. Having never fought a wild boar before, she'd been more than just a little out of her element. Although fairly certain she could've handled things herself, it felt wonderful to have someone do the dirty work for a change.

He turned to Aileen and smiled. Tuck averted her gaze at the sharp pang in her chest. Maybe staying wasn't such a good idea after all. Ian made some comment, and she did her best to take part in the men's discussion about the boar and their very physical afternoon in the lists.

Douglas rose and retired to the solar with Elspeth with several others following in his wake, while Tuck shuffled down the hall behind them on Ian's arm.

She chatted a bit with Elspeth then played Douglas in a quick game of chess, which he won. Her heart just wasn't in it. How could it be when all she could think about was Colin and Aileen quietly sitting on the other side of the room getting to know one another?

"I believe I shall take my triumph and go for a stroll," Douglas said. "Care tae join me, Ellie?"

Blushing, Elspeth took his arm and left the room. The way that randy old Scot teased the woman, the way he watched her when she wasn't looking, made Tuck downright jealous. What Ian had said about Douglas never knowing how Elspeth felt about him had obviously changed. Of course, near brushes with death tended to do that to a lot of people. They saw things differently, appreciated life more.

Strange. She'd had her share of near death experiences, but they'd always made her life harder, more unpleasant. Especially today. She knew now, without a doubt, that seeing Colin marry someone else was going to kill her.

Aileen quietly excused herself with Robert on her heels. Her voice was soft and sweet, just as Tuck knew it would be.

Tuck shouldn't have come back to the castle. She should've turned down the road and kept on going when that stupid spring didn't work.

Ian and Colin laughed at something, startling her from her thoughts. Their good-natured bickering over chess strategies almost made her smile. They were so like brothers, and yet as different as the poles. She would miss them when she left for her European tour. It would be so much better if she could figure out how to get back to her own time. At least she knew she wouldn't run into him there.

"Amelia, dear heart, you look a bit peaked. Do not tell me you took Douglas' beating that hard," Ian said with a chuckle.

"Oh no, I'm fine," she lied, forcing a light tone to her voice.

"Perhaps your encounter this afternoon with that beast has left you feeling a bit undone," he suggested softly.

The whole clan was murmuring about Colin and the boar, but she hadn't provided anyone with the gruesome details. She simply changed the subject.

"Yes, I am a bit tired," she said. "I think I'll turn in."

"Good rest to you, dear heart." Ian snatched her hand, gracefully of course, and planted a light kiss.

Colin grumbled a muttered sort of good night as she made her way to the door. Pausing, she looked back at the two men she admired more than any others in her life. She was going to miss them terribly, but she had to leave. Waiting was a wasted effort. Sure, she could use the cash Colin had promised her, but frankly, she didn't care. She simply couldn't watch him smile at Aileen, marry Aileen—love Aileen.

She made plans to sneak out after everyone had gone to bed. It was better that way. Then perhaps Colin, or rather his blasted honor, wouldn't send him running after her.

****

Aileen was a sweet lass, Colin thought after Ian left him alone in the solar. She'd make a fine wife—if he didn't break her in two in their marriage bed.

He'd used every ounce of strength he possessed to keep from gazing at Amelia. How he yearned to be as one of his guards, free to wed of his own choosing, free of the vast responsibilities his position placed on his shoulders.

"We must learn who these men in the dungeon are," his father said, breaking into his thoughts as he entered the solar.

He turned from the darkened window, leaving his foolish wishes behind and sank in a chair. "Aye. Perhaps tomorrow we should bring them up and have them face Robert. See their reaction."

His father nodded thoughtfully. "I dinnae want tae think of MacKenzie being in league with another clan against us, but if 'tis so, then we must tread carefully. This wedding may be a bit of treachery, a way tae make us lower our guard."

Relieved to see his father taking an interest in something other than his impending wedding or his aunt, Colin relaxed further into his chair. "'Tis possible that MacKenzie isna the true enemy. I canna help wondering if someone else is trying tae manipulate us all."

Ian rushed into the room. "Colin, you must come. 'Tis Amelia, she is gravely ill. She may not—" He swallowed visibly and shook his head.

Every one of his limbs went numb. He tried to rise but his body refused to obey him. How could it be? He'd seen her but an hour ago, strong and sure. True, at times during the evening he'd sensed an unease about her, but to be so ill that she might die?

"You must go tae her, lad," his father said. "We'll discuss this matter later."

"Aye," Colin said with a faint nod. Forcing his legs to

move, he catapulted his body through the doorway. His heart pounded faster as his pace quickened until he was running to Amelia's chamber, determined to beat death to her door.

He burst into her room with Ian in his wake and came to a staggering halt at the sight before him. The flashing eyes he'd come to know were closed as Elspeth stood by the bed wiping her damp brow.

His aunt lifted her head and met his gaze. "I dinnae know, Colin," she said, answering his unspoken question on whether or not she would live. "She is verra ill, and terribly sudden."

He moved slowly across the room to stand by the bed. "Fetch Maighread," he ordered.

"But Colin, the lass doesna want her," his aunt said.

Ian gently gripped his shoulder. "She's right, my friend. I do not think it would be wise."

He clamped his eyes closed as his fingernails dug brutally into his palms. "Fetch her, I say!"

Ian released him and backed away.

"You let that witch near me, and I'll deck you, Sasquatch," Amelia rasped.

He moved quickly to the head of the bed and fell to his knees. "You're sick, lass. You need her care."

She focused her weary eyes on him. "She'd rather kill me than cure me."

The freckles he tried so hard not to notice stood out starkly against her pale skin. Here was a woman stronger than any he'd ever known. A woman whom he admired, trusted, wanted. How could she come to this in so short a time?

"Fetch the leeches, then," he said, glancing over his shoulder to Ian.

Her hand shot out from beneath the cover and gripped him by his tunic at the throat. She pulled him close with more strength than he thought possible in her condition, and peered at him menacingly.

"You bring one of those slimy things near me, and I swear I'll die right now and haunt you for the rest of your life, MacLean."

A frigid cold rushed from his head to his feet. He clasped his hand over hers where she held him. "Dinnae be talking of dying, lass."

"Then let Elspeth do her job." She took a deep, laborious breath and her fingers relaxed. "I've told her what to do."

Taking her hand in his, he cradled it against his chest. She had brought his father back to him and likely knew what she was about. He would have to trust her in this.

"Aye. If that is what you want. I'll not stand in her way."

She chuckled roughly. "Taking orders from a woman? I didn't think I'd see the day."

He gently brushed one of her damp ruby red curls from her cheek. "You are more than just a woman."

"About time you figured that out."

He grinned at her cheekiness. "Aye. I have been most stubborn."

Fatigue softened her grip, but he saw the twinkle of humor in her eyes. "The understatement of the century. Now get out of here before I pop you one."

Laughter rippled through him, releasing the tightness in his chest. She was too strong to die, she would beat whatever made her so ill. "Dinnae think that because I let you have your way this time that you can be ordering me about."

She snorted softly. "Unless you want your kilt redecorated, you'd better beat it."

He glanced at Elspeth. "Bring a basin and quickly."

"I am not puking up my guts with you in the room." She shoved weakly at his chest where her hand remained beneath his. "Get out of here. Go play with your claymore."

"Stubborn female," he grumbled. "Elspeth isna strong enough tae tend you by herself." He slid his arm around her back and prepared to hold her head over the basin.

She feebly swatted at him, her strength failing at an alarming rate. "She can handle it. Leave me a little dignity, will you?" Her pathetic tone tore at his heart. Perhaps her strength, her smart remarks were nothing more than another of her masks.

The basin appeared and not a second too soon. He held her head over the container and tucked her crop of curls behind her ears. Elspeth wiped her face then took the basin away.

Resting his back against the headboard, pulling her with him, Colin cradled her against his chest. The stubble on his chin caught in her damp locks and he shamelessly relished the feel of them against his skin.

Tiny shivers engulfed her as her moist shift pressed against him. She moaned pitifully. "God, this is humiliating."

"Shh. Lie still," he said softly, sifting his fingers through her hair at her temple.

Fiona rushed into the room. "Aileen is ill as well," she said, her breath coming in quick bursts. "How shall I tend her?"

"Ach my, no. Does it look tae be the same as poor Amelia? Is anyone else sick?" Elspeth asked.

Fiona nodded. "She's terribly weak and chilled. I left one of the other kitchen maids with her. I couldna find Maighread. I though she might be tendin' tae someone else, but 'tis only the two that are sick so far."

Ian straightened from where he stood leaning against the post at the foot of the bed. "Odd, do you not think, that only Amelia and Aileen share the same malady and so quickly?"

Colin's eyes snapped to Ian's. They both had the same thought.

Poison.

Every muscle in Colin's body went rigid. "What did they eat? What did they drink at supper?" he barked at his aunt.

Her brow furrowed. "The same as the rest, but Aileen didna seem tae be as hungry as Amelia," she said with a faint smile. "She had a hearty appetite after her time in the lists this afternoon."

"It couldn't have been the boar then, if she took the meat from the trencher," he said, clenching his jaw as he looked down at where Amelia lay curled in the crook of his arm, her teeth chattering.

Elspeth worried her hands frantically. "What is it, Colin?"

"I believe they've been poisoned."

She gasped. "But why?"

183

"Someone wants a war between the MacKenzies and the MacLeans and will go tae any means tae have it."

"But why Amelia?" Ian asked. "And how did they get inside the keep?"

"'Tis possible the poison was meant for another. Elspeth, perhaps. She sits beside her at the table. As for getting inside, I dinnae know, but when I find the assassin responsible, he will feel the full force of my fury."

Amelia whimpered in his arms. He realized he was squeezing her tightly to him, but it would be the only time he would have to hold her, for he feared he was losing her. Colin clenched his jaw and bit back the anguish rising in his throat. This was his fault. He should've posted more guards, been more careful.

"We must do something for them," Elspeth cried, her hands flying to her mouth. "We canna let them die. 'Tis not their time."

"A vision?" he asked hopefully.

She shook her head as tears gathered in her eyes. Then their lives were in God's hands. He would decide if it was truly their time or not.

Time. Could Amelia have knowledge he didn't? Knowledge from the future? She had saved his father, perhaps she could tell him how to save her and Aileen as well?

Sliding his arm out from beneath her, he grabbed her by the shoulders and shook her. Gently at first, but when she failed to stir, he shook harder.

"Wake, damn you!"

"Sonofabitch, what now?" She shot him a glare and rubbed her brow. "Can't a girl get some rest around here without you bellowing about something all the time?"

A deep breath exploded from his chest. She had such spirit, such fight in her. He couldn't bear the thought of her dying, of her leaving him.

He stilled at the truth in that thought. But he would be leaving her when he wed Aileen.

"Go g-growl at someone else," Amelia groused. She tried to wrap herself more tightly in the covers to ease her shivering, but didn't have the strength.

He shook his head, clearing his mind. This was not the time to think on anyone leaving. Her life was at stake, as was his future bride's.

Wrapping her more tightly in the coverlet, he asked, "How do you treat poison?"

"Poison? Why? What—"

"Aileen suffers the same sickness you do. It canna be a coincidence. It must be poison. How do you treat it in your time? Tell me how!"

Her lip curled in a sleepy-eyed grin. "My time? Believing in the impossible?"

He gritted his teeth. They were wasting precious moments. "Answer me, woman!"

Her brow furrowed deeply as her grin faded. "Are my pupils dilated?" She huffed, apparently dissatisfied with his lack of response. "Are the black parts in the middle really big?"

He cupped her pale cheeks and withheld a shiver at the iciness of her skin. "Aye. The green is nearly gone, and you have no fever. Just this blasted chill."

"Damn, I thought it was the flu," she said, her eyes drooping.

He cupped her face firmly. "Nay, you canna die!" Sliding his fingers into the damp hair at the base of her neck, he frantically searched her face for any flicker of recognition. "You have not tormented me enough," he said roughly, hoping to reach the quick-witted woman he knew her to be with his barb.

She frowned deeply and opened one eye. "Nobody likes a smart-ass."

He glanced quickly to heaven in thanks. "You ate of the meat and drank some wine. What else? You must remember."

"It couldn't be the meat. I took it off the trencher." She faintly rolled her head back and forth on her pillow. "Must've been the wine. It was already poured when I got there."

Her eyes opened wide and met his where he continued to hover close. "That bitch," she snarled, trying to rise. "Wait until I get my hands on her."

"Lie still, you daft female! You'll not be going anywhere."

She moaned, flopping back to the bed.

"Who, dear heart? Who are you speaking of?" Ian

185

asked, quickly stepping to the side of the bed.

She rolled her head to the side to see him. "Maighread. She's had it in for me since day one. The woman's certifiable. Hadn't you noticed?"

It couldn't be. Colin knew she wasn't fond of Amelia, but to kill her and Aileen? "Why would she do this?"

"She's always wanted you, Colin," Ian said.

Amelia's quivering hand clasped Colin's arm, pulling his thoughts from the disturbing possibilities.

"I think it's more than that," she said. "I didn't say before, I didn't think you'd believe me, but I think she was intentionally pumping your father full of drugs."

He shook his head. "I dinnae understand."

She sighed and took a deep breath. "She was mixing the herbs with the wrong things, giving him too much. If she's such a great healer, like everyone says, she would've known better. She was slowly killing him."

"Good God," Ian whispered hoarsely.

"Call for one of the men. My father and Aileen must be guarded," Colin ordered.

Ian rushed to the door and bellowed into the corridor. Michael appeared almost instantly.

"Place a watch on my father, on Aileen, and another on this door. No one except Ian, Elspeth and Fiona are tae enter. Then find Maighread. I want her confined tae her chamber. And have all the wine still about in pitchers poured intae the cesspit. Dinnae let anyone drink of it, you ken?"

"Aye." With a puzzled look on his face, Michael nodded then left.

Colin looked back to Amelia, her shivering growing worse by the minute, and he was still unsure of what to do to make her well. She had to get well.

"There's a chance it wasn't her," she said.

He brushed the backs of his fingers across her cold cheek. "I've already considered that, lass."

Her brow furrowed deeply. "Or there may be two assassins," she mumbled and her lids slid closed.

A tortured cry burst from his lips as he clasped her shoulders roughly. "Nay! You must tell me what tae do!"

He ignored the pleading tone of his own voice, regardless if others saw him as weak and vulnerable for caring for her. Her eyes opened to mere slits, giving his lungs permission to breathe once more.

"Hard t-to say, not knowing what it was, but I already t-t-tossed some up." She smiled weakly. "Guess it's a good thing w-wine doesn't seem t-to like me." She took a deep breath, and continued, "But I need milk. It'll d-dilute the poison." She grimaced. "God, I h-hate that stuff. Elspeth?"

"Aye, I'm here, lamb."

"Plenty of fluids and k-keep me warm and dry. Do the same for Aileen, but m-make sure to induce vomiting first then g-give her milk."

Amelia turned back to Colin as his aunt bustled out of the room. "And you..." She looked at him for several long seconds then reached out, her fingers trembling as they brushed his lips. Her eyes filled with deep concern as they lifted to his. "There's so much I want t-to say. If I don't make it—"

"Dinnae talk that way, lass. You'll be fit as ever and tossin' my men in the bailey before the solstice," he choked out. The backs of his eyes burned, and he was terrified he would never see her again.

She chuckled softly. "You're on my list. I w-want a rematch."

"Aye, and you'll have it." He clasped her hand and pressed a kiss to her palm. Then an amazing thing happened.

She smiled, well and true—and for him.

He gazed in awe as her entire face was transformed, her eyes filled to overflowing with warmth. For the first time he saw not the woman who drove him mad with her sharp tongue, not the she-devil who tormented him by wearing tight trews, not the intelligent warrior he'd come to admire, but the woman who had wrapped him in the finest gossamer strands and lifted the barrier from around his soul.

The woman who had stolen his heart.

"Be careful, Colin," she whispered.

"Rest, lass." He released her hand, although he longed to pull her back into his arms.

Turning toward the door, he pulled Ian aside. "Guard her until I return. I wish tae speak with my father and learn of Aileen's condition. Then I intend tae see Maighread."

Ian gave a firm nod. "You can count on me, my friend."

Colin moved toward the door, eager to go about the rest of this business so he could return to Amelia.

"Colin," she called from the bed.

He paused and almost smiled at the sound of his name once again on her lips.

"Don't kill her," she said. "I want a p-piece of her myself. And don't forget to have all the f-food stuffs guarded. And you should d-double the guard at the gates."

He grinned, amazed once more by her determination, her courage, her intelligence, and her beauty. "I know what I'm about."

"That's a first," she quipped.

Chuckling beneath his breath, he hurried from her chamber. She would get well. No woman with a fighting spirit as strong as hers would let death take her easily.

Chapter Nineteen

Morning crept upon him. Colin was tired beyond belief, having spent the night searching for his cousin. But she was nowhere to be found. Her absence proved her treachery.

Wasn't it bad enough that he had someone trying to start a war, he had to have a jealous female attempting murder beneath his roof? He had not discounted Amelia's thoughts on his father's long illness either, but why would Maighread seek to harm him? He'd always been good to her, treated her as his own daughter.

The sight of Robert pacing fretfully at Aileen's door, made him pause. "How does she?" he asked.

"Your aunt willna let me in tae see her," he snapped then sighed heavily. "But she says she does as well as can be expected."

Colin nodded. "We will find Maighread, and she will pay for this treachery."

Robert nodded, obviously trying to control his temper. Colin knew how he felt, thoroughly and utterly useless. Elspeth had shooed Ian off hours earlier, and was determined to do the same to him. By Amelia's orders, no less.

With heavy feet, he made his way to his own chamber hating the overwhelming sense of ineptitude.

Halfway down the corridor, he was met by his father.

"Where is your guard, Da?"

"You're beginning to sound like Ellie, lad, with your fussin' and such. I can take care of myself against a woman," Douglas blustered, then calmed himself considerably. "And I was worried over Tuck and Aileen. How do they?"

"Robert says Aileen is doing as well as can be expected. As for the other, I dinnae know. Elspeth willna let me in tae see her." He chuckled halfheartedly. "Our guest has ordered me from her chamber."

His father laughed and slapped him on the back. "She has spirit, she does. But not tae worry. She'll recover. Now, let us fetch Robert from his watch and tend tae business."

They had a guard bring the men from the dungeons to the great hall. He watched Robert closely, but noted no sign of recognition. His father, however, had a flash of memory, and knew one of the men from the raid he'd interrupted. The raid that had nearly taken his life.

"We didna do any reiving. 'Twas you, who were doin' the reiving," Robert argued.

His father jumped to his feet. "We didna touch a hair of your cattle before you ambushed us! I'll not have you spreading lies about the MacLeans."

Colin stepped between his father and Robert. "We need tae discuss this calmly." He nodded to the two men Amelia had caught. "And I think there lies the answers tae the riddle."

The men paled considerably beneath their steely glares.

"I think that you'd best be telling us what you know," Colin said, his voice firm.

It wasn't long before they knew all.

The Campbells wanted both MacKenzies and MacLeans gone from the island. By pretending on more than one occasion to be either MacKenzies or MacLeans, they raided the outlying farms. It was a nasty treacherous business, and all for the sake of a piece of rock. Its strategic position was like gold to them, and they were willing to do anything to have it.

"And is poisoning women part of your plan?" Colin demanded to know.

"We dinnae know anything of poison. I swear it," one man said.

He had them returned to the dungeon, then turned to his father. "'Tis no doubt in my mind that Maighread is behind the poisoning."

His father nodded, as did Robert.

"We must speak with MacKenzie. He must know of this," his father said. He looked to Robert. "You must go and tell him of this business, Robert. He should know of Aileen's illness as well."

"I'll not leave. My place is here. The laird placed her in my care and I'll not leave my post. I'll send a man with the news. 'Twas my intention at first light after seein' how she fared the night."

Elspeth appeared in the doorway. "Douglas, I must speak with you."

"'Twill have tae wait, Ellie. We've much tae discuss."

"I'm afraid it canna wait," she said.

"Amelia," Colin gasped, popping up from his chair, his heart pounding against his ribs.

Robert leapt to his feet at the same time and choked out a word. "Aileen."

His aunt cocked her head with one brow raised. "'Tis as I suspected."

They both rushed toward her, barking out questions, Colin demanding to know of Amelia, while Robert insisted she tell him of Aileen.

She held up her hands to silence them. "They are both a wee bit better, but time will tell." Leaning to the side, she peered around Colin to his father. "You see now, what we need speak of?"

His father rose from his chair. "That I do, love," his father said, walking up beside her and bussing her on the cheek.

She blushed and gave him a reproachful grin.

Colin's jaw fell lax. "Love?" he asked, stupefied to see his father behave in such a way. He'd been more than cordial to his aunt, wooing her, but love?

"Aye. Your aunt and I are tae be wed when this business with the MacKenzies is done. But now you've made it a sight more troublesome."

Colin pointed at his own chest. "Me? What have I done? You canna possibly blame Maighread's insanity on me."

His father chuckled, slipping his arm around Elspeth's thick waist. "You dinnae see the truth standing before you, lads?"

Colin and Robert looked at each other, then back to Douglas. They both shook their heads, at a complete loss as to what he meant.

Douglas reached out and clasped Robert's shoulder. "Do you love Aileen true, lad? Now's the time tae speak your mind. It'll not go further than this room if that is your wish."

Robert's mouth opened and closed like a codfish.

"Aye. I see that you do. And you, son. What of you and Tuck?"

Colin stared blankly at his father.

"I'm afraid you'll have tae be clearer, Douglas," Elspeth said with a small giggle.

"Aye," he sighed. "Here's the problem, lads. Colin was tae marry Aileen and join the clans. 'Twas agreed tae some time ago, but I see now that it wouldna be for the best."

Colin shook his head. "What do you mean, *was* tae marry Aileen?"

"'Tis plain tae see that you love Tuck, while Robert here loves Aileen." He dropped his chin and peered at Colin from beneath his bushy brows. "'Twas not right tae ask you tae give up your own happiness when there are other ways tae make peace with a man. Especially now that we know 'tis not the MacKenzies who are our enemies."

Colin swallowed hard. "But—"

His father shook his head. "You've found a woman you can love, and a marriage without love has little pleasure. I had hopes you would come tae care for Aileen, as I did your mother. But I can see now, 'tis not meant tae be."

Moving to the hearth, Colin gripped the mantle. Not once that he could recall had he ever seen any overt affection between his parents. Not as he'd just seen between his aunt and his father. It was the way a strong laird had to be. He couldn't allow others to see his weaknesses, his heart. Had he been wrong all these years?

He turned back to his father, confused, bewildered, and struggling to grasp the small thread of hope.

"Your mother and I were happy, dinnae misunderstand me," his father said. "But we didna love one another." Douglas clasped his hand on Colin's shoulder. "I thank her for giving me such a fine son, but I'll not condemn you tae live out your life with a woman who isna in your heart." He chuckled and pulled Elspeth into his arms. "'Tis lovesick I am, but I mean what I say, son. As I see things, we can have three weddings, eh, love?"

"Douglas, let the lads at least do the asking first. You dinnae know the hearts of Aileen and Amelia."

"What?" he blustered. "They'd be foolish not tae take either of these braw, honorable lads tae wed."

"They're also verra ill," she argued. "They'll need time tae recover."

"Aye," he said with a sigh. "Robert, you'll send word tae MacKenzie of this Campbell business and of Maighread. We'll leave the wooing tae later, but mind you dinnae be draggin' your feet, lads." He smiled at Elspeth. "'Tis a waste of valuable time."

Colin looked at Robert and Robert at him. Then they both bolted for the door. They ran neck and neck up the stairs in the wake of his father's laughter and Elspeth's fussing about disturbing the women. Neither of them paid her any heed.

Barreling past Robert as he disappeared into Aileen's room, Colin burst through Amelia's door and hurried to her bedside. She'd fallen into a deep sleep, but shivered fiercely. Ignoring Fiona's sputtered protests, he slipped in behind her and cradled her against him as he'd done before, and she calmed somewhat.

"Colin MacLean, you'll march yourself out of here this instant," Elspeth fumed as she entered the room. "And while you're about it, you go and fetch that lad out of Aileen's chamber as well."

He ignored her as she continued to stare down at him with her stern frown and her hands planted firmly on her hips.

"We need tae change her shift and the linens," his aunt said, her voice softening. "You canna stay."

"I'll tend her," he said, wiping her damp brow and throat with a soft cloth.

"You'll do no such thing. 'Tis woman's work," she huffed. "'Tis not seemly for you tae be here. Now, be gone with you."

"'Tis my fault this has befallen her. Blind, I was, tae Maighread's treachery. I'll not leave her. I canna," he said raggedly.

Elspeth sighed, her face twisting with her decision. "Verra well. But you'll turn your head or I'll be turning it for you."

He nodded then lifted Amelia into his arms, coverlet and all, so they could change the linens. Sitting in the chair by the fire, he held her firmly in his lap. What would he do if she didn't survive? How could he bear to be without her now that he could have her?

He'd buried his feelings for so long that when his father opened the small door of hope, his heart exploded, no longer able to contain his love, his grief, his fears. No longer would he battle against a tide of emotion. He would still be strong, for the clan and for Amelia, but his strength would come from his heart instead of his duty.

Once the bed was made, he placed her against the bedding. He hesitated, not wanting to let her go, terrified he would never have her in his arms again. Straightening his spine, he turned and walked to the window, allowing Elspeth and Fiona to change her shift.

He watched the sun as it edged up into the sky. Would she wake, would she get better? The sound of her teeth chattering pained him. He wanted to turn around and hold her, care for her. His heart sank deep in his chest.

But what if she didn't want him? He wasn't handsome like Ian. Lassies liked him well enough, but he lacked the fancy words and pretty compliments. He had the feet of a giant when it came to dancing, and knew little to nothing of wooing a woman. Assuming he'd marry Aileen or another of his father's choosing, he'd never thought to learn.

"Bless my soul," Elspeth gasped.

He spun around, his thoughts momentarily overtaken by unknown fears. Gazing upon Amelia lying bare from the waist up, he noted one creamy breast bore a long jagged scar. It made him sick inside to think that she'd come so close to death before.

His aunt covered her quickly and settled her beneath the covers once more.

Placing a chair by the bed, he lowered his weary body into it and took her hand, rubbing it warmly between his.

"Come, Fiona," Elspeth said. "Let us see tae Aileen.

I'll likely have the same battle with Robert as we've had here." The door closed silently behind them.

"Amelia," he whispered, rolling her name over his tongue for the first time, the taste of it as sweet as her kiss. He pressed his lips to her hand, and rested his head on the bed, his mind repeating prayer after prayer.

He dozed for a time, but awoke to her moaning and shifting restlessly. Tears slid down her cheeks as she tossed her head back and forth.

He gently stroked her brow. "Be still, mavourneen. 'Tis but a dream."

She sobbed softly. "Don't, Papa. Please," she cried.

He scooped her up and moved to the large chair by the fire. Wrapping her tightly in the coverlet, he cradled her against him.

She calmed as he stroked her head and kissed her brow while he listened to the words of his heart. Feelings he'd never allowed himself to indulge in, words he'd never spoken to another living soul echoed loudly inside him, and yet he could not find the courage to voice them.

****

Tuck opened her eyes and blinked several times before moving. She was sitting in someone's lap. A soft snore stirred the hair at her brow as she peered at the legs beneath her. She recognized those legs. They starred in every fantasy she'd had since she landed on the island.

She bolted from MacLean's lap, clutching the blanket around her. He woke with a curse and lunged for her. She stumbled back onto the bed and he followed, sprawling on top of her. Her loud complaint became a grunt at the unexpected weight.

Holding her to the mattress, he brushed his fingers across her brow and cheeks. His gaze searched her features, almost as if he couldn't believe she was real. But she had to get him away from her. The way he looked at her, and with his mouth so close she might not get through this odd encounter without grabbing the man and kissing the daylights out of him.

"MacLean, you either tell me why you're looking at me like that, or my knee's going to connect with your sporran."

A slow grin eased over that exasperatingly wonderful

mouth. "I never thought I'd be happy tae hear your sharp tongue."

The dim light of the fire and the low burning candle by the bed illuminated his face. He looked tired, she realized. Dark shadows lay beneath his lion eyes, while a new beard hid the sharp angles of his face. She touched his jaw with the barest tip of her fingers before she jerked them back.

"Nay, lass," he whispered, clasping her hand.

His steady gaze sent a quiver running through her as he pressed his lips to backs of her fingers. The warmth of his breath brushed across her skin, bringing to life all the things she knew they could never share. All the hopes and desires she'd buried deep down inside as she watched him with Aileen. His betrothed.

In a blink it all flooded back to her. The wine, the poison—revisiting her dinner, while MacLean held her head, no less. She groaned and covered her face with her hands.

"Dinnae tell me you're still sick." He gently took her hands from her face. "How do you, lass? Tell me true."

"I'm okay. Just a little embarrassed, I guess." *And hurt that you're only being nice to me because we're friends and nothing more.*

He stood and fluffed her pillow, righted her in the bed, then pulled the covers up to her chin. And she let him, enjoying every scrap of tenderness, no matter how inconsequential.

"You've had a hard two days. 'Tis glad, I am, the worst is past."

"Two days!" Her brain slid into soldier mode. She smacked at his hands where he continued to tug and tuck at the blanket. "Stop mothering me and tell me what you did with Maighread. How's Aileen? Is your father all right? Did you put a guard on the larder and double the men at the gates?"

"Of all the women," he muttered, shaking his head. "Aileen didna drink as much as you and was much better yesterday. As for my father, he's well. Maighread, however, has disappeared." He held up his hand, stopping her before she could speak. "I have sent a small search party tae find her."

"Oh, how I'd like to get my hands on her," she growled, fisting the covers tightly.

"As would I, but you are tae stay in bed and finish mending."

"I've done nothing but rest since that witch slipped me a micky. I'm all right," she added with a huff, realizing he had no clue what she meant.

One lone brow rose sharply as he looked at her. "You're not tae get out of that bed."

"Fine. But I don't need you in here playing nursemaid. Beat it, Sasquatch," she said, waving her hand. Much more of this, and she wouldn't be able to hold herself together.

He grumbled a few curses beneath his breath as he strode to the door. "I've gone daft, tae be sure."

"Wait a minute," she called, remembering some of the things he'd said while she'd been sick.

He turned with a scowl and she grinned.

"Do I remember hearing you say you believe me? About where I'm from?"

"Aye," he said with a nod. "But not a word of it tae another soul, you ken?"

"My lips are sealed," she said, secretly thrilled that he believed her.

He shifted his gaze to the window. "The sun will be up soon, but you are not tae get out of bed," he said, waggling his finger at her. "But if you have need of anything..." He dropped his hand, his features softening. "If you should have need of me, tell Elspeth or Fiona, and they will find me."

She cocked her head and studied him closely. The way he'd held her when she was sick, the way he fussed over her now, proved without a doubt he cared for her. Something no man had ever done before.

"Thank you," she said.

His brow furrowed a moment and his lips parted, as if he wished to say something, then he straightened his back and with a firm nod strode from the room.

Snuggling beneath the covers, a smile eased over her lips. She pressed her hand to her breast and stroked the back where his lips had touched. But they were only friends. He was getting married. A sight she really didn't want to witness.

Chapter Twenty

Colin thought to retire to his own chamber, now that she was out of danger, but knew it was a wasted effort. He wanted to tell her of his heart, to say the words, but they'd lodged in his throat, stealing his voice.

How was he to woo the woman if he couldn't even admit openly that he cared for her? He had little experience in courting, and Amelia was not the sort to want flowers and pretty words. Or would she? She was a woman, regardless of her unusual skills and sharp tongue.

He walked the battlements until the sun rose, but no divine insight was gifted him. He met Ian on his way to the great hall to break his fast.

"I would think you would be happy today, but from the sour look on your face, I would say not," Ian said.

News of Amelia's recovery had obviously been spread throughout the keep.

Colin placed a hand against his friend's chest as they stepped off the stairs, stopping him. "I must ask a favor." And damned if it didn't gall him to do it.

"Of course, my friend."

"I need tae know—I need tae know how tae woo her," he spat out.

"I see. And you wish me to teach you," Ian said with a choked chuckle.

"'Tis no laughing matter, lest you care tae find a few of your pretty teeth missing."

Ian cleared his throat and slapped him on the back. "Quite right. This is serious business. Especially considering the lady in question." They crossed the hall and took their seats. "The usual will not work with her. Flowers and sonnets and the like." He tore off a piece of fresh bread and chewed thoughtfully, wearing on Colin's nerves. But at least he'd assumed correctly about the flowers.

"Perhaps a new blade, one fashioned with jewels. Although hers is rather unique," Ian said.

"Aye, 'tis true." Colin nudged him with his elbow as he lifted his cup. "Think of something else."

"There you are, my lads," his father said as he strolled into the hall. "I have a need tae speak with both of you."

"Is something amiss?" Colin asked around a mouthful of food.

"Nay, nay. Robert tells me Aileen is fit to travel and wishes to return home in a day or so." His father nodded to Robert sitting by Aileen at the far end of the table. "He will take what we've learned back to MacKenzie. If all goes well, we will meet a few days hence where our lands join along the road. There is much tae discuss should the Campbells decide tae strike openly."

Colin opened his mouth to speak, as Fiona rushed into the hall and came to an abrupt halt by his aunt. Her gaze darted to him several times as she whispered rapidly to Elspeth. His stomach roiled as his aunt's eyes widened and focused on him.

Ignoring his father and Ian's continued conversation, he got to his feet. "Fiona!"

The lass jerked at his bellow and warily turned to face him.

"What has happened?" he asked, lowering his voice, but it was with great effort. He knew, deep in his heart, that whatever bad news she had to impart, it involved Amelia.

"The lass has left," Elspeth said, softly patting Fiona's wringing hands.

Swallowing the bile rising in his throat, he quickly strode from the room toward the stable, hardly noting the men who followed in his wake. He would find her, and when he did he'd flail her hide. The woman had barely beaten death. What could've possessed her to leave?

Did she hunt for his cousin, determined to bring her to justice, or was there a more heartrending reason? One he feared may be the true cause. Regardless, he had to find her.

He began saddling his horse and turned to find more than half the garrison, Ian included, doing the same.

She'd won them over with her courage, her skills, and her rare smiles. But they all couldn't go in search of her. They were in the middle of a war. Someone had to stay behind and guard the clan and Castle Arreyder, not to mention he still had a small party searching for Maighread. They were short enough men as it was.

His duty clashed sharply with his desires. He shouldn't be going at all. He should remain here where he belonged, not traipsing across the countryside looking for a redheaded she-demon from the future. He must be mad.

Elspeth appeared by his father's side and slipped her hand into the crook of his arm. "You must go, Colin," she said softly. "She needs you."

His gaze shifted to his father. The old man smiled softly and nodded.

With that encouragement, he turned to the men, busily readying their mounts. "I dinnae need a guard."

Scowls and sputtered arguments surrounded him.

"Love has surely addled what little wits you have, my friend, if you think you shall pass through the gates alone," Ian said.

"'Tis my concern and doesna involve the whole keep. Least of all, you," he snapped, his fear for Amelia's life stealing what little patience he possessed. He should've told her of his heart, he should've forced the words passed his constricted throat before it was too late.

Ian sighed heavily. "Do you truly wish to argue over this, wasting valuable time?"

Snarling, Colin shook his head with a weary sigh. He'd be a fool to travel alone, but he didn't wish to have others privy to her no doubt strongly voiced reasons for leaving.

He singled out a select few to accompany him then mounted his horse, praying she was safe. Praying she hadn't fled because she knew of his heart's greatest desire and wanted no part of it or him.

****

Tuck had gone from a somewhat unsteady walk to practically dragging her butt along the ground. Maighread's poison had done one hell of a number on her.

"If I ever get my hands on you," she snarled, propping her shoulder against a tree.

201

Thoroughly exhausted from the effort it took just to speak, she slowly sank to the ground. Hating to admit it, she wished she'd waited a couple of days before heading out. But knowing that Aileen was fast on the mend meant the wedding wasn't far off.

The thought of watching Colin marry sweet, perfect, petite Aileen made her stomach churn. He probably wouldn't have appreciated her tossing up her cookies in the middle of the ceremony. A chuckle started low in her chest, bubbling up her throat and out into the chilly morning air. What a sight that would've been.

In a low formal voice, she said, "And does anyone here object to this union?"

"Raaalph," she drawled, ending with a snort. Colin would've thrown her in the loch for sure.

A blade appeared beneath her chin, stifling her laughter and tensing every muscle in her body.

"'Tis a fine morn for jests, but I'm thinkin' 'tis not so fine a day fer ye."

She didn't recognize the gruff voice, which instantly made him an enemy, and her the town idiot. How could she let herself get caught off guard so easily?

Damn Maighread and her witch's brew.

Her mind raced over the situation and how to best handle things, but as weak as she was, her options were extremely limited.

He jerked her to her feet and she swayed with the sudden movement. Her left breast, although hidden well beneath her down vest, pressed against his beefy hand where he gripped her arm.

His eyes widened and he snatched off her cap. "A woman, and a big one, eh, lads?"

A few guffaws echoed around her, and she realized for the first time this cretin wasn't alone. She cursed Maighread for the hundredth time.

He leaned closer as an evil grin split his lips. "I ne'er been fond of redheads, but then I isna tae particular."

Pooling her strength, she said, "Sorry to hear that, because I am." She cleanly knocked his knife from his hand and broke away from his grip with a solid blow to his jaw. In her weakened state, however, she was no match for three men and quickly found herself tied and gagged.

The one who'd held the knife wiped the blood from the corner of his mouth. "I aught tae slice ye open here and now, but I've a use fer ye."

She had a pretty clear idea of what that was, but held in her grimace. Somehow, she had to get herself out of this mess. A mess her stupid heart had gotten her into. She should've never let that stubborn, exasperating, overbearing—she sighed—wonderful Highlander get to her. If she'd been thinking with her head instead of her heart, she wouldn't have taken off before regaining her strength.

If she'd just listened to MacLean for once and stayed in bed where she belonged, she wouldn't be dangling over some goon's shoulder, with a filthy rag in her mouth, and a serious case of dry heaves.

Of course when MacLean bellowed like an old bear, as he usually did when imparting his so-called wisdom, she patently ignored his views on what women should and should not do.

But this time, the man had been right, damn him.

****

Locating her trail had been frighteningly easy. It wasn't like her, but then she was far from well. She refused to admit her lingering weakness from Maighread's treachery, but Colin knew she'd not fully recovered.

"Her tracks end here, lad," William said, his voice heavy with concern as he lifted something from the ground.

Colin slid from his horse and instantly realized what had twisted William's wrinkled brow into a mass of deep crags. It was Amelia's woven bonnet.

He gently took the cap, holding back the urge to press it to his face as he cried out in anguish. The ground revealed signs of a skirmish, three, maybe four men against one woman.

And Amelia had lost.

The only thing keeping him from falling to his knees with the intense pain squeezing his chest was the absence of blood. She was alive, or was when they'd taken her.

His fingers gripped her bonnet more tightly. Lifting

his head, he looked in the direction her abductors had gone. "We go that way."

He vaulted back upon his mount, turning his pain inward. But when he found the men who dared harm his beloved, they would know more agony than they'd ever dreamed possible.

Ian and his small guard silently followed. A mere hour later, they came upon the band's camp. Hiding their horses some distance away, they stealthily moved closer on foot, well hidden by the dense brush.

Colin spied Amelia gagged and tied to a tree at the far edge of the clearing. He cast a quick prayer of thanks to the heavens that she was still alive, but her captors would not be for long. Pulling his claymore free, he prepared to rush into their circle and swiftly remove their heads.

A strong hand clamped over his arm.

He snapped his head to the side to see which of his party was fool enough to interfere.

Ian motioned silently toward the wood across from the clearing. Another group of men were closing in on the camp, well in sight of the others. Obviously they were in league with the ones who'd taken Amelia, leaving Colin and his guard outnumbered three to one.

Clenching his teeth hard enough to make his jaw pop, he sheathed his sword. He had to use his head and not let his fury destroy the one person he loved above all others.

The newcomers spread out, posting guards as the one in charge greeted his counterpart in the clearing. He couldn't hear what was said, but could see clearly that he was not pleased.

The newcomer waved toward Amelia repeatedly, his face red with rage. He pulled his dirk and shoved the other aside and moved toward her.

"See to the others," Colin hissed as he made his way quickly toward the clearing. He didn't dare risk waiting to see if his intentions were to cut her free or take her life.

"A fine morn," Colin called as he entered their small circle. As expected the man stopped his advance on Amelia and turned.

It took all his strength not to look at her, to show the

slightest flicker of recognition. He was still too far away to put himself between her and a well-honed dagger.

Rolling her eyes, Tuck groaned behind her gag. Had he lost his mind? Not only was he outnumbered, he didn't even have his claymore drawn.

"Who be ye?" the one who'd grabbed her asked.

The man bearing down on her with the knife, spat out, "Ye dobber, 'tis Colin MacLean."

"Aye, that I am, but I dinnae know your name," Colin replied coolly.

She could see the anger lighting his lion eyes, sensed the intense fury he struggled to contain. Some of which, she surmised was for her, due to her latest blatant refusal to do as he'd ordered.

Okay, so she'd screwed up. She admitted it. But did he have to waltz into enemy territory as if he hadn't a care in the world? Didn't the man have a brain in his hard head?

The one with the knife edged toward Colin, a sinister grin on his craggy face. "Ye know who I be, MacLean. But you'll not be tellin' another soul."

Colin laughed. The big dumb ox actually laughed at the man who matched him in size and was already armed.

"Aye," Colin said, still chortling. "You be a Campbell. 'Tis a shame you Campbells have tae resort tae kidnapping our women. It doesna take much of a man tae prey on the weak. Then your visage isna a pretty one. Mayhap 'tis the only way for you tae get yourself a lass."

His grin broadened as he casually folded his arms across his chest. "Aye, an uglier Campbell I've yet tae meet, but I would think you'd find lassies well enough on your own shores. We've few beauties tae pick from here as 'tis."

What the hell was he—Tuck blinked, then blinked again. He was stalling. She carefully shifted her gaze to the far woods from where he'd appeared. If he had guardsmen with him, they were hiding themselves well.

She sucked in a calming breath, doing her best to ignore the stench from the rag in her mouth. She had to trust him. She did trust him. The man she knew, the man she loved wouldn't willingly put himself in a losing situation. He would save her life, of that she had no doubt. Then he'd probably lock her up for the next hundred or so years, but she couldn't blame it for that.

The goons grew weary of his continued babbling and sprang for him, while the one he'd called a Campbell stood by and watched. She winced as Colin took several well-placed blows, but smiled, as best she could under the circumstances, as he laid them out one by one.

Until the one with the knife decided to join in, that is. She screamed through her rag, although ineffectually, but Colin must have heard and spun around to face his new adversary.

She sucked in a disgusting breath as the swipe of the knife missed his throat by mere inches. God, she couldn't live with herself if he died because of her stupidity.

As they continued kicking up the dirt, Campbell lashed out with his blade and caught him across the upper arm. Blood oozed through the slice in Colin's shirt, but he paid it little attention.

The ropes cut deeper into Tuck's wrists as she struggled to free herself, determined to help him. She couldn't just sit there and watch. She twisted and squirmed, but it was no use. Stars popped in and out of her line of vision with the strain and she fell still, trying to catch her breath. She couldn't faint, not now.

"'Twould be a great pleasure tae kill you," Colin growled. He'd managed to get a solid grip around Campbell's neck and was close to choking him to death.

She took a quick breath of relief that he'd won against this cretin, but what about the other Campbells?

Ian and William strolled into the clearing as big as you please and took a moment to watch the fight.

"Dinnae kill the bastard, lad. He may be of use," William called.

Ian chuckled and crossed to Tuck. Kneeling beside her, he sliced her bonds and removed her gag. She spat and swiped the back of her hand across her lips. It would take a long time to get that horrid taste out of her mouth.

"What took you so long?" she snapped. "He could've been killed waiting on you to show up."

Ian chuckled softly. "Now, dear heart, we had to take care of the others first. Can I help it if the man refused to wait? He was determined to reach you before anything untoward could happen. 'Twas difficult enough talking him into letting us accompany him." He gently clasped her shoulder. "He was afraid, as we all were, for your safety, Amelia."

She opened her mouth then snapped it closed, completely lost as to what to say. Colin had saved her from a wild boar, offered her a place to stay, tended her when she was sick, and came after her when she pulled one of the biggest blunders of her life. But he'd scared her half to death!

Furious, she got to her feet then quickly gripped the small tree before toppling back to the ground. Swallowing hard against the sudden wave of dizziness, she turned and stomped up to Colin as best she could. Although she would much rather act like one of those ridiculous females and throw herself into his arms. But instead, she resorted to poking him in the chest.

"Have you lost your mind? Do you have a death wish or something? You couldn't wait a few more minutes?"

Hearing her barbs, knowing she was alive and well, the vise around Colin's chest eased. He ached to hold her, to tell her of his heart, but the daft female wouldn't let him get a word in.

"You had to risk your stubborn fool neck against four armed men," she continued, struggling to tear the lower half of his sleeve.

He ripped the cloth away, noting her pale face, but grinned as he caught sight of the emerald flames sparking in her eyes. She had a glorious temper.

Quickly wrapping the piece of cloth around his wound, she tied it off firmly. "What if your guard hadn't won? What then? We'd both be dead, you big dummy."

His smile quickly waned. She'd nearly lost her life with her foolishness, but had she fled because of him? Would she reject him once he laid his heart bare to her?

The tightness returned to his chest tenfold, spurring his anger. "I dinnae see what you're harping about. You're safe, are you not? And what in bleedin' hell were you thinking? You shouldna be out of your sick bed, you daft female."

Dropping her hands, she swayed yet managed to glare at him. "I don't need an overgrown nursemaid."

He leaned closer, his fury matching hers. "Nay, you need a keeper."

Her eyes rolling, she said, "Once—an ogre, always—an ogre." She fell against him in a dead faint.

"Blast you, lass. You'll be the end of me yet," he muttered against her curls as he lifted her into his arms.

His horse appeared by his side, a worried frown marring young Michael's features where he stood holding the reins.

"She's weak, lad. But I've no doubt she'll be fine." He knew he spoke the truth. Her fire, her courage, her infernal stubbornness would see her through the remnants of Maighread's poison.

Nudging his horse onward, Colin relished the feel of her in his arms. Every breath she took, deep and steady, every beat of her heart, strong and sure. Aye, his love would recover, but would he, if once she was well and truly healed she still wished to leave him?

Chapter Twenty-one

Tuck awoke to the sounds of a busy day below in the bailey coming through her open window. The soft feather mattress cradled her in a comfortable embrace, and she hesitated before opening her eyes. She simply felt too relaxed and didn't want to lose the rare feeling.

Well, the dreams she'd had weren't bad either. She'd latched on to the foggy but wonderful memories of being held in Colin's arms on their journey back to Castle Arreyder, keeping away any nightmares of her recent ordeal. The dinner Elspeth had fed her with a fussing Fiona by her side the evening before had done wonders as well. She felt almost like her old self.

Giving way to her need to rise, she stretched like a contented cat. She paused at the sight of her wrists wrapped in cloth. Well, maybe not completely her old self, but close enough. All she needed now was a good breakfast and some fresh air.

She chuckled softly at the noonday sun. Perhaps a good lunch instead. No wonder she felt so rested and hungry. She'd slept for nearly eighteen hours.

Elspeth bustled in, fussing and fuming at her as she climbed from the bed and dressed.

"After what happened tae you yestreen, you've no business getting out of bed."

"I know you mean well, Elspeth, but I can't just lie around. I'm fine, really. I know what I did was wrong. I should've at least waited for..." she sniffed the air and grinned, "...some of your delicious potato bannocks. Not to mention your wedding. Congratulations, Elspeth. I'm happy for you. Tomorrow's the big day, I hear."

"Dinnae you be trying tae change the subject. You're not well."

She smiled and shook her head. "I promise to take it easy." In her own way, of course. She took Elspeth by the shoulders and guided her toward the door. "Now don't you have some wedding preparations to take care of?"

Elspeth huffed, then smiled. "I can see that I'm not going tae convince you tae stay abed. But I'll not be responsible for what happens when *he* finds you up and about."

With that comment, she left. Elspeth could only mean one man. Colin.

Tuck shrugged her shoulders and went about devouring her lunch. He'd get over it. And anyway, she wasn't exactly thrilled about his part in yesterday's drama either. To think the man could've gotten himself killed trying to save her. She shuddered and quickly pushed the thought away.

After thoroughly cleaning her plate, she made her way downstairs and stepped outside. She paused on the top step, confused by what she was seeing. Aileen and Robert were saddled up and readying to leave.

"Where are they going?" she asked, glancing at Ian.

"Home. Are you sure you should be up and about, dear heart?"

She waved off his question. "Sure, sure, but what about the wedding? I mean, Colin's, not his father's."

He chuckled. "You'll find out soon enough, my sweet. If the man's got any sense."

Shaking her head at his cryptic comment, she watched MacLean take Robert's hand then wave as Aileen and her small guard rode out of the bailey.

"I don't get it. Does this mean there's a truce or what? Did she get ticked because Maighread tried to kill her?"

"Yes, there is a truce of sorts, but Colin and Douglas will be meeting with the MacKenzie in a few days. It appears the Campbells have been impersonating each of the clans, attempting to instigate a war, hoping that in the end they would be able to take over the island."

She nodded thoughtfully, recalling the odd tension between the Campbells she'd had the unfortunate luck to meet, and Colin. Yet the fact that Aileen was leaving, still in her single status, had Tuck crossing all her fingers and toes.

Did it mean Colin wasn't getting married after all? Did it mean he was free to—she stopped that thought before it could grow and get her hopes up all over again. She wasn't the woman for MacLean. That had been proven time and again. So what if he cared about her enough to risk his life and come after her, it didn't mean he wanted her as a man wants a woman—loves a woman. Is honor was everything. He felt responsible for her. End of story. And not a fairytale.

Reminding herself of the painful fact that she was never going to find that stupid happy ending Jenny had always talked about, she was determined to at least repay the kindness of Elspeth and Fiona, and so many others. She would use her skills to help keep the clan safe.

"I guess I'd better get with it, in case the Campbells decide to pay a visit," she said, ignoring the pinch in her heart.

"I do not think—"

She waved off Ian's objection and strolled toward the lists. "The guys need some more pointers, especially after watching that fight yesterday. The Campbells are definitely not wimps."

Michael greeted her with an eagerness that made her smile, and in minutes she was deep into a hefty workout, although William refused to have any part of it, the big chicken. What did they think would happen? She wasn't going to break, for Pete's sake.

"Okay, now you try it," she said, motioning for Michael to give her a good toss.

He took his stance and cleanly put her on her back.

"Good job," she said, lying there looking up at him.

"What the devil do you think you're doing?" Colin's face appeared over her, blocking out the sun.

"Enjoying the view. What does it look like I'm doing? I'm working."

She moved to rise, but found herself swept up into his arms. "Hey! What's the big idea?" She squiggled to get free, but couldn't move pinned against his chest.

"You daft female! You're not well enough tae be wrestling."

"I'm fine," she snarled, hating the feel of his arms around her, the beat of his heart against her side, the nearness of those lips. If only he hadn't kissed her. "Put me down, Sasquatch."

He ignored her as chuckles rippled through the courtyard.

She shot the lot of them a glare over his shoulder. "You guys just wait. You're going to be sore in places you never dreamed of," she called.

She jerked her gaze back to Colin's scowl as he marched into the keep. "And you, just wait until I get loose."

"Your threats mean little tae me, woman." He kicked open her chamber door then tossed her on the bed. "I'll say this but once. No traipsing through the wood, no sneaking off in the dead of night, and you are tae stay...in...bed."

He turned to the door, and she jumped up. "I'm not tired."

She was one step behind him to the door when he slammed it shut and spun around.

"You're not leaving this room." He gripped her arm firmly.

Shifting her weight, she twisted to the side and tossed him onto the bed, but with his hand still clasped around her arm, he pulled her down on top of him. She stilled at the feel of his massive form, solid and strong, stretched out beneath her.

She swallowed hard. "You see? I'm fine. I put you on your back without any trouble. Now, I've got men to train." She pushed against his chest, lifting herself up.

He gripped her shoulders, halting her escape. His lion eyes peered into hers. "How do you know, 'tis not where I wished tae be?"

She shivered with need at the deep sensual tone of his voice. He pulled her down closer and closer until his lips were but a breath away from hers.

"I want you, Amelia, but I'll not beg, nor will I take what isna freely given."

"Y-you want me?" She was stunned, thrilled—terrified.

Lifting his hand, he cupped her cheek, his callused fingers brushing against her skin. "Aye. Verra much."

He trailed his thumb across her bottom lip, his gaze following the slow, achingly sensuous movement. She closed her eyes on a rough moan then his lips met hers.

The gentleness of his kiss, a total contradiction to the others he'd given her, stole her breath. As sweet as it was, she wanted more, she wanted the fire he'd let loose inside her before. Tentatively, she touched his lips with the tip of her tongue, not sure how to tell him, but it was enough.

With a deep guttural groan, he flipped her to her back and devoured her. She'd never wanted anything, anyone the way she wanted him. Her hands roamed over his broad shoulders and down his back, feverishly exploring. She ached for the feel of his bare skin, all of him touching her both inside and out.

"Hurry," she panted, as they tugged at their clothes.

They were bare from the waist up in seconds. Tingles shot through her from the rasp of his chest hair across her nipples. He pressed delicious kisses across her shoulder, up her neck to her mouth. With a moan, she fisted her hands in his hair and reveled in every heated swipe of his tongue.

He blindly fumbled with the zipper on her pants. "How do you open the bleedin' things?" he growled against her mouth.

Smiling beneath his determined scowl, she shoved his hand aside and quickly unfastened her jeans.

With a devilish grin, he nipped and nibbled his way down across her belly and along her thighs as he slid her pants off. He paused with a curse at her boots and nearly took off her feet as he yanked them free.

In moments he was hovering over her, bare and beautiful. His long hair teased her ribs as he laved his tongue across her breast and pulled the pebbled peak into his mouth. Her body came to life. She writhed beneath him, wanting more, demanding everything.

"Colin," she gasped.

"Soon, lass."

She growled a response, going mad as his tongue and teeth tormented her. His hand drifted over the curve of her hip, then dropped between her thighs. She nearly screamed at the onslaught of pleasure from his fingers caressing her tender flesh.

Cradling his head firmly in her hands, she pulled him up to her face. "Now," she demanded.

"Aye, now," he said raggedly, then ravaged her

mouth with his as he thrust inside her.

A pathetic squeak sounded in the back of her throat, and she fell still.

He snapped up his head, a grimace on his face. "By the saints, you should've told me you were a virgin."

She let out a slow breath as the pain eased. "What difference would it have made?" She knew it would smart, but she hadn't expected it to hurt quite that much.

"I wouldna have been so rough, blast you."

"If you're trying to tell me that it's over, I just might have to kill you." It couldn't be over. There was one hellacious orgasm out there with her name on it, and she knew, deep down inside, that the only man who could give it to her was Colin MacLean.

He chuckled as he nipped at her chin and lips. "Nay, lass. The pain part is done, but not the pleasurin'."

She toyed with his hair, relishing the feel of it sliding between her fingers. "Then I think you've got some work to do."

"Aye. That I do, but 'twill have tae wait a bit until you're ready." He pressed kisses across her mouth and cheeks as he spoke, moving down her throat to her breasts.

"How long is a bit?" she asked breathlessly.

"A moment or two," he murmured against the tip of her breast, nipping and suckling.

"Mmm, then I think we're way past a bit."

He kissed her then slowly lifted his hips. She sucked in a breath at the feel of him sliding in and out, rebuilding her hunger with every stroke. Her inner muscles tightened around him, welcoming him. He groaned in her ear, sending tendrils of ecstasy spiraling through her.

"Colin," she gasped. She wriggled beneath him, eager to reach that elusive crest as her skin tingled, her heart raced, and her mind spun.

With a rash of fevered kisses, he made his way back to her mouth while cradling her bottom in his hand, angling her hips, allowing his thrusts to go deeper. Pure male heat engulfed her.

"Amelia," he murmured on a throaty moan, and drove into her one last time.

Her back arched, embracing his power, his passion,

and she detonated on the spot. His muscles quivered as he poured himself inside her, adding to the impact of her release. On and on it went, until her mind reconnected with her body and she relaxed in his arms.

Lifting his head, he rolled to the side, pulling her with him. He pressed a kiss to the top of her head, but said nothing.

Content, she lay with her cheek against his chest for some time before speaking. "They're probably wondering what happened to us."

"Aye." He chuckled. "I'm surprised they've not come tae see if we've killed each other yet."

She laughed and propped her chin in her hand. "We nearly did, but not in the way they might think."

Laughing, he kissed her long and hard then rolled her to her back. His gaze traveled the discolored skin across her shoulder followed by the tips of his fingers.

"Tell me of this mark," he said. "'Tis unusual."

She ran a finger along the edge of his cheek, marveling at how striking he was. "It's from a bullet. I got it on my last tour of duty."

His brow furrowed as he examined it more closely.

"I havenae seen the damage a firearm can make, but I have heard tell they make a verra large hole in a mon."

"There are more kinds of guns than I can name, in my time. But no matter the weapon it still hurts like hell."

He nodded, a solemn frown on his lips then lowered his gaze to her breast and hip. "And these?" he asked, his fingers gliding over her scars.

She clenched her jaw against the wave of memories, her hand instinctively covering the slash across her breast. "I had an accident when I was a kid," she said stiffly.

Lifting his head, he gazed into her eyes, deeper than anyone had ever gone.

She looked away, uncomfortable with his close scrutiny.

"Your father did this." It was a statement not a question.

"How—" she choked off the question and nodded.

"You spoke of things in your sleep when you were ill."

215

He grasped her chin and forced her to look at him. "If he were here, I would teach him what 'tis like tae know real pain."

She blinked, trying to hold in her tears.

Clasping her fingers, he lifted her hand from her breast. "These marks are not something tae be ashamed of, mavourneen. They pain me tae see, but they dinnae take away from your beauty."

She shook her head with a watery chuckle. "I'm not beautiful."

"But you are." He splayed his fingers into her hair. "I'm not good with words like Ian, I've no practice at such things. But you are beautiful, Amelia."

His gaze roamed over her features. "The green of your eyes is like summer in the glen. The way the firelight catches in your hair 'tis like the most glorious sunset. And your skin," he said, running his fingers across her shoulders and down her arm, "creamy and fern-tickled, drove me near tae madness the first time I laid my eyes upon you."

"I think those words are perfect," she said roughly, and threw her arms around his neck, holding on with everything she had, wanting him, loving him with her whole heart, and praying he wouldn't break it.

Chapter Twenty-two

Colin could barely take his eyes off her. She'd decided to wear a dress for his father and Elspeth's wedding, and was by far the most beautiful lass in the hall.

She took her place beside Fiona at the table and turned. Her gaze met his and he was struck with the urge to hoist her up and carry her back to her chamber and love her with all that he was.

"There's nothing worse than a lovesick Highlander," Ian grumbled.

Colin blinked, then turned a scowl to his friend before shoving a knife full of food into his mouth. A faint snicker or two reached his ears, and he turned to see the entire room smiling stupidly at him. With a snarl, he looked back to his meal. The whole cursed keep knew what had transpired between them the day before. The woman was barely out of her sick bed. How could he have made love to her that way?

Because it was either that or explode with need.

Shoving aside his plate, he sat back, his gaze finding her once again. His fingers slowly stroked the smooth armrest of his chair, remembering the feel of her skin, the texture of her rampant curls. He wanted her again and again, but had no right to seek her bed without the words. Words he was too much a coward to say.

Tuck found it difficult to concentrate on a single word being said by an over-exuberant Fiona. All she could see was Colin sitting at his father's right hand looking wonderful in his formal attire. His kilt, wrapped around him, his stark white shirt, his ebony hair pulled back at the nape and tied, she could barely breathe, he was so striking.

The image of his face contorted in ecstasy as they made love flashed through her mind. She never dreamed she could bring a man pleasure like that, or that one could take her so fully and forcefully and she not feel the

217

least bit subjugated. If anything she wanted him to love her again and again. She wanted to feel the weight of him pressing her into the feather bed, his arms wrapped around her, his powerful thighs spread over hers, trapping her in the sweetest embrace.

Her gaze lowered to the table. Would she ever get the chance to feel that way again? He'd slipped from her chamber after she'd fallen asleep and hadn't returned later that night as she'd hoped. There was more to what had happened between them than a mere lust filled afternoon. Wasn't there? But what if that was all it had been? What if he didn't want her now that he'd had her? Her throat tightened, threatening to block off her air.

"Tuck?"

"Hmm? Oh, yes, I'm sure your wedding will be just as nice, Fiona. If you'll excuse me." She hurried for the battlements, for the wind against her cheeks and face, where she felt the most at home. There she could shove the pain down to the deepest darkest crevices in her heart.

Too many times since coming to Scotland, she'd let Jenny's fairytales seep into her dreams. She'd been alone for so long, felt empty inside for too many years, how could she bear to have these new feelings ripped away? How would she get through life here in the sixteenth century now that he'd changed her?

"He cares," she mumbled. She knew that much, but how much and for how long?

A horrendous shriek flew to her ears on the wind. Before she could bring her head up and turn, she was knocked to the floor, the back of her head striking the stone as someone pounced on top of her.

"He is mine," a shrill voice cried.

Shaking her head, Tuck tried to clear the haze blinding her. She could barely make out Maighread hovering over her, one hand pressing down on her chest, the other raised in the air.

Tuck reached up to block the blow. Quivering against the woman's surprising strength, she could make out a dirk hovering scant inches from her heart.

"You canna have him! He is mine."

"I don't think so," Tuck hissed.

218

Shoving with all her strength, she tossed the witch off and rolled unsteadily to her feet. A wave of dizziness engulfed her. She swayed, struggling to prepare for another attack, but her vision was taking too long to clear after whacking her head against the stone.

Maighread lunged toward her, the blade high in the air. Unable to block the oncoming blow, she knew she was going to die.

A deep bellowing roar reverberated around them.

Colin. She heard his heavy feet pounding against the stone as Maighread brought her arm down. He appeared between them as the haze cleared, and she watched the insane woman, unable to stop her forward lunge, impale herself on Colin's sword.

"You—are—mine," Maighread breathed then slipped to the floor, her lifeless eyes staring up at the overcast sky.

"Amelia." Colin dropped his claymore and pulled her tight to his chest. Jerking back, he cupped her face in his hands and peered into her eyes. "Did she harm you?"

She shook her head. "No. I just have a bump on the back of my head," she said, fingering her scalp.

Ian burst from the stairway and abruptly stopped. He looked at the still form lying at their feet, his jaw clenched and his hands fisted at his sides.

Crouching down beside Maighread, he closed her eyes. "Sleep, little one."

Tuck felt a sharp pang of remorse. Ian's joking about Maighread turning him down had been his way of hiding the pain. Apparently, he wasn't the womanizing rogue he let everyone believe him to be. He'd truly cared for her.

Ian rose and turned to them. "I am glad to see you unharmed, dear heart."

She nodded, standing in Colin's arms. "I'm sorry." She didn't know what else to say in the face of so much pain.

"I shall take her to her chamber," he said, then lifted Maighread's lifeless body into his arms.

As he disappeared into the stairwell, Tuck whispered, "He was in love with her."

"Nay, mavourneen," Colin said, squeezing her tightly to his side. "But he did care a great deal for the lass. Why

I shall ne'er understand." He guided her down the stairs.

Douglas and Elspeth arrived in Maighread's room shortly after them.

"William said he thought he'd spied her among the crowd, but I didna wish tae believe him," Douglas said.

Colin lifted his gaze from the shrouded body. "Nor I, but I took care tae have the larder and foodstuffs closely guarded."

"Ach, the poor lamb," Elspeth cried, quickly covering her mouth before burying her face against his father's chest.

"I'm sorry tae spoil your wedding day, Da." Although he didn't wish for Maighread's death, knew she would've been punished severely for her treachery, he could not spare any remorse in her passing. She'd wanted to end the one life he held most dear.

"'Tis not your fault, lad. She brought her end upon herself." Douglas turned and guided a sobbing Elspeth away.

"Come. I wish tae be far away from this sadness," Colin said.

Tuck let him lead her to her room. He bore so many things on his broad shoulders, but now with the weight of Maighread's death, he seemed close to breaking. He stopped at her door and ushered her inside.

She turned before he could leave. "Your father's right, you're not to blame."

His jaw clenched. "Aye, but it doesna make it any easier."

"No. It never does." She held his gaze for what seemed like ages, hoping, wishing, praying he would take her in his arms and take away the horrid chill of death enveloping her.

"I thought—" He swallowed hard. "I thought I was tae late."

"I'm pretty hard to get rid of," she said.

He hesitated for a heartbeat, then stepped across the threshold and took full possession of her mouth. She returned his kiss hungrily, his breath filling her with life, with hope.

Laving her neck with kisses, he said, "Ach, mavourneen, I've a need tae touch you, tae feel your creamy skin against mine. Tae feel alive."

"Then why don't you?" she breathed, her legs turning to jelly.

Never had she ever thought a man could turn her into such a malleable mound of quivering female. She felt like fine plastique being molded and shaped into a powerful explosive. And when she went off, she wanted him to go with her.

He kicked the door closed and fumbled with the bolt without removing his lips from her skin. Easing to the bed, he changed his assault lower, his lips brushing across the tops of her breasts, barely visible above her bodice.

She moaned as his tongue slid into her cleavage. Maybe pushup-bras, antique or otherwise, were a good thing after all. A very good thing.

He undid her laces as she removed his kilt. Once they were both undressed, they stood for several seconds letting their gazes roam over one another.

"I'll ne'er get enough of the sight of you," he whispered.

She let out a long breath of pure satisfaction. "I think I can safely say the same."

Smiling, he hoisted her up and tossed her on the bed. Their laughter turned to heated murmurs as they came together in a raw act of possession, celebrating life at its most intimate level.

A time later they lay silently in one another's arms once their hearts had slowed. Colin tucked his love against his side, her soft curls tickling his cheek, her long fingers sifting through his chest hair, occasionally raking her nails against his skin. It felt incredible, and he was unable to contain his moan of satisfaction.

"What does mavourneen mean?" she asked.

With a grin she couldn't see, he said, "It means nettlesome shrew."

Her head popped up from his shoulder, her beautiful green eyes narrowed, her luscious mouth drawn tight. "You know what I can do to you." The corner of her mouth crept up into a teasing grin.

He chuckled at her false ferocity. "Is that a promise?"

"Looking for adventure, are we?"

By the saints, he loved this woman. He tapped the tip

Jo Barrett

of the nose. "'Twill always be so with you, but tae answer your question in truth, it means my darling."

"Oh," she said, turning a deep shade of red.

It would take some time to tear down the lies her father and others in her past had filled her with, but he welcomed the challenge. "Now, I have a question for you. What is this—Sasquatch?"

She bit her lip with a crooked smile. "You won't like it."

He peered at her sternly, then flipped her onto her back and pinned her with his body.

"Oh, all right," she said with a sigh. "It's a humanlike animal, supposedly larger than a man and covered with shaggy hair or fur. It's a legend, really."

His jaw fell slightly lax. Did she think him a beast? God in heaven, had he hurt her? What a fool he'd been! He'd taken her virginity no more than a day ago and roughly too.

"Ach, mavourneen," he said, cupping her face. "I beg you tae forgive me. I ne'er meant tae hurt you."

"What are you talking about? You haven't hurt me."

"'Tis a beast, you described. And 'tis what I've been tae make love tae you again so soon. I'm sorry, lass." He lowered his head, resting his brow against her shoulder.

Her fingers slipped into his hair. "I'm fine, and I wouldn't have traded a moment of it for the world."

"Then you dinnae hurt?" he asked, lifting his head.

She shifted, just so, beneath him. "What do you think?"

He let out a hiss as his rigid shaft brushed against her moist heat.

"Think of Sasquatch as an endearment," she murmured, nipping at his chin. "You're big—and strong—and legendary."

Her long luscious legs rubbed against his. "But I dinnae have fur," he muttered, rapidly losing the ability to speak.

"No, you don't." She ran her tongue along his throat.

He clamped his eyes closed and swallowed hard.

"But you hadn't shaved for a good while the first time I saw you," she said. "And you're the biggest man I've ever known." She tasted the edge of his lips then rubbed her

222

mouth against his with the lightest of touches.

Much more of her torture and he would be lost. "Think you can win my good favor with your kisses?"

"Oh, my arsenal is a lot bigger than that." She squiggled lower, embracing the tip of him between her supple folds, then pulled back.

He growled low and long. "You intend tae drive me mad, woman."

"Somehow I have the feeling..." she shifted again, pulling him in further before drawing back once more. "...that we'll both go crazy."

His lips met hers hard as he thrust forward, not allowing her room to retreat. He wrapped his fingers between hers above her head as she surrendered to him. It was the sweetest gift she could ever give him, his warrior woman, and he gave of himself in return, completely and with all that he was.

Chapter Twenty-three

"What think you, Colin?" his father asked, pulling his attention back to the important conversation at hand.

"'Tis a sound plan. Upon our return to Arreyder, we'll place men about the isle to keep watch. The Campbells willna set foot upon Mull without our knowing."

The MacKenzie nodded in agreement, much calmer than he'd been at the beginning of their meeting. He'd cast threats and accusations back and forth with his father for some time before finally acknowledging they had a far more deadly enemy.

The peace between the clans had lasted for generations, but that didn't mean his father and the old laird liked one another. On the contrary, they'd been, at best, tolerant of one another over the years, but each had the good sense not to let their personal dislike affect the clans and the safety of their people.

The meeting ended, and they turned their mounts toward home. Although the Campbells and their devilish cunning were at the forefront of Colin's mind, another problem plagued his thoughts. A certain woman would likely try and skin him alive when he returned to the castle.

He'd spied her listening closely to the discussions between he and his father regarding the meeting of the clan lairds over the past few days, and insisted she be included. She argued that her knowledge of strategy and war would be of help, that her fighting skills alone would be of great use in case the Campbells ambushed them. None of which did he even begin to consider.

He could not allow her to place herself in danger. She, however, hadn't taken his decision to heart. Knowing her as he did, he suspected she might take it in her female head to follow them. So, he locked her in her room before she'd awakened that morning.

Hence, he had a problem. How was he to deal with a

furious female who could put him on his belly faster than he could blink? A sigh slipped from his lips. That was the smallest of his troubles, however. The image of Amelia lying peacefully in her bed after they'd made love appeared before his mind's eye. More than anything, he wanted to stay with her, but could not. There were plans to be made, things he needed to see to.

He sniffed at the blatant lie. He was running from her like a man afraid of his own shadow. Although he'd made love to her, several times, succumbed to the intense desires that plagued him for weeks, he had yet to tell her of his love. Fear was not a stranger to him, but in this instance he felt more the fool.

She'd responded to his touch, offered her body to him in every way, but what of her heart? He grimaced at his sorry state. She'd reduced him to a sympathetic dolt. He'd never be the hard man he was before. If she were to reject his offer of love, he would be of no use to his clan. There would be nothing left of him but a shell of a man with a shattered heart.

The woman was everything he could ever want or need. She challenged him at every turn, and he enjoyed those challenges beyond pleasure. He would not let his fear of her breaking his heart rule him any longer. He would tell her of his feelings after he faced her wrath.

Lifting his gaze to the keep in the distance, he murmured a prayer for strength, nearly choking on the words.

"Daft, she is," he said, then kicked his horse into a fierce gallop.

****

"Lock me in my room. Ha! We'll just see about that," Tuck murmured, locating another meager toehold in the wall.

She'd pounded on the door, screaming her lungs out for hours, but no one answered her. The beast had threatened them all with a flogging.

Damn the man! He knew she was capable, he knew she could fight and strategize with the best of them, but the stubborn ox refused to listen. Couldn't he understand she needed to be there with him to watch his back?

"If anything happens to that big ape—" No, she

refused to think that way. Nothing was going to happen to him. "Not on my watch."

Cursing beneath her breath as her bleeding fingers struggled to keep a firm hold between the stones, she stretched out her foot, reaching for the next toehold. Why couldn't that stupid vine have reached her window? It would've made the climb a snap, but noooo. She had to have the only room a cockroach would have trouble getting into.

She snarled low and long. "When I get my hands on you, Colin MacLean you're going to wish—" She squeaked as a thick arm wrapped around her waist and plucked her from the wall.

"Damn you! Have you no sense?" Colin bellowed as he plopped her down in front of him on his horse, his heart slamming against his ribs.

"I was almost at the bottom," she snapped. "If I hadn't been so busy thinking up new ways to kill you, I would've realized how close I was and jumped down." She squiggled in his arms. "Now, let me go, you—you blasted Scot!"

"So you can find another way tae get yourself killed?"

"I have a lot of rock climbing experience. I wouldn't have been killed. And I wouldn't have been scaling the damn keep, if you hadn't locked me in my room!"

He narrowed his eyes at her. "If you ever do such a daft thing again I'll paddle your backside."

"You and what army?"

"You'll do as I say, like it or no!"

"Well I don't like it and I'll do as I please. When are you going to get that into your thick head?"

Colin climbed down from his horse with his arm firmly around her waist. "You'll do as I tell you, woman, and I'll not have any of your sass."

"Don't count on it." She laid him out in the mud at the base of the stairs to the main hall, flat on his back.

The men burst out laughing as they rode into the bailey. Shooting them a steely glare, they fell silent, but he knew he'd not heard the end of it.

Amelia stood at the top of the stairs, her fists on her hips. "When are you going to learn? I do not need a babysitter!" She turned and stomped into the keep.

Knowing she was ever ready to fight, not willing to give her another chance to use one of her nasty tricks, he quickly plowed forward, spun her around, and tossed her over his shoulder.

She grunted as the air rushed from her lungs. At least he'd have a few moments of peace without her harping in his ear. But he knew the battle wasn't over.

He gritted his teeth against the sheer terror that had engulfed him as he rode within sight of the keep. Pushing his horse as hard as he could, he'd prayed she wouldn't fall.

His steps faltered as he climbed to her chamber. It was his fault that she did such a fool thing and would have been his fault if she'd died.

He sat her on the bed without a word, his heart lodged firmly in his throat. How was he to keep her safe if she wouldn't do as she was told?

She bounced back up, glaring hotly at him. "Your warlord tactics won't work on me. Not this time. Now, get out of my way."

"Not 'till I beat some sense intae you."

"Oh, you just try it," she snarled.

"Blast you, woman, I don't want tae fight you, but I'll not have you risking your life!"

"That's a load of bull! All you want is control. My life doesn't mean a damn thing to anyone." She spun away, her arms wrapped tightly around herself.

He snagged her by the shoulders and jerked her back around. "Your life means everything tae me! I love you, you stubborn female!"

Her mouth opened in a small rounded oh, but no sound came out.

Letting out a disgruntled sigh at having told her of his heart in such a way, he said, "Sit, so I can tend you."

He eased her onto the edge of bed, hoping the next words from her lips wouldn't break his heart. He turned to the basin by the hearth and moistened a cloth. Kneeling before her, he took her hands in his and bathed her bloodied fingertips.

"No one's ever loved me before," she said, staring at him as if she'd never seen him before.

He looked up into her watery eyes. "Then 'tis way

past time."

A small smile touched her lips. "Then I guess I love you, too."

He grinned, barely containing his immense joy. "You guess? You canna do better than that?"

She laughed. "I'm new at this so you'll have to be patient."

"I'm not known tae be a verra patient man, lass."

Smiling, she said, "Really. I hadn't noticed." Her lips turned down slightly. "Colin, I don't know how to do this. I don't know how to be in love."

"Shh, mavourneen." He rose up on his knees and kissed her. "We'll find our way together."

Never had he felt such completeness with a woman. The women he'd bedded before were nothing like his Amelia. The fire in her hair was in her soul as well. They would have strong children, in mind and body.

If she would have him. Her love for him was a gift indeed, but he wanted more. He wanted her forever.

"Amelia, I wish tae—I want—" He let out a frustrated breath that stirred the curls alongside her face.

She cocked her head. "What?"

She was so beautiful, her cheeks a rosy hue, her lips well kissed, and her eyes filled with warmth. He nearly forgot what it was he wanted to say.

He took her hand and brought it to his lips. "I want you always by my side." Afraid of what he would see in her eyes, he dropped his gaze to their joined hands. "'Tis a simple thing we can do by consent. 'Tis the old way. We've no need for a priest tae make us husband and wife in my eyes, but if you wish it, I will find one."

Her silence stripped him to the core, but he had to face her decision whatever it may be. Slowly, he lifted his gaze.

"I, Amelia Tucker," she said shakily. "Take you, Colin MacLean, to be my husband. I promise to love and honor you for the rest of my life." She paused with a soft sniffle. "Is that what you mean?"

"Aye," he said, his voice breaking. His eyes misted over and he blinked to clear them. "I, Colin MacLean of the clan MacLean, take you, Amelia Tucker, tae be my wife. I promise to be a loyal, faithful, and loving husband tae you for as long as I live." He kissed her, then pulled her into his arms and held her close.

Never had he dreamed such a thing would be possible, not for him. He'd envisioned a life without emotion, without love.

"Colin? I don't have any sort of dowry or anything." She pulled back to look up at him. "I'm not even Scottish. Will your father approve of you marrying me instead of Aileen?"

He chuckled deeply at the sound of worry in her voice. She didn't know that whether his father approved or not, 'twas too late for anyone to naysay their joining. He'd loved her thoroughly and with great pleasure more than once, and once was all it took. She may be carrying his babe at that moment.

"It isn't funny, you big ape," she said, punching him in the stomach.

He pushed her down to the bed and gently snagged her injured hands, pinning them above her head. Ah, the fire snapping in her eyes did marvelous things to him.

"I'm not laughing at you, love, but the situation. Although I wanted you, I wouldna go against the agreement with the MacKenzie," he said, watching her scowl deepen. "But my father saw that I didna care for Aileen. I couldna hide my heart from him or Elspeth. He didna want me tae marry without love."

Her scowl faded as her eyes focused on his chin. "And, um, Aileen wasn't disappointed?"

He grinned and nuzzled her delectable neck. "Nay. She loves Robert as he loves her. All has turned out for the best." He nibbled across her chin to her lips. "Now if you dinnae mind, I've other things I'd rather *discuss*."

He took his time loving her, touching her, savoring the feel of her skin against his. His lady wife. His heart.

Hours later, Colin escorted Amelia to the solar, her hand trembling in his. This magnificent woman, capable of dealing a fatal blow to a man twice her size, was afraid his father would reject their marriage although he'd tried to assure her countless times while they made love.

Elspeth lifted her head from her stitchery. "Did you have a nice rest, dears?" she asked, a distinctive twinkle in her eye.

Amelia's face burned brightly.

"I would say so, by the color of Amelia's face," Ian said with a hearty chuckle.

Colin shot him a glare, then pulled his beloved with him to his father's side where he sat across from his so-called-friend at the chess table.

"I have news of some interest tae you," he said. "Amelia has consented and is now my wife." He lifted their joined hands, displaying his ring on her finger.

His father stood. "Is this true, lass?"

She nodded jerkily.

The old man slapped him on the back then stole a kiss from his stunned bride. Elspeth hugged her with tears in her eyes.

Ian pressed a hand to his chest and bowed before her. "My heart may never recover, but I congratulate you." He leaned close for a kiss, but paused at Colin's low snarl. Chuckling, he took her hand and kissed it.

"Wonderful," his father said. "We'll have a grand feast to celebrate the union." Elspeth slipped into his arms. "The solstice should serve us well. We have much to rejoice over and will need the longest day of the year tae do it. Peace, love, and mayhap an heir in the near future to carry on the clan MacLean."

They all laughed, except Amelia. Her hand fell limp in his and the warm blush had disappeared from her cheeks.

"What is it, mavourneen?" he asked.

She lifted her wide-eyed gaze to his, her mouth opened and closed silently. Her head slowly waggled from side to side, then she darted out the door.

He started after her, but was stopped by his father's hand on his arm. "Leave her be, lad. She's overcome by all this excitement," he said jovially. "Come and sit. There is much we need tae discuss after our meeting with MacKenzie this morn."

He let his father lead him to a chair. Something was wrong. His instincts had never failed him, but it would have to wait. He'd ignored his duty long enough that afternoon. His wife, and whatever troubled her, would have to wait a few more minutes.

****

Tuck stared out her window over the Isle of Mull twisting the ring on her finger. The Celtic knots inscribed in the wide band were nothing compared to the knot of pain in her heart.

"The solstice," she murmured. Why hadn't she remembered?

On the solstice the water sprite returned to the magical waters of the burbling stream, leaving his heart sadly broken.

Tears slid down her cheeks as Jenny's story and its terrible ending echoed in her mind.

"It isn't fair," she cried softly. She'd only just found him, learned to love him and be loved in return. How could she give him up now?

The image of the goon at Raghnall Castle pressing his gun into Jenny's side flashed before her mind's eye. If she didn't go back, Jenny could die, but if she did go back, her heart would shatter.

Warm hands slipped around her waist and pulled her back against a solid chest. She closed her eyes and leaned into Colin's strength.

He pecked a gentle kiss against her temple. "What ails you, love?"

She clenched her teeth against the pain. "I remembered how to get back to my time."

He eased away, leaving her cold inside. She wrapped her arms around herself and gathered the strength to explain everything.

She turned and looked up at his stoic face. "There are things I didn't tell you."

Gripping the bedpost, he turned away, his profile grim.

"I was guarding a woman, a very wealthy woman," she said quickly, eager to tell him so he'd understand. "There had been kidnapping threats made. That day, at Raghnall Castle, we were attacked." She swallowed down the lump of failure threatening to choke off her words. "We struggled, but my client, Jenny, decided to help." A smile teased the edges of her mouth at the memory.

"She jumped on the guy's back, and well, in the scuffle I got pushed into the fountain. The next thing I knew, I was sitting in that field near the spring." She took

231

a deep breath and dropped her arms, releasing the steady grip she had on herself. "Then I met you. I have to go back, Colin."

He turned from his study of the bed, the bed where they'd made love and consented to be husband and wife, his amber eyes colder than the chill stealing down her spine.

"I forbid it," he said firmly.

"What did you just say?" She couldn't believe what she was hearing.

"You're my wife, and you'll do as I say!"

Her brittle hold on her emotions snapped like a twig. "I don't believe this. Haven't you been paying attention? No one tells me what to do. Not you, not anybody."

"You'll not be going, and I'll hear no more on the subject!" He spun away and stormed out of the room, slamming the door in his wake.

"Damn you, Colin MacLean," she whispered roughly.

Tears slid down her cheeks as she turned back to the window. Why couldn't he see that she didn't want to go, but that she had to? It was her duty. He should understand that. He almost married someone he didn't love because of his responsibility to the clan.

She twisted the ring on her finger. But he married her, Amelia Tucker, bodyguard for hire instead. A woman who was nothing like the ones he knew. She could never follow his orders blindly, could never be the subservient woman he was accustomed to. Only in bed did she give him that power over her, and that she gave with her whole heart.

It had all been a horrible mistake. She knew that now. She should've never let him so close. She should've never let him near her heart or any other part of her anatomy. It was a good thing she was leaving. What could she have been thinking to fall in love with the man?

"The solstice can't get here soon enough," she mumbled between sniffles.

****

Over the next several days they didn't so much as look at one another, and managed to never be in the same room at the same time. Elspeth and the others had noticed, but remained silent, apparently hoping that whatever had transpired would run its course. Yet Colin knew it would never be so.

He made his way to the top of the keep after yet another exhausting day in the lists, but it didn't dull the pain. She wanted to leave him. The truth hurt him more than the deepest thrust of a finely honed claymore.

Bile rose in his throat as he paced the battlements. He felt betrayed. After they'd loved one another, spoke of the future and their life together, how could she do this? Did the words mean nothing to her? Had she lied to him from the beginning?

Accustomed to suppressing his feelings, he couldn't begin to grapple with the flood of conflicting emotions overwhelming his thoughts. Part of him wanted to hurt her as she had him, while the other wanted to pull her into his arms and hold on with everything he had. He could force her to stay, but what purpose would that serve? She would hate him then, if she didn't already.

Lifting his head to the heavens, he wished for the days before she'd stormed into his life, when he'd known the course of his future, when he'd had control of his heart. A bitter smile eased over his lips. And yet, to have never known love, or the feel of her beneath him, the taste of her lips, the sound of her voice, soft and pleading as he brought her pleasure. Nay, he would not change the past. If only he could change the future.

The solstice arrived and the celebration went as planned although Tuck and Colin hadn't said one word to each other for more than a week.

Holding back the tears the well wishes brought to her eyes, Tuck was amazed at how these people had become such a large part of her life in so short a time. She was going to miss them terribly. Even an irritating, overbearing, hardheaded Highlander. What a lamebrain she was, trying to convince herself that loving him had been a mistake. As if she could've stopped the inevitable.

She stole a quick glance at him beside her where they sat at the big table. He looked wonderful and yet just as miserable as she was. Returning her gaze to her food, she stabbed a bit of meat with more vigor than necessary. For the first time in her life she wanted to compromise but couldn't. Jenny needed her more than Colin did.

Jo Barrett

Her insides knotted. Pressing her hand to her stomach, she tried to blame the twist in her gut on her period, which had come earlier that morning, but knew it was a lie. She'd always been lucky where that was concerned, and suffered little to nothing when it came around in the way of discomfort. It was more of an annoyance than anything. No, losing Colin was partly to blame for the pain, but the rest lay in her secret hope her period wouldn't come for a while. Like nine months.

Although it wasn't right to take his heir away, it was a part of him she would have with her in her own time. She idly wondered what sort of mother she'd be.

"Not a very good one," she whispered to herself. Having had no good role models in her life, the prospect was pretty dismal. Yet, she wanted to be one. Something she'd never considered before, it simply didn't fit into her lifestyle, and after all, she needed a man for that. Something she'd been convinced would never happen. Strange, how loving one man could bring about so many changes in her. Jenny wasn't going to recognize her when she got back, she thought with a rough chuckle.

"I know not what has occurred between you two, but I wish to Heaven you would end this feud," Ian grumbled by her side, pulling her from her depressing thoughts.

"Nothing's occurred. We just had a difference of opinion, that's all." She slipped the tasteless bite of food into her mouth and chewed.

He scoffed. "If this is what things shall be like around here on a regular basis, I may actually have to find another place to lay my head. Before Colin removes it from my shoulders permanently."

Her head snapped up at his comment, then to Colin who was intently listening to something his father was saying

"What do you mean, permanently?" she asked.

"He's been like a madman in the lists. When he's nearly killed off his garrison, he chooses me as his opponent. I've never seen him so agitated." He took her hand and pressed it to his chest. "I beg you, dear heart. Make peace with your husband so the rest of us may live to see another day."

Just talking about the man brought parts of her body

234

to life, flooding her thoughts with bittersweet memories. She'd never felt so rotten in her life, but almost smiled at Ian's exaggerated plea.

Pulling free of his grasp, she said, "I'm sorry he's being such an ass, but I can't help you. Unless you want me to show you a few moves."

"Uh, no. I do not think 'twould be wise to beat him in a match, although I'd sorely like to try. It would only serve to anger him further."

"Then you're SOL."

He gave her a puzzled glace.

"Shit out of luck," she said flatly, not caring in the least that she'd shocked him with her crudeness.

The festivities during the feast grew a bit rambunctious with the bagpipes playing and everyone dancing, except her and Colin. She watched him, wanting to catalog everything about him, but turned away whenever he looked in her direction. There was no doubt he'd detect in her eyes that this was the last time she would ever see him again. During their argument, he'd failed to ask her when she would leave. In all likelihood, he'd probably try to stop her once he realized her intent. She almost wished he would.

The sun crept across the sky, and it was time to go. With one last glance at her husband, she silently stole out of the great hall and made her way up the stairs to her chamber. She changed into her jeans and gathered her things. Looking around the room, where she'd been happier than she'd ever dreamed, tears burned the backs of her eyes.

Her ring glinted in the sunlight streaming through the window. Twisting it off her finger, she laid it gently on the mantel. He would find another woman to love, another wife, one from his time who would do as she was told.

Wanting to leave him something of her own, she bent over and unstrapped her knife from her calf. If archeologists found it in the future, they'd be confused as hell, but she didn't care. She laid it alongside the ring and turned toward the door, then paused. With a grin, she set the last of her Gummy Bears beside her knife and left the room.

With all the revelry going on, no one noticed her slipping out the door and through the gates. It was better this way. Saying goodbye would tear her up inside.

Swiping at her tears as she made her way through the woods, she knew somehow, deep down, that the spring would work this time.

In minutes, she stood on its bank, the sunlight sparkling on the dappling water. She stared into its meager depths then looked back to where Arreyder Castle stood, hidden from view by the woods.

"I'll love you forever, Colin," she whispered.

As she took a deep breath and lifted her foot, the sound of heavy feet tearing through the forest made her pause. She turned to find Colin standing at the edge of the wood, his chest heaving with his quickened breath.

She swallowed the lump in her throat, but it didn't stop the tears from silently sliding down her face. "Don't try and stop me, Colin. I have to do this. I could never forgive myself if Jenny was hurt or died because of my selfishness, because I want nothing more than to stay here with you."

"I know." He quietly crossed to her. "You gave your word tae her before you gave your hand tae me, but when you said you knew the way back, everything I'd feared from the moment I realized I loved you seemed tae be coming true. It tore at my heart, and I fought back the only way I knew how. I shouldna have said what I did. 'Tis your duty tae protect the lass." He swallowed hard. "Forgive me, love. I beg you."

A tremulous smile spread across her lips. "You're forgiven. Just don't let it happen again."

His lips turned up at the corners with a rough chuckle. "'Tis the solstice that you remembered," he said, a sorrowful frown quickly replacing his smile.

She nodded.

He looked to the sparkling water, his jaw clenching and unclenching. "I'll not stop you." He turned his misty gaze to hers. "Although I wish tae with all my heart."

She flung herself into his arms and buried her face against his chest, muffling her sobs. He held her tight, and she knew he cried as well.

He cleared his throat. "You left something behind."

Lifting his hand, he pulled her ring from his pinky. "This belongs here," he said, sliding it onto her finger. "For always."

"I wish—I—"

"I know, mavourneen. I know." He kissed her.

Ian burst into the clearing. "Colin, the Campbells are—" He stopped and smiled. "'Tis about time you both came to your senses."

"What about the Campbells?" Colin asked.

Ian's smile faded. "They are landing in Mull Bay. We must hurry to join the MacKenzies."

"Let's go," she said. She took a step toward the castle then was tugged backward.

"Nay," Colin said. "Your duty isna here."

"You need me. I've got to watch your back. I've got to—"

"Nay, love, though it pains me greatly," he said solemnly, shaking his head. "You must go tae Jenny. She needs you. 'Tis your duty tae return."

Her eyes filled once again. He was right.

She looked at the spring, then back at his handsome face. More love than she ever thought possible filled his eyes. Love for her.

"Who is Jenny and return to where?" Ian asked.

She stepped up to the handsome Englishman and took a deep breath. "I'm trusting you to watch his back," she said tearfully.

He nodded firmly. "As always, but where are you going? I do not understand."

"I'm going to miss you, hotshot." She pressed a quick kiss to his cheek then turned back to Colin.

"I love you," she said.

"And I love you."

They looked at one another for several long, painful heartbeats then she pressed her lips to his and moved to the bank.

"Remember me, mavourneen," he said, his voice breaking over the words.

"Always."

Tears streamed down her face as she stepped into the spring. Sunlight reflected off the water, sending stars darting across her line of vision.

Chapter Twenty-four

"Holy Mother, Mary and Joseph," Ian muttered. "Where—what—tell me there is a good explanation for what I just witnessed," Ian said.

Colin unclenched his fists and swallowed down the grief threatening to choke the life out of him. "She has returned tae her home."

So many times since she arrived, she had placed herself at risk, and with each new threat he thought he had truly lost her. But this way, he knew she was alive—somewhere in time, and hopefully out of danger once she saved her friend.

He grinned tightly with the thought. Aye, she would save her, and many more like her. That was what his wife did, she saved lives—and souls.

He spun on his heels and trudged through the wood to the road where he'd left his horse. Ian followed without a word. Riding swiftly to the castle, he could think of nothing but how much he wanted to tear something apart. His anguish was far beyond containment.

He slid from his mount then bounded up the keep's stairs in twos, meeting Elspeth at the top. He looked into her gentle eyes, full of worry for his bride. It was she who had told him of Amelia slipping away from the celebration.

"I've no time for explanations. She has returned tae her home. You were right, Aunt. 'Tis tae far for me tae travel."

Hurrying up the stairs to Amelia's chamber, he retrieved her gift, having left it behind in his haste to reach her before she disappeared from his life. Her blade would always be at his side since the woman of his heart could not be.

The men gathering in the bailey, ready for battle, grew quiet as he joined them. He led them to Mull Bay in silence. The Campbells would taste his wrath, his grief.

They would not take from him the only thing he had left. His home.

****

Tuck blinked away the stars and for a heart-stopping moment thought she was still with Colin. Then she realized the massive figure in front of her was a statue. Not her husband, not her love.

She looked down at the gravel path beneath her wet boots, a little confused to not be standing in the spring. Apparently she hadn't found the exact spot but at least she had the right spring.

"Jenny," she rasped.

Taking off in a fevered run, she rushed down the statue walk, through the ornate garden to the fountain. Rounding the hedge, she came to a screeching halt at the sight of Jenny giving the kidnapper a few good whacks with her purse. He toppled over to the ground out cold.

Several security guards rushed across the small courtyard as Tuck shook off her amazement and hurried to Jenny's side.

"This man assaulted my client. I'd like him held for the authorities," she said, snapping her bodyguard ID in their faces.

One man nodded as they hauled the man to his feet. "We'll take him tae the manager's office."

"Fine. We'll be there shortly." She turned to Jenny as they carted the man off. "What the hell do you have in that thing?" she asked, pointing at Jenny's purse.

She blinked her big brown eyes, then smiled sheepishly. "A few pennies?"

Scowling, Tuck snatched her bag and shoved her hand inside. Her mouth fell open as she pulled out several rolls of pennies. "How many wishes were you planning on making?"

Jenny shrugged and adjusted her glasses. "Considering the number of wishing wells in Europe, I thought it best to be prepared."

Tuck handed her back her purse, shaking her head with a low chuckle that grew to all out laughter. Tears leaked from her eyes, a mix of bittersweet relief and utter torment. She didn't have to come back. Jenny hadn't needed her to save her after all.

239

"Are you feeling all right, Tuck?" Jenny asked warily.

She cleared her constricted throat. "I'm okay. Come on, let's get this over with. I want to get out of here." She took Jenny's arm and escorted her inside, unable to bear the sight of that damn fountain any longer.

After a lot of paperwork, interviews, and a phone call to Jenny's father, they were finally headed back to their hotel.

Tuck watched the Isle of Mull grow smaller as the ferry carried them away. Hidden in her vest pocket, she ran her thumb over her ring where it sat on her finger, feeling a small bit of comfort in its existence. It hadn't been a dream. He'd been real, and she missed him more than she thought possible. A part of her was dead inside, empty.

Jenny slipped up beside her, and she swiped away the remnants of her tears before she could see.

"Are you sure you're feeling all right?" Jenny asked. "You haven't been acting quite yourself."

Tuck forced a smile to her lips. "I'm just tired. I, uh, guess I'm catching a cold or something."

"Tuck, you don't get tired nor do you ever get sick."

"Look, I'm fine. Okay? I don't need a mother hen."

She spun around and went up on top to see if she could catch a glimpse of Arreyder Castle in the distance. It would be the last time she ever saw the massive stone structure. She could never go back. It would kill her to be where she wanted to be, but not when.

Hours later, after writing up a formal report for Jenny's father, she stood in her room trying to concentrate on her exercises. It beat the hell out of crying herself to sleep, but it wasn't working.

Disgusted, she grabbed her wallet, shoved it into her back pocket, and made her way downstairs to the hotel bar. The thought of getting good and drunk held definite appeal.

"A shot of your best whiskey," she said, taking a seat at the bar.

The tumbler appeared before her in a matter of seconds. She hefted the glass and tossed the contents down her throat. Her eyes teared up a little as it burned on the way down, but that was nothing compared to what her thoughts were doing to her insides. She'd never feel the same way again, but she wouldn't trade what little time they'd had together to relieve the pain. Although she could try and dampen it a bit.

She slapped the glass down. "Another," she said with a nod, and again she tossed it back. She wondered how many it would take to make her numb.

"White wine, please," a soft voice said beside her.

No need to look, she knew who it was. "Leave me alone, Jenny," she said wearily.

"Not until you tell me what's going on." Jenny smiled her thanks to the bartender and took a sip. "You've been acting strangely all afternoon, and I know for a fact you don't drink."

"I do now." She waved at her glass, and another whiskey appeared.

"Considering what happened this afternoon and knowing your background, I've concluded that your current behavior has nothing to do with the incident involving that man."

"How very astute of you," Tuck said, and sipped her drink this time. She felt Jenny's eyes on her, studying her like a specimen. Sniffing derisively, she said, "Hell. Why not? Maybe if I tell someone, it won't seem so unreal." *Or maybe it will hurt all the more.* Clenching her teeth, she looked at her client. "What I'm going to tell you goes no further, understood?"

"Perfectly."

She shook her head with a wry grin. "But you're not going to believe a word of it, so I guess it doesn't really matter."

Jenny cleared her throat and adjusted her glasses. "I assume this has something to do with the fact that you are now wearing a ring I know you didn't have before. That your hair is approximately one point two inches longer than it was when we left this morning, and that your boots were wet instead of the seat of your jeans as they should have been after the altercation with the assailant."

A low chuckle slipped from her lips. "You're a hoot, Jenny. I gotta tell you. But yeah, it has to do with all that." She took a sip of her whiskey then said, "I was that water sprite in your story."

She cut a glance at her client, expecting some reaction, but got only an expectant stare. The woman wanted details, and she wouldn't be satisfied until she'd heard it all.

Taking a deep breath, Tuck let it all spill out. "I fell in the fountain and ended up in fifteen eighty-four. I was there a couple of months, which explains the longer hair. My boots were wet because the only way back was through a spring, the fountain having not been built yet. As for the ring, I met and married—" she cleared the pain from her throat as the light caught on the metal around her finger. "I married Colin MacLean," she added softly.

"Fascinating," Jenny breathed. "May I see the ring?"

Puzzled that it sounded as if Jenny believed her, Tuck pulled off the ring and handed it to her. Her bare finger turned icy. Just like the rest of her.

Jenny cocked her head as she shifted the band in the light for a closer look. "This is a beautifully crafted piece. At the very least sixteenth century, but I suspect much older. I surmise this ring was handed down from generation to generation several times."

Propping her elbows on the bar, Tuck clenched her hands into fists and bit down hard on her knuckles. "Yeah, he said something about it belonging to his mother." She desperately tried to hold back her tears, but there was no stopping them. "I need some air," she choked out.

Tossing some cash on the bar, she sped out the door into the night. Breaking into a run, she fled down the street to the water. She couldn't run from the past, from the decisions she'd made. She had to live with them, but they were killing her.

Her stomach slammed into the railing at the edge of the walk along the shore. She screamed with pain-filled rage, then buried her face in her hands and sobbed. How could she live the rest of her life without him, knowing that he was dead to this world, this time?

Small delicate fingers pulled her hands away from her face. Jenny looked at her with soulful eyes then slipped her arms around her. Tuck hesitated only a moment before resting her head on Jenny's shoulder. For the first time in years, she bawled like a baby.

****

"Colin, damn your eyes, man! Are you trying to kill me?" Ian demanded.

Colin lowered his claymore until the tip touched the ground. His other hand shook with the fierce grip he had on Amelia's blade. "You shouldna come up on a mon that way!"

Ian growled a curse beneath his breath. "Have you not noticed that we've won, you bloody Scot? The Campbells are defeated."

Colin blinked a time or two to clear the stinging sweat from his eyes. The Campbells were laying down their arms. The smell of blood permeated the air, as did the sounds of injured men. He idly wondered how many he'd killed.

His rage at losing the one who held his heart had gripped him fiercely. He wanted others to hurt as he was hurting.

Ian clasped a hand on his shoulder. "'Tis over, my friend." He pointed to his father and William where they stood speaking with the MacKenzie.

The Campbell laird had already retreated to his boat. The men left behind would be sent along as well, but with a warning never to set foot on the Isle of Mull again.

His gaze fell to her blade still clutched in his fist. No longer black, but red with Campbell blood. He shrugged off his friend's hand and strode to his horse.

Ian matched him stride for stride. "Dare I ask where you are going?"

He didn't bother to answer, knowing his friend would follow, watching his back as she'd bade him to.

The ride was not long, but painful. He guided his horse through the trees to the little spring where he'd last held her, mere hours ago. Once he slid off his mount, he moved to the water's edge and washed away the blood. Crisp and clean, he scooped handfuls of it up and doused his head and body, wishing to God it would numb the pain in his soul.

Had she been in time to save the young woman? Did she remember him in her world or had her trip through time stolen him from her thoughts?

He sat by the spring for long hours, watching the light flash across the water until it grew late.

"'Tis time to go back," Ian said quietly. "There is work still to be done and some celebration, I'll wager."

"Aye." He rose and mounted his horse. "But I dinnae think there is enough whiskey in all of Scotland tae ease me this night."

"We shall see, but before you slide too deep in your cups, I wish to hear the tale."

Colin nodded and explained what he could, telling him what his love had told him as they made their way back to Arrevder.

"Amazing," Ian said with awe. "Perhaps she will return one day. Knowing Amelia, if there is a way, she will find it."

"I dinnae know, but I can hope."

Chapter Twenty-five

"Wake up!"

Tuck's entire body jerked and bounced. She peeled open one eye to find Jenny jumping up and down on the bed. "Go away," she grumbled, and rolled over to go back to sleep the sleep of the dead.

Dead drunk, you mean, a voice murmured in the back of her hazy brain.

After bawling her eyes out on Jenny's shoulder, she returned to the bar, bought a bottle of whiskey, and retired to her room to complete her sojourn into an alcohol-induced oblivion.

"Wake up, Tuck. You've got to get up. We have things to do, and we've only got six months," Jenny said, her voice unusually excited.

"If you don't quit jumping on the bed, I'm going to baptize you with the contents of my stomach." She moaned although the bed had stopped moving. Maybe she'd better head for the bathroom while she still could.

Stumbling to her feet, she felt her way blindly across the room. The cool clean porcelain called to her like a long lost friend.

Several minutes later, Jenny sighed as she handed her a damp washcloth. "I told you not to do it, but you refused to listen to my thorough explanation of what alcohol does to the body in such massive doses."

"Yeah, well, hindsight's twenty-twenty. At least I slept." She washed her face, then pressed the cloth to her throat as she settled back against the wall, her legs stretched out before her on the floor.

"No, you were unconscious. There is a distinct difference."

"Unconscious is good. As a matter of fact, it would be really good if I could be unconscious some more." She climbed to her feet, grabbing the sink for balance. "Why don't you go find a museum to visit or something? I'm

245

going back to bed."

"But you can't," Jenny whined, making Tuck flinch.

"Please, drop it to a normal level. Subnormal, if possible."

"Tuck, you're not listening. We have to prepare you for your trip back."

Tuck crawled between the sheets and sighed as she laid her head on the pillow. "I don't have much to pack. Didn't ever really take it out of my bags."

With a huff, Jenny flopped down on the side of the bed. Tuck grimaced at the sudden bouncing.

"I'm talking about getting back to Colin," Jenny said.

One eye popped open and located her tormentor. She was serious. Letting out a long puff of air, she said, "There is no going back, Jenny. You know the end of the story."

"That has no bearing on this."

It hurt to scowl, but she managed. "Spit it out. In simple English."

"You traveled back in time and returned to the twenty-first century on the solstice. In theory you should be able to do it again."

Tuck propped herself up on her elbows, ignoring the pounding behind her eyes. "You said six months."

"Winter solstice. If my calculations are correct, you should be able to travel on either of those days. Nighttime, of course, after the sun sets for the winter solstice, and daylight hours for the summer solstice. However, we can attempt to send you back before sunset to prove or disprove the theory."

Tuck eased back down to her pillow, her gaze focusing on the ceiling. To go back, to be with him again, to live out her life as his wife—it didn't sound believable. She chewed her lip, trying not to get her hopes up.

Jenny tapped her ring where it sat on her finger. "You have nothing to lose."

Yes, she did. The last of her sanity. If she tried and failed, it would destroy her once and for all.

But if she didn't try and there was the slightest chance..."I'll do it," she said, her heart racing with the possibility.

Jenny snatched back the covers. "Good, then get out

of bed. We've got a lot of work to do."

"Hey!" She grabbed her aching head, really wishing she hadn't yelled. "I've got six months," she hissed through clenched teeth. "What other kind of work could I possibly have other than sleeping off this hangover?"

"You don't want to go back empty-handed, do you? If I had the inclination to live in the late sixteenth century, there would be a few items I would think were necessary to take with me. Items not available in that time period. However, you can't exactly drive a car into the fountain at Raghnall Castle."

"Okay, so I pack a bag—a backpack. That won't take me six months. Now, can I go back to sleep?"

She pulled the covers up to her neck and snuggled onto her side, willing the image of Colin to the forefront of her mind. She could dream happy dreams for six months. Then she would know how the rest of her life was going to turn out. Like hell or like heaven.

"Tuck," Jenny huffed loudly. "A backpack is a fine idea, one made of leather so as not to be too conspicuous, but you still have work to do. We have to fill your head with every piece of knowledge we can that will aid you in that time period." She jerked the covers away again. "Consider this reveille, Sergeant Tucker."

With a groan, she crawled out of bed, but only because she knew she'd dream of Colin when she went to bed later that night. And because Jenny wasn't about to leave her new project alone.

The weeks dragged by as her self-appointed professor bombarded her with more and more information. Jenny had her commit to memory significant events in time and the lead players, so that she could use the information to keep her new family safe.

That part wasn't so bad. Tuck definitely saw the advantage to knowing who was on which side and who would come out on top after a war. It was the rest of the work that drove her batty.

She stuffed her brain with a plethora of topics from agriculture to zoology, and prodded her through a rigorous medical program, doubling her knowledge and skills. She prayed she wouldn't have to draw on the latter knowledge often. It was going to be tough enough knowing she couldn't just run down to the corner drugstore for cough syrup, or hightail it to the hospital for a broken bone. No x-rays, no penicillin, no surgeons.

"Why don't you come with me?" Tuck asked. "We could use a real doctor, a real surgeon. As a matter of fact, there's this kid who could use your expertise."

Jenny paused in her rifling through yet another massive book, and looked up. Tuck could see the spark of interest in her eyes, but she shook her head.

"No, I couldn't. I have my father to deal with, and believe it or not, he isn't in the best of health." She snapped the book closed. "Besides, I couldn't live like that. It's too rough for me."

Tuck laughed. "You'd miss your MTV, is that it?"

She smiled. "Actually, I'd miss the Learning Channel, but that's not it. I would be beyond frustrated in that atmosphere. My studies are too complex. I need access to my lab, to various forms of equipment still considered experimental in their own right. I wouldn't be happy in the past."

"But you like the romance of it," Tuck said with a grin.

Jenny's eyes turned dreamy. "Oh, yes. The chivalry, the grandeur, it would be something to see. And I would like to help the child you mentioned, but it would be an endless process. There would always be another person in need, and I'm only one woman."

Tuck sighed. "You're right. But maybe you'll come visit someday. The, uh, portcullis will always be raised."

They both laughed, lifting their spirits.

"I've been thinking," Tuck said. "Why fifteen eighty-four? And why did I get shot back before the solstice instead of on it? And why did I come back to a slight second after I left?"

"Excellent questions," Jenny said, taking off her glasses. "I've asked myself the same." She chewed on the end of the frames, her eyes narrowing as she concentrated. "I would like to test my theory."

"And that would be?"

She lifted her far-off gaze and focused on Tuck. "I've determined that the date you arrived was the spring equinox. As for the year, and do...not...laugh, I believe your wish had something to do with it."

She curled her lips in against her teeth, trying not to snort, but Jenny obviously saw the humor on her face. "Sorry, that's a bigger piece for me to swallow than this whole time travel thing."

Waving her glasses, Jenny said, "Hear me out. What were you thinking when you tossed your coin into the fountain?"

Tuck blinked, but remained silent.

"I thought so." She slipped her glasses back on. "You had that time period or possibly even a Highlander in your thoughts, and I added to that image with my story. Which I undoubtedly wouldn't have told, nor would it have existed if you hadn't gone back. So, it was predestined, in a way, a loop in time."

"We're back to that fairy stuff, aren't we?" Tuck asked with a small groan.

"Well, perhaps not fairies, so much as you landed *when* you most wanted to be. Now, as to the rest of my theory, I believe you can only step into the time loop on the solstice and out of it on the equinox."

"Whoa, whoa. I didn't arrive here on the equinox."

Jenny sighed thoughtfully. "Let's see if I can explain it more simply."

Tuck smirked. "Please do."

"Think of it like the ferry. A perpetual loop, yet with a stop along the way. It begins on the mainland, stops at the isle of Mull then returns to the mainland. You left here on the solstice, landed in the sixteenth century on the equinox, then ended your trip when you began, on the solstice."

"So you're saying that if I leave on the winter solstice, I'd arrive on the fall equinox. Then *if* I chose to come back on the solstice, I'd arrive here seconds after I left?"

Nodding, Jenny looked off into the distance. "Yes, but I'd prefer to test my theory, if you're willing. I'd like to see if you can step into the loop on the equinox, which I believe would place you on the summer solstice. Always falling backward in the year since you are traveling back in time."

Tuck nodded, her thoughts running like terrified sheep through her brain. "But what's to guarantee that

I'll return to the right year?"

"There are no guarantees. But as I said, I believe the year is up to you, and I don't believe you can begin on the equinox."

Shaking her head, her heart pounding excitedly in her chest, Tuck said, "I don't care. I have to try. If I get back on the summer solstice, I can help fight the Campbells."

Jenny nodded sagely. "Then we'd better get back to work. Your study time just got cut in half."

****

Sadly, however, Jenny's theory was correct. She couldn't travel on the equinox. Tuck felt nearly as horrible as when she realized she hadn't needed to come back to the present to save Jenny. But she had another chance. Dozens of chances. She wasn't going to give up. Ever. She'd try every equinox, every solstice, until she found a way back to Colin. Back to where her heart was.

Winter arrived on the little isle of Mull and so did Jenny and Tuck. Raghnall Castle was closed for the season, but that didn't stop them.

Tuck worried her bottom lip. If the rest of Jenny's theory was correct, and she arrived on the fall equinox in the right year, it would be months after the fight with the Campbells. That thought terrified her. Would Colin be there, would he remember her, would he still be alive? She considered checking the history books, but according to Jenny, that much detail couldn't be trusted. Only the larger events.

"Well, here we are," Jenny said excitedly, crouched behind the bushes at the edge of the castle grounds.

Tuck grinned. She was like a kid on Christmas morning, but she had some bad news for the mousy scientist. "You have to stay here, Jenny."

When they'd arrived on the fall equinox to test her theory, the guards had thoroughly searched Tuck's large leather pack and were beyond confused by the items they'd found. She'd made up a story about hitchhiking across Europe and they bought it, but Jenny had stuttered and stammered. She nearly blew the whole thing. Who knew how she'd handle getting caught trespassing in the middle of the night after watching her friend disappear into a fountain.

"Stay behind? Are you insane?" Jenny squeaked.

"I won't risk you getting caught. You don't know how to lie."

"I can lie, I just prefer not to," Jenny said with a sniff.

Chuckling, Tuck said, "Right. Like you did in September when the guards searched my pack."

"I wasn't prepared for your story. A rather good one, I might add."

Tuck took a deep breath. "You know as well as I do, that if you get caught after I disappear, your scientist-professor brain will take over and you'll be expounding on the *fact* of time travel. You'll either be taken away and locked up, or some other lunatic will believe you. Then what'll happen to history?"

"Hmm, you have a good point. Astonishing that I hadn't come to that conclusion first," Jenny said, straightening her glasses. "If people started traveling whenever they liked, there would be total chaos. And, thinking as you would, someone with a evil mind might decide to change the course of history to suit their own purposes."

Tuck's brow furrowed painfully. "My knowing stuff, changing the future for the clan MacLean won't hurt anything will it?"

"Not on the scale say changing the outcome of World War II might have. Just do your best not interfere too much. Don't let Colin become Scotland's king, for instance."

She gave a quick nod of her head. "Gotcha. Low key. No problem. Now, stay put. If I'm not back in fifteen minutes, you'll know it worked."

"Or you got caught."

Narrowing her eyes, Tuck said, "You're going to follow me, aren't you?"

"Naturally. I wondered how long it would take for you to come to that obvious conclusion. I have to see for myself if my theory is correct."

Shaking her head with a weary sigh, she said, "Come on, but keep close to me and do exactly as I say."

They made their way to the fountain beneath a sickle

moon. That tingly feeling, the sense of knowing something was going to happen, buzzed around Tuck like a swarm of bees.

"Do you feel it?" Jenny whispered.

Tuck stopped abruptly several paces from the fountain and turned. Jenny plowed into her with a grunt.

"Feel what?"

"Nothing. Never mind," Jenny said, shaking her head. "It's merely the anticipation."

"Yeah. Anticipation." And fear that they'd both be going to jail, instead of her going back in time.

Jenny hugged her then shoved her toward the water. "Hurry, before the guards make the next rounds."

"I think you're enjoying this too much," she muttered, holding back the surge of tears threatening to choke her. This might be the last time she ever saw her friend.

Jenny's lips quivered and her eyes shown in the dim light. "I'll admit this is exciting. More so than when that person attacked us in this very spot." She swallowed. "Now, get going. You're holding up science," she said shakily.

Tuck grinned and gave her a quick hug. "See ya in the history books, Doc." She turned and stepped into the water.

Chapter Twenty-six

"You cannot go on like this, my friend," Ian said, casting a shadow over Colin's face.

He ignored him as usual, slipping one of Amelia's delicious treats into his mouth. What a shame he could find no cook who could recreate them, if only their taste and not their odd shape.

Savoring the morsel, he let his gaze wander over the little spring. He'd had some men clear a wide path through the wood so he could more easily arrive by horseback whenever the mood struck him. Which, as Ian was so wont to point out, he did every day.

For hours, he would lie back against the sweet grass and watch the clouds pass overhead. He listened to the music of the burbling spring and imagined it was her voice he heard. The soft words she spoke while they lay together, the steady beat of her heart drumming in time with his. All the things he remembered and cherished about her.

And on those days when it rained, he imagined the thunder and lightening to be her as well. Her waspish retorts, her fiery temper, her burning passion. He relived them all time and again, but soon, the fall colors would be gone and winter would be upon them. He wouldn't be able to lie here and remember, the bitter cold would drive him indoors.

Ian kicked his foot, knocking it off the log he'd propped it upon. "Get up, you lack-wit whoreson."

The twig between his fingers snapped. "Watch your tongue, Sassenach."

"What I'm watching is a Highlander who's gone as soft as a newborn babe's arse."

Colin flung out his arm and brought Ian to the ground. Throwing a few well-placed blows and receiving a few in return, they rolled about the clearing, pummeling one another.

"I'll break your nose, you bleedin' Sassenach. Then the lassies willna find you so pretty," Colin said between grunts and blows.

"You couldn't break my nose with your incredibly hard head much less your flabby fist, you beef-witted Scot."

Ian gained the upper hand as they rolled, pinning him for the moment, but Colin would win as he always did. It had become a game of sorts, one he appreciated, as it took his mind off of Amelia if but for a few short moments.

Once they were through thrashing one another, he would feel better and would be ready to return to the castle and bear another night alone with the memory of her sweet skin against his, tormenting him.

"You wouldn't be losing if you'd bothered to take a few pointers from your wife," a familiar voice said.

They both fell still as a shadow fell over them where they lay. Slowly, Ian lifted his head for a look at the intruder, while Colin tilted his back, his heart pounding in his chest.

A redheaded angel stood over them, a cocky grin on her rosy lips, with both hands resting on her hips. The sunlight flashed off her ring, blinding him for a moment. He prayed she wasn't an illusion created by his lonely heart.

The vision sighed. "Ian, if you don't get off my husband, and soon, I might have to hurt you. You look a little too cozy, if you catch my drift."

"Huh? Oh! Yes, quite right, quite right." He scrambled off, leaving Colin lying there with his mouth open.

"He's all yours, my lady." Ian bowed grandly. "I shall make myself useful back at the castle," he said, backing away.

The sound of horse's hooves faded and still Colin could not move. He could only gaze up at the woman standing over him.

His wife.

Her hair had grown considerably since she left some months ago, now lying across her shoulders in wild disarray. His fingers twitched, aching to feel the long lazy curls slip between them.

She slipped off her pack and sank to her knees by his side. "Are you comfortable?" She grinned, a devilish sparkle in her eyes. "I wouldn't want to disturb your rest."

Lifting her head, she shaded her eyes as she glanced at the sky. "It's a beautiful day. A little on the nippy side, but a good one for being lazy."

In one swift move, he pulled her to his chest and rolled her to her back, pinning her beneath him. He drank in the feel and look of her. Her flaming curls spread against the late autumn grass, her warm sweet breath brushing across his face, her heart beating in tune with his.

She was color, where there was none, she was sound, where there'd been only the wind and water, she was life, where there'd been only loneliness.

And she was his.

"Tell me I'm not dreaming, mavourneen," he begged, his throat tight.

She ran the tips of her fingers along his jaw to his lips. "If you are dreaming, please don't wake up."

On a moan, he pressed his lips to hers and knew she was real. She'd come back to him. Somehow she'd found a way, leaving behind wonders he could never imagine. An easier life than he could ever give her.

He rained kisses across her cheek to her ear then simply held her as his eyes dampened, afraid the future would rip her from his arms.

She gripped him, whispering roughly. "I was so afraid I wouldn't find you. Afraid I'd end up in the wrong time, the wrong place. That the Campbells would've—"

"Nay, lass. I'm here and whole." He raised his head and marveled at the sight of her once more. "I never dreamed you would return, although I wished it with all my heart."

She smiled tearfully as she slipped her fingers into his hair at the nape of his neck. "I didn't know I could come back. Jenny figured it out. She helped me be where I wanted to be."

"Then the lass is well?"

She nodded.

"Glad I am tae here it. But—" He glanced at the

spring burbling alongside them. "You left so much behind. Your friend, your work, so many things."

She took his face in her hands and turned him back to her. "You weren't there. None of it was any good without you." A wide bright smile spread across her face. "And we can always take a little trip if we want to."

He thought on it a moment, then said, "I'm not sure I want tae test that particular form of travel, but if you ever wish tae go back—"

She silenced him with a finger to his lips. "I don't want to go back. This is where I want to be. This is my home, my family. This is where I belong."

"Then here is where we'll stay." He kissed her softly.

"I've missed you so much. Make love to me, Colin," she whispered against his lips.

He grinned. "Do you not fear catching a chill? Or that we'll suffer an untimely interruption from some verra nosy kinsmen?"

"I think Ian will keep them away as long as we show up at the castle before dark. And as for a chill, somehow I don't think you'll let me cool down enough to catch one."

"Aye. You have that aright, love," he said, starting them on a slow sweet journey.

Epilogue

"I don't care," Tuck whined, a sound completely foreign to Colin's ears.

He knelt before her where she sat in the large chair in the solar and took her hands in his. "But love, what do you expect me tae do?"

"I don't know, but I can't do this without her." She sniffled.

"Ach, mavourneen." He gently laid his head atop her rounded belly. She'd made little sense these last months as the time of their first-born's arrival neared. "You'll be fine, the babe will be fine. Have faith, love."

Her fingers splayed in his hair and he moaned, but quickly curbed his growing desire. Making love to her was more than awkward at this late date, and they both feared for the babe's welfare.

But soon, he silently chanted to himself, he would have his wife back and an heir. He often had a hard time containing his immense joy at the turn his life had taken and was thoroughly teased by his men and Ian, but he paid them little heed. How could he be angry when he was so happy?

"I'm afraid, Colin," she whispered. "There are so many things that can go wrong."

He lifted his head and peered into the emerald depths filled with worry. "And having Jenny with you would ease your mind?"

She nodded. "But I can't go to her. I'm afraid to travel like this, and—and I want our baby born at home."

A scowl settled over his brow. "Nay, you'll not travel through that hole in time carrying my son."

Her chin tilted up. "Don't you dare order me around, Colin MacLean. This is my *daughter* too."

He grinned at her quick show of temper and pecked a kiss on the tip of her nose. "I want *our* child born here as you, and we both agree 'tis not safe tae travel in that way

Jo Barrett

in your condition." Climbing to his feet, he said, "Which leaves only one alternative. She must come here."

"You're not going after her, so don't even think about it."

"Leave you now?" He crossed his arms over his chest and eyed her. "I'm beginning tae think that being with child has rattled your wits. Perhaps we aught not have any more bairns. Nay, I'll not make love tae you again if this is tae be the result."

"Like that'll ever happen," she said with a deep chuckle, tossing back her head and sending her long wild curls sliding over the fabric of the chair.

How he longed to love her thoroughly and see that mane of fire spread across his chest, but other matters took precedence over his increasing longing.

He returned to his place at her feet, gently cradling her belly in his hands. "I'll send someone, an emissary."

She lifted her head. "Who? No one knows—" A crooked grin stole across her lips. "Do you think he'll go?"

"Aye, love. He'd lay down his life for you—for me."

She giggled. "Jenny's gonna' freak."

He gave her a perplexed look, lost in her use of such an odd word. When would he ever learn them all?

"I mean, she's going to be totally stunned. He's what you might call her idea of a knight-in-shining-armor."

"That rogue?" he asked chortling heartily.

"Did someone call?" Ian asked, strolling into the solar, a teasing grin on his too-handsome face.

Colin exchanged a knowing glance with his love then rose. "Aye, my friend. We were just speaking of you." He clasped him across the shoulder and guided him toward the large window looking out over the island. "Amelia and I are in need of a favor."

"Anything. You have but to ask."

Ian glanced at Amelia sitting in her chair, struggling to raise her feet onto the stool, but he made no move to assist her. All knew of her determination to do things for herself. She reminded them more often than not.

Ian smiled. "Ah, you have finally decided on the child's guardian. 'Twould be an honor."

Amelia paused and looked at Colin, then bit down on her bottom lip, holding back her laughter. Although they had agreed on Ian as their child's guardian, he would never guess what they truly wished of him.

An idea flashed between him and his wife, and Colin turned back to his friend. "Aye, Ian, we wish you tae be the bairn's guardian, but 'tis Amelia's wish for the babe tae have two such protectors. Unfortunately, the one we've chosen isna here. We would like you tae fetch her back in time for the birthing."

"Of course I'll escort the lady," he said, and took Colin's hand in agreement. "Where shall I find her?"

"She lives in the U.S.," Amelia said, watching Ian closely.

"The—you mean to say you want me to—to—good Lord." He paled and slumped in a nearby chair.

"Will you do this for me, my friend? I know 'tis a lot tae ask, but Jenny is a healer from Amelia's time. She wants her here tae make sure the babe comes intae the world safe and hale. I'll understand if you doona wish tae do this."

Ian swallowed hard then got to his feet. "Nay. I said I would, and I shall." He turned toward Amelia. "I am your servant, my lady. Tell me what to do."

Look for the sequel to Highlander's Challenge, coming in the spring of 2008.

Can Ian bring Jenny back in time to help deliver Amelia and Colin's baby? Or will something or someone get in the way?

A word about the author...

Jo currently resides in North Carolina with her patient and supportive family while she juggles her writing career and her position as a programmer analyst. In her early years, she wrote folk songs, poetry, and an occasional short story or two, but never dreamed of writing a book. She didn't even like to read! But one fateful day, she picked up a romance novel and found herself hooked. Not only did she discover the joy of reading, but the joy of writing books. These days, if she isn't tapping away at her computer on a story of her own, she has her nose buried in the latest romance novel hot off the presses, and is enjoying every minute of it.

Visit her website at www.jobarrett.net

Made in the USA
Lexington, KY
26 April 2010